THE MINES

DANIEL YUSCHICK

ISBN: 978-952-94-1884-8 (Paperback)
ISBN: 978-952-94-1886-2 (EPub)

- 1 -
THE STORIES

So what if she was intrigued by the macabre? It wasn't merely the imagery and aesthetics that fueled her imagination but also the underlying stories they told. Tas Fredericks was always expected to gravitate toward the glitz and glamor, the shiny and new, but her interests drew her to the history behind the façade. Just her and her morbid curiosity.

When she was a kid, each school year started the same way. Teachers asked students to talk about their summer breaks and every year there would be at least one or two classmates who'd brag about their trip to Disneyland. The stories were the same every time. The lines for the rides were long, but the wait for Splash Mountain was a full-day affair. They took pictures with their favorite characters and, without fail, burned to a lobstery red in the weeklong sun.

Every single time.

Not long after the years of enthralling Disneyland stories came the tales of debauchery over spring break in Myrtle Beach as if it were the only destination. A cooler of

Corona, eight people to a room, somebody broke up, others got together, and again, more sunburns. Despite her slight aversion to the sun, she again couldn't connect with the idea of the trip. It was a place she didn't want to go to do things she didn't want to do.

Instead, she flipped through the latest issue of *National Geographic*. The photos were extravagant and, to her delight, partnered with vivid stories. She had learned about remote villages in South America, wildlife in the deserts of Africa, and the celebration of death in Indonesia. Those were the stories she wanted to hear and, more importantly, tell.

If her curiosity was a tinge morbid, why was that such a bad thing? She wasn't so much interested in death itself as she was the surrounding stories. As she sat on the plane destined for home, watching a clumsy couple struggle to fit their luggage into the overhead bins, she was intrigued by what the story of their deaths might look like.

The man beside her made a comment she didn't catch, but when she glanced over, he was awaiting her attention. "I'm sorry," she said, taking out her earbuds.

"Oh, my bad. I was asking if that couple's ever been on a plane before. But it's less funny the second time."

"No less true, though."

The couple adjusted their bags into place and the woman lumbered to her seat while the man searched for their flight essentials—a sweater, book, sandwich, and a bottle of water.

Tas's neighbor continued. "I mean, either take that stuff out before getting on or move out of the aisle and do it."

She wondered if his only dimension was dry, observational humor about others. "Yeah, I don't think they're aware of those options."

Should I put my earbuds back in? What's the etiquette for this conversation?

"I'm Bobby," he said.

"Hey. I'm Tas."

"So, New York, huh? You heading home? Going to visit?" His voice trailed off, and he leaned onto the armrest between them.

"Neither," she answered. "Just a layover before heading home."

"I was gonna say, you didn't sound like much of a New Yorker. What brought you to Iceland?" Bobby shifted in his seat and wiped his hands on his legs.

"Also a layover. I'm coming from Helsinki," she said. "What about you?"

"Yeah, a couple buddies and I came here for the week." He pointed his chin toward the others a few rows back. "Lots of hiking. Checked out the Blue Lagoon and some stuff like that. But how was Helsinki? I've never been."

"It was great," she said, surprised at the genuine excitement in her voice. "I've always wanted to visit and I'm glad I finally did."

"I'll be honest, I don't know the first thing about it. What'd you do there?"

Given his quick summary, she thought he'd be looking for a short bulleted list as well, but she struggled to paint with broad strokes. She learned in the days of Disneyland and Myrtle Beach that her list of places of interest usually differed from others.

"Pretty much ran around," she said with a light shrug. "Checked out an island fortress in the archipelago, ate lots of chocolate, that kind of stuff. I guess the main thing was visiting a nearby lake that's pretty notorious."

"A notorious lake, huh?" His eyes widened as he shifted again to face her better.

"Totally." With some uncertainty, she elaborated. "It's where Finland's most infamous unsolved murders happened. Four kids went camping and only one came home."

He stared for a moment, waiting for a punchline or smile that never came. "Wait, you're being for real?"

"For real."

"Why would you visit a place like that?" There was a slight edge to his voice. "That's a thing, isn't it?"

It was *a thing*. She was somewhat bothered by it having a name like it was being fetishized. Like there was normal tourism and then, "Yeah, dark tourism."

"That's it," he said snapping his fingers. "I actually watched something about that recently. Seems weird. I mean, no offense."

Offense taken. "No worries. It's cool."

Bobby leaned back and ran his hands along his cheeks. "But isn't that disrespectful of the victims?"

Not this again. "I don't think so. It's not like I'm going there and mocking them or disturbing the grounds or anything. The park is open to the public. Anybody can go there."

He was clearly torn on the issue. His head slightly bounced from side to side as if mentally straddling the fence of his opinion.

"Look," she added. "People visit movie locations all the time. I don't think it's much different."

"Movies are fake though," he said.

The roaring engines of the plane speeding down the runway silenced their conversation. As it climbed through the heavy, low-hanging clouds, the city lights vanished.

Tas knew where the conversation was heading and didn't care to debate or argue. "Well, I'm going to try to doze off." She gestured to her earbuds.

"I'm sorry. I didn't mean..."

"No, it's cool," she said, popping them into place.

When she closed her eyes, she pictured looking out over Lake Bodom. The spring had yet to melt all the ice, and the leaves danced with the cold breeze that blew through the trees. The ground squelched under her boots as the frosted nature around her thawed. In a clearing ahead stood a bright red cabin perched on a hill overlooking the shimmering lake below. It was peaceful and serene. The air was crisp. That early morning moment was far too beautiful for such a tragedy to seem possible.

The area felt familiar as she moved toward the bank holding out her phone to align grainy black-and-white crime-scene photos with the present-day scenery. When she matched the same ghoulish trees stretching overhead, she placed where she stood. The area was small and flat and, in that moment, covered with frost and mud. When she'd glance down to her phone, the pictures showed a ravaged and mutilated tent, blood-spattered and gashed open in the same spot.

No amount of research could have prepared her for the surreal experience of standing amidst the murders. She empathized with the victims but couldn't relate to the terror they must have experienced. She couldn't imagine being there, fighting for her life. Nor would she want to.

A light morning fog rolled around the edge of the lake and crept onto shore. She stood still, admiring the contrast between the beauty of the park and its violent past. But the solitude was disturbed when a jolt ran through her body.

From the window of the plane, she saw the runway. They had landed, and the pilot spoke over the crackling speakers welcoming the flight to New York and giving them the rundown on the time and weather. She and Bobby nodded as they left and she made her way to her final gate.

One more flight to go.

When she arrived in Raleigh, she walked outside the airport and found her friend Dean Ericsson already waiting. "Look at you being early!"

"Only because I didn't want you to lecture me about it. 'If you're ten minutes early, you're on time,'" he said in a mocking tone.

"And if you're on time, you're ten minutes late. I know, I know." She couldn't help it; her father had passed the motto down to her. He was always diligent, and she admired that despite the constant frustration it caused. It was part punctuality, part selfishness, but the proverbial worm could be anything, and she preferred being a bird with choices. "It's good to be home, though. Thanks for the ride."

"No problem," he said, merging into traffic. The airport was always a chaotic mass of confusion. Cops tried to organize it with their waving lights and incessant whistles, but it was beyond saving.

Once on the highway, she filled Dean in on some highlights of the trip. She'd face far less judgment from him. In fact, no judgment at all. If anything, he met her stories with a reserved interest as if his intrigue was a guilty pleasure. There was a little wanderer inside him, yet it preferred living vicariously through others.

Being back stateside meant her self-imposed blackout from work emails was over. A rush of notifications flashed onto her screen as she descended into inbox hell.

"Leave it," Dean said. "It's still the weekend."

But she continued to scroll until she found it. "Yes!" Her face beamed as she turned toward him. "So you know that exhibit I've been expecting? It was delivered while I was gone."

"Nice! That's the mining one, right?"

"Yeah. The evolution of mining practices in Africa."

As the curator for the history museum, she was responsible for acquiring exhibits and shows. It was a way for her to bring the remote parts of the world to her and it wouldn't get much more remote than desolate mining towns in 1900 South Africa.

She clenched her phone in both hands. “I’m super excited about this one since I don’t know anything about that area.”

“I don’t think anybody does.”

And that was part of her excitement. It was one thing to learn the stories but another to share them. She wanted to show that there was more to the world than the same ten places on every bucket list.

Morbid curiosity. Dark tourism. Whatever you wanted to call it, she wanted to tell the stories people had never heard and would never hear again. That’s what it came down to for her: keeping those stories alive.

“Home sweet home,” she said as they pulled into her apartment complex.

“Glad you made it back safely.” He put the car in park and slouched into his seat. “If you’re not too beat, Mike and Syd suggested drinks later.”

Tas looked into her side-view mirror to confirm she looked as rough as she felt. “Sounds good, but I’ll seriously need to freshen up first.”

A mischievous grin grew across Dean’s face. “Yeah, that’s probably for the best.”

“Oh, shut up!” She pushed him away from her and against his door.

“Anytime. I’ll text you in a bit.”

There was no need to ask where they’d meet. It’d be the same place as the countless times before. Not every experience had to be unique. Some stories were meant to be told over and over again and drinks with friends was one of her favorites.

- 2 -
THE NIGHT

Did it defeat the purpose of running the heat with the window down as she drove? Absolutely. But with the sun still bright, there weren't many better ways to drive through downtown joined by the conversational banter of a podcast. Tas enjoyed simple moments.

The brewery's parking lot looked as if the entire city had the same idea. She pulled her dulling gray sedan, well, 'satin charcoal', the salesman had boasted, between two newer BMWs with a tinge of self-consciousness. Her car had acquired its fair share of nicks and chips over the years and it looked worse tucked between two sparkling status symbols.

"Chalk it up to character," she'd joke.

With a press of her fob, the car locked with a quick beep and flash of its headlights, a feature the salesman mentioned in the event she wasn't aware of it being standard in literally every other car. She turned toward the building and stopped to appreciate the latest mural that brightened the lot. Painted boldly in the accentuated style of boardwalk caricatures, a donkey and elephant fought to paint the state of North

Carolina red and blue with the tagline "Gerrymandering is Vandalism."

After snapping a quick selfie with the statement backdrop, Tas made her way toward the entrance.

"Tas! Over here." Dean waved her over to the patio where he sat with Mike and Sydney.

The weather was gorgeous but still a notch below sitting outside comfortably. Luckily, a tall patio heater stood next to their table where an empty seat and full beer awaited her.

She turned to Dean with narrowed eyes. "You took a sip, didn't you?"

The group broke out in laughter leaving Dean to defend himself. "I told you guys she'd assume I did it!"

Mike raised his hand and owned up to the party foul. "It was me. But thanks for blaming him, anyway."

"Typical." Tas's default response that, with her self-proclaimed mastery of inflection and tone, had hundreds of potential meanings. "You know the first sip is the best one," she said, lifting the glass to take the next best sip. "Still so good, though. This has to be my favorite porter in the city."

Sydney raised her glass. "Welcome back, globetrotter. Dean was filling us in on the trip. But tell me, do they drink that garbage beer of yours over there, too?"

Tas knew right where she was going. "You mean those IPAs you drink so much?"

"She has a point, babe," Mike said, showcasing his beer as if it were some coveted prize. "Black-as-my-soul imperial stout."

All the craft breweries in the city were great, but Tas hated the culture and hipster badge of honor that came with drinking the most extreme beers. And leave it to Mike to embody that toxic mentality as if drinking was meant to be a challenge or competitive feat.

She cleared her throat and diverted. "Did you guys see the mural in the back?"

"I like it! It was here last time, too," Sydney said. "It made me want to pull up the old John Oliver segment about gerrymandering again."

While Mike and Sydney handled most of the political discussion Dean and Tas chimed in occasionally, choosing to enjoy their beers in relative silence.

When Tas finished the last, and worst, sip of her beer, the waitress approached their table with a notepad in hand.

She's good.

"Another round?" The waitress smacked her gum and twirled a pen between her fingers.

"Y'all want to split a couple pizzas?" Sydney asked. "I could go for pepperoni."

Dean asked, "Can we get banana peppers on one?"

The group stared at him not saying anything. Their eyes, accusatory and shunning, said everything they needed before Mike broke the disapproving silence.

"Come on, man. We've been over this."

Dean slouched back on the bench in defeat. "Fine," he said to the waitress. "Two pepperonis, I guess."

The waitress flashed a smile that looked more irritated than amused. "I'll put that in and get you guys your drinks." She swept the strands of hair from her face and turned toward the kitchen.

Tas noticed the pack of cigarettes peeking out from the waitress's back pocket. *Maybe she needs a smoke break.*

The sun was retreating behind the skyline to the west; with the dimming light came an extra chill. The lighting that hung above the patio during the spring was still down for the season, and the faces of those with their backs to the sun became shrouded in ever-growing shadows. Tas rubbed her hands back and forth along her legs for some warmth, awaiting the pizza that couldn't be there soon enough.

It was peak dinnertime, and the patio was packed creating a din of conversation and laughter that brought the evening to life. A table of college students dressed in their matching red-and-white school pride had several beers between them and scattered playing cards filling in the gaps. Another table of men dressed in casual suits had undone their ties, which hung loose from their necks—the universal sign that business was over. And if their ties didn't give it away, seeing them huddled around a game of Mario Kart settled any doubt.

The street that ran next to the patio was also busy that time of day. Groups of runners in "Run Club" tops ran along the park and toward downtown while young families pushed kids in their strollers with Whole Foods bags in tow toward the latest apartment developments. Tas loved the city, but its character was being torn down and built back up as "urban luxury" apartments and condos.

She checked her watch.

Probably near bedtime for those kids.

"God, Tas," Mike said. "Just check your phone like a normal person."

"Cause you're so normal, huh? What's so wrong with checking my watch for the time? That's literally its job."

"I've got a sundial somewhere around here if you'd prefer that."

Sydney smacked his shoulder, a playful smile on her face. "Don't be mean."

He let out a big huff, crossing his arms like a punished child. Playful enough, but like Tas's jokes and reactions, often rooted in truth. Mike was an only child, and both of his parents were executives at tech companies. He grew up being thrown into sports that doubled as childcare and coasted through school and college merely based on his athletic achievements. It was easy for the school to look the other way when he was helping the basketball team sell tickets.

Yet despite his athletic build and experience in sports, they weren't his passion as much as a means to an end.

Instead, after school, Mike used his father's connections to get into the business development department at his company. Tas respected him for not being the stereotypical jock, but she'd been lying if she said she didn't harbor slight resentment for how easily most things came to him.

The brewery door opened, and the waitress backed out and propped it with her backside and cigarette pack. Carrying a large pizza in each hand, she turned from the doorway and stepped down to the patio in a single easy motion learned from making the trip countless times. She set the pizzas down and pulled out napkins and silverware from her apron. "I'll be right back with the plates."

The fresh-baked smell of the pizza tempted Tas. There's a reason Trophy was the group's default place. Mike would fight tooth and nail that Lilly's had the better pizza but the three-to-one vote always ended up with the group right where they were.

Steam rose from their dinners in enticing waves against the chill air. Tas was entranced by the heat haze and drifted off into thoughts of her upcoming exhibit and to the sprawling sands of Namibia. Stretches of wooden carts filled with combinations of equipment, miners, and gold were being pushed from the dark mouths of mines. But the faces of the men didn't seem exhausted from the strenuous labor. They looked scared. The bodies in the carts were injured and mangled with broken limbs hanging over the sides. Blood ran down bodiless arms before it dripped and dissipated into dark brown splotches in the sand. She could see the gore. She could see the terror.

She could see...

"A-yo, Tas. Look alive." Mike snapped his fingers toward her. "First time eating?"

She shook her head and watched the sands of her daydream scatter away like the shaking of a snow globe. "Yeah, my bad." The others were already eating, and as she slid a slice onto her plate, she couldn't help but see the pepperoni under the cheese as the blood that ran through the sands in her mind.

"You all right?" Dean asked quietly enough, but his soft tone didn't mask his concern.

She looked over at him and smiled almost imperceptibly. "Yeah."

"And Mike, if you say one damn thing about the sauce this time..." Tas trailed off to leave the impending threat to his wildest imagination.

"I won't. I promise," he said. "Besides, if I'm going to comment about anything it'll be that baby."

They followed Mike's tilting head to the table where a baby sat with its parents.

"I mean, who brings a baby to a brewery?"

"Maybe they didn't have a sitter," Sydney suggested.

"Maybe they should drink at home then," Mike said, instinctively tensing for another one of Sydney's smacks.

"Don't. Be. Mean," she scolded, not missing the opportunity.

The conversation continued and the trays of pizzas emptied. Dean had gone quiet as if he'd retreated into his head. Tas knew he could shift from sociable and funny to quiet and observant. She wasn't much different. But as he bounced his legs and cracked his fingers below the table, she couldn't help but think he seemed anxious.

The waitress came by with the unmistakable odor of smoke clinging to her. She gave a relaxed smile and handed out the checks. "Y'all have a good night."

Mike stood from the table and stretched his arms toward the sky and Sydney threw her purse over her shoulder. "I got to get this one home," she said. "Any more drinks and he'll either pass out or get handsy and I'm not trying to deal with either tonight."

She wrapped her arm behind Mike and looked up at him with a smile. "Let's go, big guy."

"Are you good to drive?" Tas knew she sounded like the mom of the group but she couldn't help it.

Sydney tossed her hand in the air and gave her keys a jingle as she started across the street. "I'm good."

Mike and Sydney got into their car, its engine revved to life, and Sydney pulled out with a wave and a smile. Moments later, it was nothing more than shrinking taillights blending into the city.

"I'm parked in back," Dean said, gesturing to the back lot.

"Me too."

They walked from the patio around the building and back to the parking lot.

"You got a hectic week ahead?" Tas asked.

Dean nodded with an exhausted sigh. "Yeah. The navigation portion of the app worked a couple weeks ago. Tommy 'optimized' it," he said with air quotes. "Then Friday, I'm testing it out in the field and it all went to shit. Nothing worked."

"How does that even happen?"

Dean shrugged and forced a small laugh of disbelief. "Hell if I know."

The parking lot was almost empty, and the homeless were mulling around the alley on the far end, their black garbage bags at their sides and their brown bags in their hands.

Dean leaned against Tas's car and was nothing but a silhouette with the streetlight glaring down behind him. "It's whatever though," he said. "But I should get going." He tapped the trunk twice and pushed himself away toward his car. "Have a good night."

Tas pressed the fob and gave a final wave. "You too. See ya!"

The heat came to life as she started up her car. Again, she cracked the window to have the night's crisp air wisp through her hair. The true crime podcast resumed where it had left off discussing the unsolved murders of Villisca, Iowa and she wondered if there was a clever little label for her taste in podcasts much like her travels. *Dark tourism. Whatever.*

She turned to grab her seatbelt and watched Dean race through the lot. "Slow down, tough guy." A man crossed her rearview mirror, staggering through the space behind her. Once he had passed, she tossed the car into reverse, backed out of the space, and headed home.

She took her exit and drove down the darkened ramp tucked between two massive walls of evergreens. The light at the intersection was red, and she looked for any oncoming cars before coasting into a right turn. She was a chronic California stopper. A few blocks later she turned into her neighborhood, a street of townhomes that had seen their prime decades before she'd ever called it home.

Once inside her place, the door swung closed behind her. "Water and ibuprofen," she reminded herself. Even though she'd only had a couple of beers, her body needed some care before the week. She made her way to the bathroom for the painkillers and to the kitchen to wash them down with a swig of chocolate milk. She may have been too old to drink without caution, but she'd never outgrow chocolate milk.

Or any chocolate, really.

"My love of chocolate is the only reason I run," she'd tell others.

With her presleep care taken, she walked up the carpeted stairs with small shocks of static and slight wobbles of the wooden banister following each step. In her bedroom, she lit a few candles on her nightstand making the room nice and cozy.

The weight of the flights and beers smothered her the moment she slid beneath the heavy duvet. It was pointless having lit the candles. She blew them right out and sank her head into the pillow.

She waited for sleep to take her, but an uncertain anxiety settled over her and kept it at arm's length. Something was off. The sudden rush of uneasiness held her through her tossing and turning. It held her from the calming, silent clearing of her mind.

It held her until she wasn't even aware it had let her go.

- 3 -
THE DREAMS

Dean wanted to run to his car, but Tas might have been watching. What would she have thought? Instead, he took hurried steps while tapping his fingers against his thumb.

It's gonna be okay.

But was it?

The whole night had been familiar. Déjà vu. He'd often taken notes of his settings and surroundings as if working through a mental checklist. Because in a sense, he was.

A subtle chill trickled down his neck and he grabbed the keys from his pocket. There was no telling when a particular list would be triggered and, God help him, completed but it was significant when one was. His heart would race and his legs would grow restless. A string of otherwise meaningless events could unfold and bury him beneath a raging anxiety.

A night out at Trophy wasn't uncommon. But once the games of Mario Kart grew rowdy and Mike joked about the baby, Dean could no longer shake the looming dread. He had to remind himself; there was no point in stressing until he found the entire list.

Or until it found him.

Dean was opening his car door when his heart raced at the sound of footsteps behind him.

"Excuse me," a man said.

Dean turned to find a haggard-looking old man in multiple oversized jackets with a wild, untamed beard approaching.

"Can you help me out? I'm a veteran." The man held out his hands, dirtied and calloused. "Could you spare a couple bucks for the bus? I need to get up to New York."

Check.

"I... I'm sorry," Dean said. "I don't have—I have to go."

A tightness wrapped around Dean's chest. His body rushed with feverish heat and chills raced along his every nerve.

He needed to get home.

Dean's mind wandered to his notebook. Not one containing development notes for work, backtracking the issues breaking his app's navigation, but his personal notes. The words and recollections meant for his eyes only.

Green lights led the way to his downtown apartment. He didn't mind the mass construction throughout the city. There was a sense of peace whenever he'd step into his spacious open floor plan with clean lines, crown molding, and pillars framing the living room archway. Many found the style tacky, impractical even, and underneath it all, so did he. But when the apartment's soft lights warmed up the rooms, there was a calming effect, and that night he needed any amount of comfort he could find.

A trail of melting slush followed Dean as he rushed through the foyer into his bedroom. He leapt onto the bed and stretched to his nightstand to hit the light and throw open its drawer. Inside was a slight amount of bric-a-brac—matches, tie clips, condoms, collar stays—all scattered around several notebooks. On top of the small pile was one with a black

Moleskine cover and elastic strap keeping it shut. He reached for it and flicked the strap aside.

The pages slid from beneath his thumb like a flipbook as he hurried to the last entry. Every page was written in the same black ink with a date, day, month, year, centered in the top margin. When he reached the last entry dated March 10, 2019, he scanned the contents of the page and flipped backward. January 17, 2019. He ran his fingers down the lined sheets, tracing the letters so intently the slightest ridges where too much ink had pooled bumped beneath his finger. Weeks and sometimes months would pass between entries, but he came to a page dated October 13, 2018, where his scanning finger found the braille-like ridges he was searching for.

The words he had hastily scrawled dared him to read, and with a deep breath, he did.

"At Trophy with everyone. There's a couple with a baby and a table of men playing video games. A homeless veteran asks for bus fare to New York."

With beads of sweat along his hairline and in the dim light of his bedside lamp, those were the words he had scribbled after being rattled from his dream that October. He didn't immortalize every dream in writing, only the ones that were real enough to touch, that fractured the divide between subconscious and reality. Not every detail survived the split-second transition to being awake, but he'd capture the pieces that clung to his memory, dug their claws into his mind to stay long after he'd open his eyes.

Nightmares weren't necessary to create the deep connection. When he sank to such a level of dreaming, it was as if he was drowning under fathoms of tumultuous ocean. A pressure would hold him in place, squeeze his chest, and strangle him. Those dreams were more than dreams. They were like fiendish puppeteers pulling his strings, stretching him to be in two places at once.

When the dreams released him, he'd spring from his bed in a suffocating panic. His lungs would burn as they begged for air. Jitters and restlessness rushed through every limb. There was an anxiety, a terror, something looming that he didn't, and couldn't, know. In those moments where his body was shocked to life, he'd never believed he was closer to death.

With sweaty hands, he grabbed the pen and scratched an "X" into the page. He traced the lines over and over with more pressure until the center was a lightless pit of black ink. After dating the page, he closed the book and ran a hand through his hair.

It was debilitating to relive his dreams. His mouth went dry, and a migraine tightened around his head. It was no small feat to stand and remove his clothes and stagger to the bathroom.

The white tiles on the floor glared under the bright light and shot daggers of flashing pain into his eyes. Their chill rushed from his bare feet through his body forcing his muscles to constrict further. Tension built in the back of his neck and shoulders while his stomach twisted as impossibly as his thoughts.

When he was weighed down by the overwhelming fear that something was missing or that he hadn't prepared for some unknown event, he'd spill two Xanax from their bottle into his shaking hands. Their dry, chalk-like taste made him cringe, but he liked to believe they'd calm him quicker without water.

He was preparing for a night where sleep would be elusive.

Back in his room, the Moleskine cover was smooth in his hands. There was always a temptation to revisit other pages, especially during his attacks. But opening the book would only deepen the stress. He wrapped the elastic strap around the cover and hid the book back in his drawer.

Out of sight but an anvil on his mind.

Dean reached for his phone and scrolled through previous texts and clicked on an unsaved number. "Can we meet this week?"

Send.

With his mind screaming against his skull, he had to steady himself from the outside in. He killed the light and lay on his back with his hands clasped over his chest. No noise. No lights. He longed to be free of his senses as he struggled to find peace within the world that bore down upon him.

Behind his eyes, a projection reel of memories flickered to life. To find peace, he'd revisit one of the few times he'd ever breathed it in.

Years ago, during that window of optimism between college graduation and reality, he found himself sitting atop a sand dune well away from the families with screaming kids and the parties with screaming drunks. After carrying around his laptop bag for four years, compliments of his Computer Science major, he had all but forgotten the sensation of wind against his back and free unencumbered shoulders. In that moment, it was only him, the crashing waves, and the squawking of the seagulls that flew above the tide.

A storm had recently passed. Its dark clouds rolled north along the beach and over the pier. In the distance, the Bodie Lighthouse stood strong like an anchor with a black-and-white-striped tower that led up to its light. Each rotation sent the beam far through the sky and into the foreboding clouds as if it were single-handedly pushing them away.

The sun had all but set, yet the horizon clung to the last rays of fiery light. Dean stood to feel the breeze wash over him. After a humid thunderstorm, the crisp wind was refreshing—a welcome reprieve from the ravaging mugginess. With a deep breath, he curled his toes into the sand and breathed in every bit of peacefulness his lungs could fit.

"Hey! We got it started!"

Down from where he stood and closer to the shore was Tas, waving her arms high and pointing to the fire that was stirring. The flames were young and growing hotter and brighter. The thought of them receding down to ash never crossed his mind as he left the solitude of the dune to take the last empty seat next to Tas.

When he sat down, she was already midstory with Mike and Sydney.

"I've already mapped it out. It's about three hours outside of Prague."

"Will you rent a car?" Sydney asked. "How will you get there?"

"Nah. It's Europe. I'll take buses. They'll take me almost the whole way." Tas paused and took another drink. "It's only a short walk from the last bus to the church."

Dean popped the cap from his beer and tried to catch up. "Wait, what's this?"

"I'm going to Prague next month," Tas said. "I booked my flights and everything today. There's a church there, well, ossuary that would be amazing to see."

"I don't even know what that is."

"It's like a church but when there's not enough room to bury all the dead, they bring the skeletons inside. This place is decorated in bones. Thousands of them," she explained, stretching her arms outward as if their distance apart quantified the number of bones.

Dean shook his head. "And that's how you want to spend your vacation?"

"Do you even know me? Of course!"

Mike took another drink before chiming in. "Yeah, dude. Haven't you heard? She wants to see the weirdest, most morbid shit she can find."

"Something like that." Tas ignored his mocking tone. "This just interests me so much more than somewhere like Paris."

"Now, you're crazy," said Sydney. "Paris is at the top of my list. If only someone would get off his ass and take me."

Mike returned Sydney's look with one of his own.

Tas continued. "The catacombs would be cool though. Oh! That reminds me."

"Of more dead things?" Mike asked.

"Not quite. But did you guys know about the underground mall back home buried under Cameron Village? It was closed back in the eighties, I think. I would love to find a way down there to see it."

"How'd catacombs remind you of a damn shopping mall?"

Dean looked around, letting the surrounding conversations fall away. There were only a few people on the beach. Most wore hoodies or light jackets to combat the breeze that rolled in with the tide, a problem he didn't have near the fire. Separated from the others taking an evening stroll on the beach, Dean watched as an older man with a metal detector scanned the sand along the shore.

The man had a straggly build with flip-flops and loose beige chinos rolled several inches above his ankles. His jacket was zipped end to end and his Carolina Panthers cap tucked behind his headphone-covered ears. His movements were steady, almost a cadence: two steps forward, rotate left, rotate right, return center. He came up empty one spot at a time. Over and over again.

"Do you think he's ever found anything?" Dean's voice sounded directionless and shallow.

The group stopped their conversation and followed his stare. They turned to face the man and his tireless search.

"Hell no," Mike said with more than a hint of condescension. "There's no treasure here. Look at him. Does he look like he's found anything worth a damn?"

"Not everybody values the same things," Tas said. "I doubt he's looking for much of anything."

"Then why bother?"

"He could find anything. Say he found a key. Who's key was it? What did it open? What if it unlocked something more than some person's closet? He'd never know. It could be anything. The best stories are always the ones you have to discover." Tas's eyes sparkled as she spoke.

"Says the girl with a fresh BA in history!" Sydney lifted her bottle and the group followed to toast her accomplishment.

"And to the old man," Mike added.

"The old man."

They took their drinks and gave the treasure hunter a final stare before turning back toward their makeshift firepit.

Tas picked up where she had left off. "It's more than the history itself, though. It's the chance to see things few others have. Like ossuaries, caves, remote islands, even that underground mall. Not everybody sees those places. I mean, there are still tribes in the rainforests living completely separate from modern life. Medicine, technology, culture, everything. It blows my mind."

"Well, I think it'd be cool to visit one of those small fishing villages in Greenland. There's like fifty people total," Sydney said. "It'd be crazy."

Mike's eyebrows raised as he shook his head. "Y'all are the crazy ones."

"I can see that," Dean said. "Not the crazy part but the feeling of experiencing something totally different."

"Exactly! Everybody's seen pictures of the Eiffel Tower or seen it in movies. We know its history and what it looks like. What about some undiscovered cave system in Vietnam or something? Underground, away from the people who aren't looking for it. I bet you that guy would find it." Tas pointed to the man and his metal detector, who still walked with the same rhythm farther down the beach.

The remaining clouds had been pushed away leaving a clear dark sky above. Starlight shimmered on the waves off the coast and danced with the waves that crashed to shore. Their roaring fire had burned down to glowing embers, and the beach was all but empty. It was almost all their own.

Sydney and Mike moved from their chairs to architect their dream sandcastle.

Dean and Tas stayed by the fire, trying to stoke a little more life out of it. He always felt secure in their silence—safe—but that night he wanted to break it. He looked over at her, her face relaxed and expressionless staring out at the water.

"So aren't you scared to travel alone?" Dean asked.

"I guess, a little." Tas reached up to take the sunglasses from her head so she could rework her ponytail. "But it's something I want to do. I don't want to wait around for things to happen. It's like I'd be holding my own dreams hostage if I waited for the right time or the right person."

She placed the sunglasses back on her head and turned to him with a smile. "Know what I mean?" Her voice was soft, nearly overpowered by the breaking waves.

"Yeah. It's awesome you're doing that. I mean, before you, I'd never known about these kinds of places much less seen them. I'm not going with you, but you know what I mean."

"Well, next time I consider going off the grid, you should come along. You could use some excitement."

"And not live vicariously through you?"

"Where's the fun in that? Where's the fun in staying here?" She gestured her arms outward making him think she didn't mean the beach or even North Carolina but *here* as in who they were in that moment.

"You're right."

"So yeah, you should come with me next time," she insisted.

Dean chuckled and took another drink. "Maybe I will."

Tas looked over to see Sydney and Mike tossing balls of sand at their masterpiece. "Not a fan of sandcastles?"

"Just testing its integrity," Mike said, winding up for another assaulting throw.

Dean looked away from the barrage on the castle and turned his attention to Tas. If she knew he was watching, she didn't show it. Her curly ponytail waved in the wind and her eyes shimmered in the crackling fire.

Her eyes.

There was a strength inside them, a passion that made them warm, almost enchanting. She leaned forward with her elbows on her knees and hands in her hoodie. *How can she be scared going to Prague alone and still walk right into that fear?*

She didn't have all the details, but she never needed them. "I'll figure it out," she always said.

He saw more than mere passion in her eyes; there was life.

The memory washed away, and he was back in his bed. His heart had slowed and from the relaxing tension in his shoulders to his settling legs, a soothing calm settled over him. The anxiety seeped from his body, dissipating into the darkness as if carried away by the ocean breeze. The acrobats in his stomach, flipping and twisting, had settled, and he finally reveled in the peaceful comfort of his sheets.

A flashing light from his phone pulled his attention to an awaiting text.

"I could meet tomorrow. How's 3:00?"

With a quick thumbs-up confirmation, he silenced his phone and nestled the covers under his chin. Sleep could put the night out of his mind completely or thrust its panic upon him all over again. He closed his eyes and slipped away into the gamble of which it would be, counting the stripes on the lighthouse he'd hoped would ward off the storms of his own.

- 4 -
THE VULTURES

Monday mornings always received a bad rap. Few seemed to find the beauty of a spring morning where the sun peeked through the blinds to awaken with its warmth. Tas was never one to sleep with the curtains closed. She would rather wake up with sunshine than fall asleep in total darkness.

From the light shining into her room, she knew the alarm was only minutes away from buzzing. Her duvet had been strewn across the bed and bunched around her legs. The night had provided sleep but little rest.

Once she stirred awake, Tas's mind would spring to life with the day's agenda. Even a loose plan would allow her to be more productive and motivated.

I need to check the exhibit's construction plans, lead the school tour at 10:00 a.m., and verify the show's pieces in storage.

When her phone played the soft piano melody, she rolled over to dismiss the alarm. The screen disappeared and revealed a string of missed calls and texts from Sydney.

"We were in a wreck last night. I'm okay. Mike's banged up some," read the first text.

The brightness of the screen burned her eyes and left her vision blurry. She jumped to the edge of the bed and rubbed her hands over her face. Did she read what she thought she did?

When her vision became clear, she read the text again. The words carried no tone, no context but pulled her heart with the weight of an anchor.

Tas's hands shook as she rushed to call Sydney.

Sydney had no sooner answered when the dam of Tas's thoughts broke through.

"Syd! Are you guys okay? What happened?"

Sydney sniffled and gasped for air. "I don't even know," she said. Her voice choked and fought back tears. "We were going down Dawson, and some guy ran a light. He pretty much T-boned us on Mike's side." She paused to blow her nose and took a deep breath. "His head went through the window and there was so much blood. Oh God, I hope he's okay!"

Sydney broke down into helpless and sorrowful cries.

Tas pictured her sitting alone and drained, her forehead resting in her palm with tears falling to the floor.

"Syd. Hey. You're okay." Tas tried to remain calm hoping it would offer even the slightest reassurance. "Where are you?"

Another heavy sigh followed by more sniffles. "We're at Rex."

"I'll be right there. Don't worry."

Before the call disconnected, Tas was on her feet. She texted Dean the news and rushed to throw on jeans and a hoodie. No more than a minute seemed to pass before she was in her car reaching into the center console for a mint to mask any morning breath. Once on the road, she called her boss.

"Good morning, Ms. Fredericks." Sam's tone was polite with an underlying hint of sarcasm that didn't go unnoticed.

"Hey Sam. Sorry, I know it's early but I have to come in late today. An emergency came up." She spoke with urgency as if every action was accelerated. "Could you cover or get someone to handle the kids' tour this morning?"

"Ms. Fredericks." He cleared his throat. "Tas, another emergency? This isn't much notice and puts me in a bind."

His tone was all too familiar. *Emergency*. No, that wasn't the first frantic morning call she had made nor was it the second but three such calls in as many years seemed reasonable to her. Unfortunately, reason was not one of Sam's better traits.

The first time had been when her tire blew on the highway. She'd dropped her head to the steering wheel, clenched onto it at the ten and two positions, and cried a few stressful tears. When she had settled her breathing, she called Sam. He seemed more understanding especially compared to the second time she had disturbed his morning routine with bad news.

That situation was less an emergency and more a stark realization that she was no longer twenty-three. Sydney had turned thirty that weekend, and they celebrated by going out Saturday. What had started as dinner and drinks at her favorite spot downtown turned into a long night of drinks, arcade games, and more drinks at the speakeasy.

Beer before liquor, never been sicker.

She knew the rhyming words of advice yet threw caution to the wind. The night ended when the lights of last call illuminated the bags under their eyes. There was no more hiding in the dark corners sunken deep into the plush leather chairs. They stumbled to their Uber and said goodbye to a successful celebration.

Back at her apartment, all the water and painkillers in the world couldn't save her from the next morning. When Monday rolled around, she learned she couldn't be saved from that morning either. With her face smothered under an ice pack, she flapped her hand around the bed until she found her phone to call Sam about her weekend flu.

"It must have been something I ate," she suggested, with little conviction.

Sam had grunted as confirmation and wished her his best.

Regardless of those times, she considered Sydney an emergency and would deal with Sam's attitude.

"I know and I'm sorry," she continued. "But I have to do this. I'm not sure how long I'll be, but I'm running to the hospital now."

Sam relented. "No problem. We'll figure it out."

"Thanks, Sam! I appreciate it."

"And Tas," he said, right before she hung up, "I hope you're all right but I also hope, for both our sakes, this isn't an ongoing habit."

Her eyes rolled. "No, sir. Thank you."

She had to pick her battles with Sam and at that moment, she chose to fight her way down Route 40 instead. The stop-and-go rush hour would cripple the highway soon and she hoped to reach her exit before it did.

The sunshine that greeted her that morning had since been overtaken by thick, thunderous clouds. They loomed far in the distance, but she knew the rains were inevitable. She flipped her headlights on in preparation and passed a slow-moving semi on her right.

By the time she had arrived at the hospital, the clouds were overhead and unleashing an assault of heavy rains. She checked her car for an umbrella but came up empty.

Typical.

She put up her hood, pulled it tight against her head, and raced from the parking deck to the entrance.

The cold fluorescent lights that greeted her did little to warm her from the downpour. A trail of puddled steps followed her along the tiled floor as she made her way to reception.

"Hello. How can I help you?" The receptionist turned to greet her without taking her hands from her keyboard.

"Hi. I'm looking for Sydney Wheeler and Mike Carver. I'm a friend. Can you tell me what room they're in?"

The woman turned back to the computer and continued typing. "Looks like Sydney Wheeler has been discharged. But Michael is in room C-343."

Tas looked around for any sign pointing her in the right direction.

"The elevators are down that wing," the receptionist said, gesturing around her desk. "Third floor and to the left."

The elevator's call button glowed with a soft shade of green. She had always judged others who'd press the buttons multiple times, whether at an elevator or crosswalk, and never understood the pointless urgency until then. The tapping of her foot patted like a metronome until the elevator arrived with its cheerful ding. She rushed to the doors as they opened, unaware she was committing another act she so often judged, standing in front of doors too eager to get in, blocking the others' way out. The elevator finally emptied and closed her inside.

The doors were barely open before she darted into the hall. C-327, C-329, C-331—she raced down the hallway until she had the doorknob of C-343 in her hand.

In a chair next to Mike's bed Sydney sat with her elbows resting on the rails. She jumped at the sight of Tas and ran toward her with open arms.

"Tas!"

Tas wrapped her in a comforting hug and pressed their heads together. "I'm so glad you're okay. How's he doing?"

Sydney opened from the hug to face Mike. He lay there in the bed asleep with a bandage around his head and gauze covering his right cheek. His hands were flat along his sides attached to monitors that beeped and blinked in a rhythm.

"They said he'll be okay. I just can't stand seeing him like this. He's just... why?" She buried her face in her hands. "Why didn't that asshole stop?"

"I'm so sorry," Tas said.

And what could she say? There was nothing that could make everything better, so she held onto the silence for another minute.

"Do you know anything about the other guy? Like was he drinking?"

Sydney answered with an edge. "Of course."

They stood there looking at Mike lying helpless on the bed. Tas knew the next part would be difficult. "Did they give you a breathalyzer, too?"

Sydney looked sharply at her but calmed before she answered. "I was under the limit. We were at Trophy a few hours, plus the pizza. I was fine."

"So what happened?"

"Well, we were heading home like normal." Sydney moved back to the chair and ran her hands through her hair. "Mike and I were chatting about whatever and I turned onto Dawson. We came to the Hillsborough intersection with all the people walking around, and as we were going through, I heard a horn and then crash. The back side of the car spun out from under us.

"The guy hit us around the back passenger door so it's not like he was hit head-on," Sydney said, nodding toward Mike. "But I think the airbags were slow to deploy because of that. They did nothing to keep his head from going through the window.

"Once the cars stopped, people started gathering around with their damn phones. Somebody called 911 before I even realized what happened. I looked over to Mike, and he was leaning against his door and out of the window. He was awake, sort of, but really groggy and out of it. I stayed in the car with him until the cops and everyone showed up."

From the door came a couple of light taps before it clicked open. A nurse walked in and stood at the near side of Mike's bed. She flipped the metallic cover of her charts and scanned the top page. "Hey there. So which one of you is Sydney?"

Sydney stood from the chair. "That's me."

"Hi. I hope you're feeling okay," the nurse said with a warm smile.

"Just shaken up."

"I bet. All things considered, you two were lucky. As for Michael, here, we're still awaiting the MRI results, but it looks like he escaped anything major as well. Tell me, does he have a history of shoulder problems?"

"Yeah, he dislocated it a few times playing basketball."

"Okay. He was complaining of pain and numbness in his arm so we suspect a subluxation of his right shoulder but again, can confirm that when the MRIs come back."

Sydney placed her hand on Mike's shoulder gently and breathed a sigh of relief.

The nurse closed her charts and tucked them under her arm. "In the meantime, you should probably head home and rest up. But do you have any questions you'd like to ask first?"

Sydney shook her head. "Not right now. Thanks."

"Well, yeah, in that case, go on home and rest."

The nurse left the room and Tas grabbed Sydney's hand. "Come on. I'll drop you off at your place. You can get some sleep and wait there until they release him."

Sydney leaned over the bed rail and kissed Mike's forehead. "Rest up, big guy."

Outside, the rain continued its onslaught as they drove to Sydney's apartment. Hailstones that sounded as large as fists smashed onto the roof of the car while its wipers fought with futile results against the downpour. Tas drove at a crawl, hunched over the wheel with her eyes glued to the blinking hazard lights of the car in front of her. The entire highway flashed like fireflies creeping through the darkness.

"I hope my insurance will cover a rental." Sydney spoke in a droning, flat tone with her head against the window. "No idea how long our car will be in the shop."

"They would have to, I'd think," Tas said. "It's not like it was your fault."

"I feel like it was though." Sydney laid her head back against the seat and closed her eyes.

The rest of the white-knuckle drive was in silence. By the time they arrived in the parking lot, Sydney was fast asleep.

"Hey, we're home," Tas said gently.

When they reached the apartment, Sydney dropped her jacket to the floor and kicked off her shoes. Without the adrenaline and chaos of the morning, she seemed exhausted, laboring with every step toward the couch. Sad whimpers of soreness escaped her as she collapsed onto the plush, cloud-like cushions. She wrapped herself in a large brown blanket and immediately drifted off to sleep.

In a room decorated with photos showing Sydney's excitement and life, Tas couldn't help but think how empty she looked on the couch.

Photos of Sydney and Mike basking in the sun at the beach and bundled up in the snowy mountains stuck to their fridge with North Carolina magnets. Framed on the wall was a picture from the day they moved in, arm in arm in front of their door. Mike dangled the keys between them while Sydney stretched onto her tiptoes to give him a kiss on the cheek. Their pictures captured so much warmth in an apartment that suddenly felt more like a cold vacuum than a loving home.

"You gonna be okay? Do you want me to stay?" Tas asked.

There wasn't much of a reply. Sydney tossed under the blanket and mumbled a response that sounded dismissive.

"Well, I'll keep my phone on me, so if you need anything you let me know, okay?"

That time there was no mumbling. Sydney was out.

Tas checked her phone. Dean had yet to read, much less reply, to her text, but more alarming was the time; it was almost lunch. Sam's voice was already playing in her head.

I figured you'd have taken the full day at this point.

The museum needed her more than Sydney did that afternoon, but the acidic weight of guilt still sat in her stomach as she stepped back out into the storm to leave.

. • • • .

The car's radio droned on about some furniture store clearance sale when Mike had heard enough. He stabbed his finger at the power button and huffed back into his seat.

"What's with you?" Sydney asked, keeping her focus on the road.

Mike scrolled through his phone, not to pay attention but to fidget. "I swear I always pay when we go out," he said, continuing to scroll.

"Wait, really? That's what has you in a mood?"

"Yes, really." Mike looked over. "I swear, like eighty percent of the time I pay even if it was your idea to go out."

Sydney wrapped her hands around the steering wheel with irritation, the color draining from her knuckles. "How many times have I told you I'm happy to pay? You never let me."

"Yeah because I don't want you telling your friends I'm some broke-ass mooch or something."

Sydney laughed but there was no humor in it. Only disbelief. "I literally can't win with you then."

"No. What I meant is that you don't even offer to pay. You expect—"

A car horn blared to steal his attention and drop his stomach. Everything happened in mere seconds. There was the horn and screeching brakes, the skidding on the road salt, and the heart-stopping impact.

His body jerked from side to side as he screamed. Shattering glass, burning rubber, and a deafening explosion. Mike caught a quick glimpse of Sydney before his head was thrown into his window and his world fell quiet and black.

The city crept back into view, first in flashes then in a blurred, distant fog. The distorted ringing in his ears reminded him of every fire drill when he'd walk down a hall below a shrieking alarm. The sound reverberated through his head with a pounding pressure.

He noticed the scorching pain burning through his shoulder next.

Against his body's painful protest, Mike lifted his head from the shattered window, sending shards of glass around him, and slumped back against his seat. Pain radiated throughout his entire body followed by crippling waves of tension. His mind wandered through the chaos before it settled on a faintly familiar odor, something like gunpowder.

Mike leaned over against the door and caught his reflection in the side-view mirror. Blood streaked over his face, painting it in layers of drying brown and fresh crimson. The streams ran from his head, maneuvering around the shards of glass that dug into him, before dripping down his neck and pooling above his clavicle.

The windshield was cracked and spidered. Its web distorted the alien crowd in front of the car—a swaying group of shadows illuminated by the blue tint of their phones.

Blood and dust clumped together to cover his arm in a sticky, graying muck. He stared into it unaware he was working a shard in his cheek back and forth until it slid out with a slight tug. The piece looked like a bloodred mosaic tile. He flicked it out of the broken window where it disappeared into the soundless night.

A hand grabbed onto his left shoulder, shocking his system back to reality. Like he had removed a pair of headphones, all the chaos rushed and consumed him.

Welcome back to reality.

"Mike! Oh my God. Can you hear me?"

Sydney's eyes were wide and glassy revealing helpless terror behind them. She clenched his shoulder and knee as if pulling him from his semiconscious state.

"Mike, say something," she begged.

His voice strained the only question he could think to ask. "What happened?"

With a sigh of relief, her head dropped. When their eyes met again, the terror in hers had been replaced with concern. "We were in an accident. Do you know my name or what day it is?"

Mike's head dropped.

"Mike. Hey! I need you to stay with me."

The dryness in his throat burned as he answered. "You're Syd. And yeah, it's Sunday."

The dark of the night began to flash with the red and blue lights of the speeding paramedics and police. Their sirens overpowered everything around them.

"What's happening?"

"We were in an accident," she said. "Some guy hit us. Do you know where we are?"

He lifted his head, again with screaming protest. A few of the little shops and buildings looked familiar before his eyes focused on the nearby street sign.

"Hillsborough. We're near the park."

The ambulance parked close by and the police cars surrounded the crash. While a few officers worked to push the crowd back to a safe distance, two others approached the car with their flashlights. They swept their lights over the scene assessing the situation as they approached. He could see them already putting together a mental image of how everything played out. An officer stood at his door and his light beamed into the window and across his face.

Everything washed away from his view. He could only see white.

"Follow my light," a man said in an even, calm tone.

A clean-shaven doctor sat at his bedside waving a penlight in front of him. The raging sirens had been replaced by the pneumatic sounds of medical equipment. The bright lights pushed the nighttime of his memory away and shifted the room into focus.

"There we go. Much better," the doctor said, clicking off his light. "I'm Dr. Rhiner. Do you know where you are?"

There was a coldness to the room. The bed ran parallel along the windowed wall, but with its blinds drawn, he wasn't sure of the time of day. His head throbbed. Each pulse shot splitting pain to his temples. Aches and soreness riddled him all over, but it was something else that worried him most.

"Where's Syd?"

"She's all right. She was released and taken home earlier," the doctor said.

Mike rushed to sit up, oblivious to the pain it caused. "What do you mean? She's not here?" The concern that had tightened in his chest deflated to disappointment.

How could she not be here?

"Don't worry. She's fine," said Dr. Rhiner. "We told her that going home and resting was best while we awaited your test results. Do you remember what happened?"

How could he not? The pain, the shock, the blood—of course he knew.

"We were in a car accident."

"Yeah and luckily, it looks like you avoided anything major."

The news didn't make him feel lucky.

"Your MRIs show a subluxation of your right shoulder. It looks like you've had some problems with this before?"

"Yeah. I dislocated it a couple of times in college."

"Okay. Well, this shouldn't be as rough as it was then. We can prescribe you some medication for the pain and look into some physical therapy as well."

Mike was too distracted to give much thought about the diagnoses. "Yeah, that's fine. But did Syd say when she was coming back?"

"I'm sorry, I don't know. Maybe she told one of the nurses."

"Can I have my phone?" Mike asked.

Dr. Rhiner grabbed it from the table along the wall and handed it to him. "We'd like to keep you here a little longer. After that, you should be fine to go home and rest. Someone will be in again soon to check on how you're doing."

He returned his chair to the table. "Is there anything else I can do or answer for you?"

Mike didn't lift his eyes from his phone. "No, thanks."

"All right. Well, somebody will be in shortly to check on you and get you on your way."

Mike waited for him to leave before calling Sydney.

Voicemail.

He tried again, and again the automated voicemail message played. They would rarely call each other, and it was rarer when there was no answer. He'd have to settle for a text.

"Hey. Where are you? I hope you're okay."

He focused on the message, but before its status changed to read, a flash of pain darted behind his eyes. It was his body telling him it needed to rest. He slid the phone under his pillow and eased himself back down.

Behind his eyes were the flashing images of shattered glass and the blood that covered him. They had kept him on the edge of sleep, teasing him with its mercy only to stir him awake again. Each time the memories had pulled him from rest, he'd shift in the creaking bed and check his phone. And each time he found no reply.

Where is she?

Darkness rolled into the back of his mind like vultures circling his growing doubt and sense of abandonment. He tried shrugging it away, but with every passing check of his phone, the uncertainty grew.

He imagined Sydney walking through the door and greeting him with a loving smile. She would bring a sense of strength and assurance in a time he needed it most. But the black outstretched wings of his vultures dimmed his optimism as insecurity festered.

There was a sense of terror in the inevitable. He could only keep the winged scavengers at bay so long before reality set in and they would attack.

And their wait wasn't long.

A soft knock on the door jolted him awake.

"Sydney?"

Mike's heart sank when a nurse walked in with a pleasant smile but not the smile he'd been wishing for.

"Looks like you're all ready to go," the nurse said. "Let's get you out of here."

As the nurse helped to collect his things, Mike sent another text to Sydney.

"They're releasing me. Do you have the car? I need a ride."

The sense of unraveling continued and his vultures relished in his fading hope.

At reception, Mike completed the final paperwork before being led to the lobby. There he sat in a room full of people waiting to get in while he was waiting with a growing disdain to get out.

As a last-ditch effort, he texted Tas. "Hey. Is Syd with you?"

His doubt coiled around him as he awaited a text he didn't expect to receive. He was embarrassed, infuriated; he was alone. The reality of the accident settled in as though every bruise and gash raged at once.

Where was everyone when he needed them?

He pulled up his apps and hailed himself an Uber—the fail-safe. If his friends wouldn't be there for him, at least some stranger would be. And if he was lucky, and that was a big if, maybe the driver would offer him the sympathetic words he needed to hear.

Mike stepped out into the parking lot, his head low and shoulders slouched, where the vultures could finally feast on any hope that clung to its last breath.

The ride home provided Mike time to stew in anger. He took long, steady breaths and clenched his hands to mask a rage that burned as indiscriminately as wildfires. Their apartment—his apartment—came into view, and his muscles tensed as if he feared what was inside.

But he was the one to be feared.

When Mike slammed the front door, Sydney shot out of her sleep and up from the couch. He moved straight to the kitchen for a beer then to his chair. His eyes were tight and focused as he popped the cap from the bottle with the edge of the coffee table. "So, I just had to Uber here from the hospital."

The tension was already icy and growing colder every moment.

"Baby, I'm so sorry," Sydney said. "How are you feeling?"

"Medically, fine, I guess. Personally, pretty pissed off. I woke up in the hospital and nobody was there. And I had to Uber home because nobody was answering their damn phones."

"Tas dropped me off this morning and I've been here since." Sydney searched around but couldn't find her phone nearby. "I guess I've been out the whole time. I didn't hear you call."

Mike called Sydney and the soft ringing of her phone came from near the front door. "There it is," he said, hanging up from the call.

Sydney ran to her jacket to grab it. "I'm so sorry! I didn't hear it."

She returned to the couch and her eyes scanned over the bandages and cuts that would probably become scars. "The nurse suggested I go and Tas was there to bring me home. I'm sorry I wasn't there. Uber would have been our best bet anyway though until we get a rental."

"That doesn't matter. I woke up in the hospital and you weren't there. I don't exactly remember what all even happened, but when I needed you, you were here sleeping."

He took another big drink from the bottle, already half-finished, and slammed it down on the glass tabletop. It's a wonder the bottle or table or both didn't shatter. Jaw tight, he glared at her. As usual, it didn't matter that Sydney was also quite sore and tired from the accident or that she'd accidentally left her phone in her jacket before she dropped off to sleep. All that mattered was that once again, he wanted to be right at any cost—even if it meant hurting her.

"You let me down, Syd."

She sighed with exhaustion. "I know."

Sydney reached for his hand, but Mike pulled it away. She recoiled back onto the couch. "Can I do anything for you?"

"You mean other than fix my goddamn shoulder? No, I think you've done enough."

"Mike, I'm sorry." Her hands trembled, and she looked at him with sorrowful eyes. "I want to make this okay. You're right. I should have been there."

He choked back another angry response and finished his beer in a final gulp instead. It was tough being so pissed when she was so apologetic. But he wanted her to feel sorry. Sorry enough that her remorse would justify his rage.

The silence between them hung as he cracked into another beer.

Sydney cleared her throat, but her voice still sounded frail. "So what did the doctors say?"

"Well, my shoulder's fucked up again, and I think my ribs are bruised. So yeah, good old-fashioned pain meds and rest."

"Should you be drinking if you're on medication?"

He took another drink but never took his eyes from her. "They said to rest, and this is how I'm choosing to do that. Had you let me rest last night and not make me go out, we could have avoided all of this. It was your idea to go out. You were driving. The least you could have done was be there in the fucking room when I woke up to apologize."

"You're right." Sydney shook her head, dismissed her gut response that would have surely escalated the argument, and whispered again. "You're right."

She stood from the couch and took short, apprehensive steps toward the bedroom. "I'm sorry," she said. And she closed the door behind her all but a crack.

Mike finished another bottle and chucked it onto the table.

Good. I feel more rested already.

The furious storm had emptied him. It ripped through his body and left behind only the rubble of his original hurt. But that was what he did. The anger would flash in a violent and bright explosion leaving behind more damage than it had repaired.

It wasn't long before his exhaustion pulled him to the couch and down onto the pillow. His eyes fell shut and again, he saw the vultures circling overhead. They were always there drifting in the wake that trailed each explosion.

He rubbed his eyes until the vultures were gone and only endless black enveloped him. Then he was out—yet another victim of his storms.

- 5 -
THE LETTER

The rain had barely relented by the time Tas made it home from Sydney's. The remaining drizzle was refreshing on her head where a headache tightened. She locked her front door behind her even though it was midday and the neighborhood had few issues with crime. Some old habits never died.

Another habit was her reliance on leftovers. It was difficult cooking for one, so instead, she often did so for four. Bringing the leftovers to work saved her a few bucks and from awkward lunches with coworkers.

Every day around noon, someone would tap on her door. "Hey, Tas. We're all heading out to China King. Want to join?"

"No, thanks." Then, with a small justified smile, she'd add, "I packed today."

Tas preheated the oven and slid the Pyrex of salmon pasta to the middle of the rack. While lunch was baking, she went to shower and freshen up for the day.

The water heater in her place always took a minute to kick into gear. She reached for the ibuprofen again and rubbed her temples. Despite her days being so routine-driven, she liked to consider herself flexible. Her late start would force her to work that evening and make up the time. But there was comfort in knowing she did the right thing. She was there when Sydney needed her.

After a minute, the shower was ready and so was she.

Showering was her favorite time to zone out and think. As she splashed the hot water over her face, the tension behind her eyes loosened and her mind drifted. Sometimes it would wander to nothing in particular, but that day, she considered her small circle of friends and her sense of loyalty to them. Their problems, their achievements were all greater than hers. She strove to be their biggest fan.

When she stepped out of the shower, she ran her hands across the steamed mirror—squeaky clean. She examined her reflection. The bags beneath her eyes had sunk deeper over the years and her laugh lines were beginning to look like the price she had to pay for her twenties. Some days she thought she wore her thirties well, but today wasn't one of them.

Her attention soon moved to the world outside an upstairs window. The trees had yet to flourish, and the storm had cast everything in dingy and damp shades. Rainwater weighed the grass down and puddles merged into tiny ponds. She imagined summer restoring the yard's beauty full of colors and children playing soccer while their parents grilled.

The oven's timer pulled her from her daydream. She grabbed her lunch and put the morning behind her knowing she did what she believed was right. Only Sam and their inevitable exchange loomed before her. She stepped outside, locked her door, and drove to the museum.

If you weren't looking for it, you'd surely walk right by the history museum and never know. At first glance, its towering blocky columns and nondescript gray stone looked less like a museum and more like a generic government building. But to settle any doubts of passersby, above the front stairs, the large stone façade was engraved with the words North Carolina Museum of History.

Once the museum's glass doors shut behind her the world outside fell quiet. Even if the street swelled with rush hour commuters, the commotion and pace of that world was kept at bay once inside. The lobby was quiet and still, with a warm low light that welcomed her. Tas loved watching the city from inside and the contrast of the peace around her and the bustling chaos just beyond the doors.

The tapping of her shoes followed her across the lobby where she scanned her badge to enter the administrative wing. The hall was less inviting despite the tall windows that ran along the side opposite all the offices.

Sam was packing up his laptop as she walked by.

"Ms. Fredericks. Glad to see you made it in."

The fact he almost sounded genuine threw her off. "Thanks. Sorry again for the hassle. I hated missing the kids' tour. You know I love those."

"I know but Erica covered for you." The concern he'd expressed a moment ago now sounded resentful. He swung his bag across his shoulder and checked his phone. "Well, I have to get running,"

"All right. Sorry again. Have a good day." She raised her hand in a half wave and walked back toward the storage area.

"Oh, one last thing," Sam continued as he locked his door. "Erica covered for you today, but I know she'd jump to fill your shoes longer if need be. Try not to put me in that position, yeah?"

The shivers of disdain tinged the back of her neck. Tas loathed when he'd ask a question with the answer he wanted to hear. "Yeah... yes."

They turned their separate ways and she replayed his threat in her head, dissecting its tone and message. Her body flushed at the fear of being fired. How could he make her feel so wrong about something she believed was right?

People have lives outside of work.

Once to the storage room, Tas swiped her badge and laid her things on the small table by the door. It's not that the room was remarkably large, but it had a way of making her feel small. Towering shelves lined the walls with an assortment of items. It seemed each holiday's decorations had their own section. The boxes of Christmas lights sat next to the Halloween props she would help set out every year.

Each October, she'd host the Spooktacular Trick 'r Treat event. Kids would come dressed up to enjoy an after-hours tour of the museum. She'd dim the lights and give the cleaning staff the night off. Nothing said haunted, spooky museum like paper-thin layers of dust. Ghosts and goblins walked around while most displays had volunteers handing out candy. Blame it on the increasing paranoia in the community, but parents had been very receptive to a safe evening inside of a history museum rather than letting their children run the streets unsupervised.

When Tas checked her phone, there was still no response from Dean. Not hearing from him for a few hours was never uncommon, but a whole day certainly was. After sending him an update and replying to Mike, she silenced her phone. She needed to focus.

Tas walked across the concrete floor toward the pallets. Her shadow shrunk and grew as she crossed the room, the center of which was bright, fading out toward the walls. From the large shipment that stood almost as tall as her, she grabbed a sturdy box to begin. She set it on a long bench on the far side of the room and carefully placed its lid to the side keeping it aligned with its box. In her defense, she considered her attention respectful and caring, but she knew her desk was just as organized and balanced.

Everything had its place.

The box had been neatly packed, filled with layers of Bubble Wrap and packing peanuts. The first item was labeled as a canteen from the Village Deep Gold Mine in South Africa. Three years as the curator, hundreds of exhibits and shipments, and she still marveled when holding history. Her imagination drifted to the expanses of sand, the loads of equipment, and the laboring men wiping the sweat from their foreheads and massaging out the pain from their backs. She could almost smell the rust and steel of the equipment. There was a fascination behind each piece and the story it carried.

Tas's sense of wonderment never faded.

The chips and dents that decorated most of the collection were riddled with history, one she could feel. The room was quiet and her mind wandered as she opened a small crate of railroad spikes. She thought of the time when the trains they enabled were revolutionary.

What were those days like?

After the first box was emptied and verified, she began moving the items to the empty shelves—their next stop on the journey to the exhibit. She grabbed the railroad spikes, six in all, and carried them in cupped hands. A weird sensation tickled across her hand and inched its way to her wrist. She stopped immediately and flung her hands outward, dropping the spikes to her feet, but the momentum hadn't shaken the spider from her arm. Its long legs seemed to wrap around her wrist. She jerked her arm again and slapped the grayish brown spider with her free hand.

When she knocked it to the floor, it mechanically moved its crab-like legs toward the shelves. She stomped at the ground, missing the first time but connecting the next with a gut-curling splat. The spider's body exploded beneath her shoe. Its legs stretched out from beneath her foot like the Wicked Witch of the West. They jerked as the brain's nerves fired off its final futile attempts of escape. Tas caught her breath and wiped her shoe along the cement watching the trail of remains that followed.

Goose bumps covered her arms as her body crawled with imagined creatures. It took several minutes to shake free of the jitters.

"What the hell?" She ran her hands along her legs a few more times to rid herself of the creepy crawling sensation before returning to the bench. When she did, the emptied box was crawling with a few more spiders. She hurried to shut the lid but stood in shock. Like a pregnant woman's belly that moved as the child inside kicked, the packing peanuts were bending and shifting as more spiders crawled their way around. The terror entranced her. When she came to, Tas threw the lid into place and ran it over to the large garage door. She smashed the button to lift the door, and when it opened enough for the box to fit, she kicked it out into the cold air.

With the door shut, she leaned her back against the wall. The imagined crawling of more spiders tickled over her still. Their long prickly legs had crawled into her mind. She felt covered inside and out.

Tas rushed out of the room.

The restroom door swung open and the motion lights flickered to life. She ran the water as cold as it would go while splashing her face and neck. If only she could wash the feeling from her mind as well. She grabbed a handful of paper towels and buried her face. How did she not notice the spiders earlier? Was she bitten? Were they venomous? She couldn't shake the image from her mind—the packing supplies moving like calm waves hiding the turbulence and terror underneath.

But how they got there and how she hadn't noticed no longer mattered. They were gone and with any luck, the cold would do them in. She had lost enough time already and, creeped out or not, she had to continue her work.

A few hours later, she came to the final box which looked to be no bigger than a traditional box of paper reams. She checked her inventory list and only a couple of small items remained. After confirming the final pieces and storing them on their shelves, it seemed everything was coming together. Tas was ecstatic when she bid on and won the exhibit. Seeing it in person filled her with pride, a sense of accomplishment.

Once she organized the empty boxes and moved them out of the way, she clicked off the lights and went back to her office.

On her desk sat a package: a brown padded envelope with her name handwritten in a heavy black marker. Not the most common packaging she received at the museum.

The glue beneath the flap ripped as she slid her letter opener underneath. From inside, she pulled out an aged notebook, dried and weather worn. Across its cover in a handwritten script, "Kolmanskop."

The name was familiar. Quite a few pieces in the show were taken from the mining town, but as she scanned her inventory list, the notebook was not included. Was it simply forgotten or was it not meant for the exhibit? Why had she received the piece separately?

She shook the package and out fell a folded note.

Dear Ms. Fredericks,

My name is Jon Martin, a tour guide here at Deutsches Historisches Museum in Berlin. Our museum recently carried the same African mining practices exhibit that I have seen will be on display soon in your location.

I have mailed you a journal written by my grandfather, Heinrich Engel, who worked at the largest mine of the era, Kolmanskop. We were unable to add it to the show here, but I send it to you in hopes it can find a place in your exhibit to tell my grandfather's story.

I am happy to help and assist with anything further. Email me anytime.

Thank you.

Tas wasn't sure what to make of the letter or the journal, but they were nonetheless intriguing. With a gentle touch and great care, she eased the journal open. The paper cracked like the movement had awakened it. The pages at one time bore lines that had since faded and became almost indistinguishable with creases and cracks.

To her disappointment, the pages were written in German. She could make out a few words, but it had been years since her two language semesters in school. The date at the top of the page aged it at just about a century, 1921. She didn't understand why German was used in Namibia, so she turned to the web for research.

Recent articles touted Kolmanskop as a remote ghost town and photographer's dream and from the pictures, they weren't exaggerating. But Tas wasn't interested in the present-day town. She wanted to know about its past. She wanted to know about the journal.

With a little digging, she learned Kolmanskop was a small diamond-mining village in the southwestern region of Namibia. Shortly after the initial discovery of diamonds, Germany rushed to claim much of the land in the region and sent along laborers to examine it further. The prospect of the desolate area containing value drew skepticism, but the lifeless desert offered unbelievable riches. Reports were sent of men walking along and picking loose diamonds up from the sand, more than they could have ever imagined. With that, the town became a magnet of wealth, technology, and those trying to cash in.

Tas was hooked. Her heart raced with excitement and intrigue, which grew with every article she read and photo of the abandoned, sand-filled buildings she saw. But she needed to go home before she became so distracted she'd be forced to sleep in her office.

Though she didn't expect much sleep.

When her spirit stirred, her mind didn't rest. She'd spend the night stuck in bed with a wild imagination running through Kolmanskop.

- 6 -
THE NIGHTMARE

Dean left his window cracked open to let in the sounds of the early birds singing. The first rays of morning sun warmed the sky, signaling the end of his tumultuous night where he rolled around all night battling endless waves of anxiety. The tide would cease allowing him a chance to fall asleep, but the winds would change and he'd wake again with his stomach churning.

His eyes were heavy and his body uneasy. The day that awaited him on the other side of his alarm was not one that encouraged him to lumber out of bed. There was a weakness and depression that seemed beyond his control.

So many mornings he woke up and told himself it would be a good day where he'd put forth a positive effort. But there'd be no lying about effort that morning.

His phone vibrated and chimed a solitary bell. Without checking the text message, he held the power button down until the screen faded to black. Not only did he intend to make no effort that day, he didn't want others around him to do so either. He wanted peaceful, silent solitude.

It had taken time for Dean to accept what it meant to be an introvert. Socializing and being friendly were never the issues, but those interactions wore him down. He recharged in silence. He found his strength when alone. Spending time on his own doing nothing was how he kept his head clear. Not until he had his panic-laced dreams did the attacks begin.

The first dream, while innocent enough, still haunted him. He couldn't breathe and his throat clenched shut. A pressure wrapped around his chest, squeezing his lungs dry. Those thoughts dug their way out from his memory every time he'd turn off the light.

Living in the South, waking up to a snowy morning was only a notch below surprising, but that's exactly how the first dream began. Like any normal day, he had gone out to his car for work but found a smiley face drawn in the couple of inches of snow—one of the neighborhood kids, no doubt. It was a frigid morning, with winds that cut to the bones as he scraped the ice from his windshield.

He missed working from home.

No other headlights lit the road that morning. If the city wasn't shut down from the snow, it would be later when the roads became sheets of ice. As he white-knuckled through a few small neighborhoods, he continued to drive alone as the only blemish in the blistering whiteout.

The blinking of his signal ticked away as he sat at a red light, which whipped around in the gusting winds. That's when he noticed the figure moving along the crosswalk.

The man wore two different beanies, navy and gray, with a long winter jacket on top of a hoodie. He had tucked his baggy sweats into calf-high boots. The scarf wrapped around his neck didn't cover the entirety of his scraggly beard decorated with its fair share of icicles. But what caught his attention was the brown bag he carried.

"You can't drink all day if you don't start in the morning," Dean said to himself.

At that moment, the man stopped and lifted his eyes from the ground. The crosswalk flashed its warnings, but he bore them no mind. A burst of wind pushed him off balance, and once he staggered to his footing, he was facing Dean's headlights—a listless stare through the beams. The light changed and the man's body tinted with its green but he stood braced against the weather.

The man seemed entranced as he knocked back another drink and wiped his mouth on the collar of his jacket. Dean could only watch as he tilted his head toward the ground, the whites of his eyes exploding from his dirtied skin and drab attire. The crystals in his mustache and beard cracked and fell away as a smile, devious and feral, stretched across his face.

Dean clenched the wheel, oblivious to the grip until his hands beat with the pulse of his racing heart. The heat he had blasting seemed to chill as if the outside air was forcing its way through his vents. He was too frozen to blink, and he watched as the man took his first lumbering step forward. The man's smile seemed inhuman. His eyes looked furious and alive. And Dean could do nothing but watch.

The man's legs churned as they carried him through the swirling snow closer and closer. Dean shook himself free of the frost and clenched his eyes as tightly as he could. "Go away. Go away. Go away," he repeated, to himself, willing the moment to end. The wind whirled to a voracious pitch, shaking his car with a furious ease. A crack screeched its way across his windshield, menacing and methodical, before his body constricted at the sound of it shattering.

Dean crashed awake, landing on his hands and knees on the bedroom floor. His burning lungs gasped for air. Goose bumps rose along his arms and down to his fingers, which dug into the carpet to keep the world from spinning. That wasn't a mere lucid dream. It was something deeper. Darker. It felt real.

When his head stopped spinning, the pounding began. He moved back to bed, massaging his fingers along his temples. There would be no more sleep that night. The pressure and chills of something that awoke inside of him would keep him from rest. He could only shake so much of the dream aside. Some pieces stuck in his mind like the tiny shards of his windshield.

When he walked to his car that morning, the cuts dug deeper. On its hood was the childishly drawn smiley face waiting for him all over again.

There were no warm feelings of children playing that time, only foreboding dread. As he sat alone at the red light once again, he awaited the break within the white out. Without fail but not without apprehension, the man in layers staggered against the storm.

Dean tapped his fingers on his wheel. "Don't stop. Don't stop." Yet despite his wishes, the man stopped and braced against the wind. It was his dream all over again, but there would be no waking up. Their eyes met and the man's crooked smile made Dean's heart flurry with fear.

But as the light changed to green, the man turned back across the road. It took a moment for Dean to thaw from the terror and creep onto the highway. His body trembled and his mind ached.

He'd never forget that dream or the day it became more than one. That was the start of his panic attacks, his anxiety, everything. He struggled to think of the cause. Why then? After all the years, why start then? There were no traumatic triggers. No underlying stress erupting inside of him. He went to sleep like any other night and awoke never to be the same.

It had been a couple of years since his first attack, but as Dean lay in bed that morning, dwelling over the night before at Trophy and his latest dream to come to life, he was thankful he had found Dr. Vauras. It was at her recommendation that he document the dreams that woke him up in a sweaty panic. Writing the notes down gave him focus when he was thrown awake, short of breath and nauseous. It also gave him a sense of control as the writing became therapeutic and the extremes of his attacks lessened.

He remained in bed, too tired to eat yet too anxious to fall back asleep. With his eyes closed, the wind whipped through the trees until their thrashing leaves sounded like the rain that would soon follow. The thunder broke and rolled in from the distance and the morning light shrank behind the darkness of the clouds. The chaos outside brought a calm to the dark seclusion of his room. But at some point, he'd need to freshen up. He didn't want to go see Dr. Vauras looking as terrible as he felt.

After a quick shower, he made himself a sandwich as a late lunch. From the kitchen, he looked through the open floor plan of the rooms. The space usually inspired comfort in its cleanliness and balance, but his solitude painted it in a different light that day.

"I'm wasting my money," he said. "I don't need half this space."

He was right. His quality of life wasn't tied to the mass square footage of his apartment. There was no need for the large living room with a full couch, love seat, and monster TV. What good was a master bedroom with cathedral ceilings if he spent his nights on the floor in cold sweats? A bathroom with two sinks and a walk-in closet—what was the point? The apartment didn't make him happier or have more friends. There he was, eating a sandwich on his own no different from when he was a teenager. The whole place suddenly became cavernous and cold.

Nothing made him feel more alone than being in need.

Dean wanted to simplify his apartment, his belongings, stress, and anxiety. He wanted to simplify his life. But he'd fight that battle another day. Making a mental note to look for some potential places online after his appointment, he threw his plate into the sink, washed his hands, and headed to the door.

Fifteen minutes later, he was pulling into the modern business park. In addition to all the luxury apartments, new business centers were also sprouting up all throughout the city. Dean made his way toward a tall, dark-glassed building that could have been mistaken for any other. For being such a liberal and technology-driven area, the city planning and architecture remained uninspiring and safe.

Dr. Vauras's practice was on the fourth floor and when he entered, her secretary, Hanna, greeted him. "Hey there, Dean," she said, with a warm smile. She carried an energy that would never make him think it was near the end of a long day.

"How have you been?" she asked.

That was such a leading question considering where they were.

"I'm good. Just coming by for my appointment."

"Of course," she said. "Grab a seat and I'll let Dr. Vauras know you've arrived. Could I get you anything?"

"Water would be great, please," he said, taking a seat.

The waiting room was empty and quiet with only the slight tin of Hanna's laptop speakers filling the air. Despite the sleek appearance on the outside of the building, the office inside was rather traditional and cozy. Small tables decorated mostly with colorful flowers accented the dark gray walls. Hanna's desk housed a couple of small plants and an assortment of lit candles giving the room a soft ambience. A small bulletin board advertised various social groups and brochures covering a range of topics from social anxiety to parenthood stress.

Hanna approached and handed Dean a bottle of water. She gave another smile and made her way back to her desk. He glanced around the room while the sound of papers shuffling and nails clacking on the keyboard told him she'd returned her attention to her work.

The magazines were the same subscriptions as before when he would have weekly appointments—just newer issues.

The covers made bold claims of quick life fixes. "Ten Ways to Empower Your Morning" and "Know Yourself Five Minutes at a Time." The headlines promised quick fixes to problems that had likely been ingrained over years. They read better than realistic alternatives though.

The heavy wooden door across the room opened with an aged squeal. Dean looked up to see Dr. Vauras emerge with a few papers in her hands. She dropped them off with Hanna before directing her attention to him. "Dean, it's wonderful to see you again."

When they shook hands, she covered his with her left. "Come on in and get comfortable," she said. "Let's see what's been going on."

They walked into her office and she shut the door behind them.

Dean walked alongside the wall-length bookcase littered with hardbacks organized by title and topic. He sank into the overstuffed chair and stared beyond Dr. Vauras's desk at her degrees with a renewed surprise that she had earned her PhD in 2003. As she sat in the chair facing him, he thought her short light hair added to her youthful style and energy. She didn't have the personality he would have associated with psychiatrists. But that was sort of their thing. Psychiatrists needed to be chameleons to form trusting bonds with their clients.

"I'm sorry for texting like I did last night," he started, shifting in the chair.

"I'm glad you did." She leaned back pressing her hands together at their fingertips. "So what's going on?"

"It happened again." He fumbled with his bottle of water before taking a sip.

"What did? Another dream? Tell me what happened."

Dean curled one leg under the other and replayed the previous night for her. He explained the events in detail ending with the man asking for bus fare. "I rushed home when he asked for it. I was already panicking."

"And when was it that you originally had the dream?" She kept her tone soft and genuine, inquisitive not interrogating.

"October of last year."

"What about that day comes to mind?"

"Nothing other than the dream." His fingers mindlessly tapped on the water bottle.

Dr. Vauras switched her crossed legs and shifted in her chair. "Have you experienced any other dreams since we last met?"

Dean's eyes jerked about before he answered, "Ummm, one, yeah."

"Care to tell me about it?" Again, she kept her fingertips together and narrowed her eyes.

"Well, the dream took place at work. I only remember being in a meeting in a specific room and then hearing some song I didn't know," he said. "Then one day at work, a meeting was moved to that same room at the last minute. A few minutes into it, one guy's cell phone rang, and it was that same song."

"Had you heard that song before? In your dream, could you hear the lyrics?"

"I must have somewhere, but no, I don't know the song." He twisted the bottle's cap off and on again and again. "But when I heard it, I recognized it."

"How did you react to that happening?"

Dean picked at the wrapping on the bottle. "I went to the restroom to rinse my face for a bit and tried to relax. But it wasn't as intense as last night or else I would have had to go home right away."

"So you washed up and tried to calm down. Did that help?"

"I guess, a little. I ended up leaving though 'cause I wasn't able to focus anymore."

"Okay." Dr. Vauras paused and looked upward. "Then things settled down again until last night. What do you think made last night so intense?"

"I have no idea. Maybe because everyone was involved. It wasn't just me, you know? Like it's one thing for my dreams to involve only me, but what if they could affect others, too?"

She tapped her middle finger and thumb together, working through a thought before returning her eyes to his. "Dean, do you believe these dreams foreshadow events, or do they create the events?"

His hands came to rest on the bottle and he paused. "I don't think I follow."

"Well, for example, do you believe your coworker's phone was going to ring before you had the dream? Or do you think it rang *because* you had the dream?"

"I've never considered it like that. I have no idea."

The silence in the room returned. Dr. Vauras waited patiently while he gave the question more thought.

"Like predetermination, you mean?" Dean began following the thread. He didn't believe a person's life was set, but could his dreams challenge that view?

She took the idea further. "If you believe in it, then that would answer the question. Your coworker's phone was going to ring whether you dreamt it or not. But what if it wasn't meant to?" She sat forward, resting her elbows on her legs. "What if you dreamt that event into existence? It hadn't happened yet. It wasn't supposed to happen, and nothing was set. Then you dreamt it and that set the wheels in motion."

"So whatever I would have dreamt, that's what would have happened?" He continued picking at the bottle's wrapper, uncertain about the conversation.

"That's possible. Or if you believe in predetermination, then it wouldn't have mattered. That phone was going to ring, regardless." She paused again and rubbed her chin. "But let's pretend we know predetermination doesn't exist. If you dreamt that event into existence, what if that meant you could change your dreams prior to their fulfillment?"

"What do you mean change it? If it happens, it happens." Dean's tone hardened.

Dr. Vauras remained controlled. "Think about the meeting and your coworker's phone. Had you thought about that dream when entering the room, you could have suggested that everybody ensure their phones were off. The phone would have rung but no ringtone would have played. By remembering pieces of the dreams and writing them down that could give you a heads-up on that possible situation and put you in a position of control."

"That's not how it works." His aggravation ignited at the mere suggestion of altering the dreams. "If these dreams keep coming true"—the wrapper tore from the bottle—"so will the nightmare."

The nightmare.

When Dean had first come to Dr. Vauras to discuss the traumatizing nightmare, tremors shook through his body and his eyes darted around the room. He had fallen silent in that session but couldn't keep the visions from flooding his mind all over again.

"I want this to stop," Dean cried, his eyes clenched shut.

"Dean, it'll be okay. Tell me about the nightmare." Dr. Vauras leaned forward.

He buried his face in his sweaty hands "I had a fucking nightmare. That's what I remember."

"And it affected you differently from the other dreams?"

Lifting his face again, he wiped away a few stray tears. "If all my other dreams are coming true, why not this one, too?"

"We don't know that. We're still learning about this." The calm tone of Dr. Vauras's voice was straining with an underlying urgency. "Can you tell me what happened?"

"I remember seeing Tas."

Everything was dark.

"What was she doing?"

Screaming, hurt, and scared.

Dean fell silent. His mind retreated back into itself as the flashes of the nightmare broke free from the darkest corner that had contained it.

"Were you two together? Where were you at?"

Tas, where are you?

Dean said nothing. He sat up, walked to the window, and stared out at the rain. The storm hung over them seemingly motionless. The thunder rumbled the earth, and the lightning zigzagged through the sky. He felt as far away as the reaches of the clouds.

In a near whisper, barely audible above the winds, he said, "I need to tell her."

What had begun in his subconscious had spread throughout him like a plague. If his dreams foreshadowed predetermined events, no matter how scared he was of his nightmare, nothing would compare to the debilitating terror he'd endure when it came to life. But if his dreams created the events...

"Tell her what, Dean?" Dr. Vauras stood with him, but her focus was on him and not the storm.

The lightning struck and illuminated the room. His face flashed momentarily in the light, and in the window's reflection, it bore a single expression.

Guilt.

"I need to tell her about my nightmare," he said as he hurried out of the room.

Dean raced from the office and out into the lobby. As he threw open the last door and raced down the stairs, he heard the desperate, muffled cry from Dr. Vauras.

"Dean! Let me help!"

Her echoing words were in vain. She couldn't help him. He didn't need it.

Tas did.

- 7 -
THE JOURNAL

"Ms. Fredericks!" Sam clapped his hands, grabbing Tas's attention.

Tas had fallen into her imagination and didn't hear him approach. She had been staring out into the garden behind the museum with eyes atop bags puffier and darker than normal. A night of wind and rain all but promised a deep, restful sleep, but the previous night her mind ran rampant with thoughts of Kolmanskop and the journal. Still, the bright blue skies and their painted clouds rejuvenated her energy.

"Hey. Sorry." She shook her head. "How's it going?"

"Everything all right?" Sam asked. "Where are we with the exhibit?"

"Well, I verified the shipment last night with the manifest. Today, I have to track down some extra content for our marketing and check in on the construction."

She saw no reason to tell him about the journal. Not like he would have cared anyway.

"Good," Sam said. "Keep me updated. I like to know how things are progressing. We need this to be a successful showing."

They didn't need it to be successful; *she* did.

There was a game she had to play, a professional waltz where she had to find her place before taking the lead in rhythm. Before she could expand the museum's offerings, she had to whisk through some of their tired staples. Every spring saw the hosting of the Porsche History of Design exhibit. Car enthusiasts would use the parking lot as an impromptu vintage car show before, and after, visiting. They would compare the curves of the bodies through the decades and debate performance pros and cons. Engineers of hindsight.

While she found the show dull, it was safe, Sam's favorite type.

But not every regular show was drab in her opinion. She was partial to shows that focused on industrial innovations and few did that better than the First in Flight exhibit. North Carolina touted plenty of aviation history and she loved telling those stories. The exhibit was engaging and the interactive displays often entranced the children. There was no connection like touch and she emphasized hands-on learning at every opportunity.

It was when she'd deviate from the tried and true that Sam was most critical, and no other show had put him on edge like the latest. Tas believed she had earned and deserved his trust to branch out given the steady increase in attendance each year she'd been there. However, Sam remained skeptical and was quick to credit the rise to population growth.

Tas couldn't control his opinions or his attitude. She could only control her work. And if she ever wanted to branch out and take the lead again, she needed her latest work to be a big draw.

Every new show came with its share of pressure but she always handled it the same way. She took a pragmatic approach, breaking large events down into small, controllable steps to keep her focus narrow and progress consistent.

Tas sat at her desk, tucked her dark curls behind her ears, and sat her cup of tea to the side. It was time to take her first step.

The journal.

With great care, she opened it and skimmed the first page. The bleached sun spots faded the lines and handwriting. The creases and wear of the pages dated them like the wrinkles of a person of the same age. She was unable read the text herself, so she transcribed the words of the past into a translator. The result wouldn't paint the perfect picture, but glimpses into the past were better than none.

With the first page transcribed, she looked over her laptop into the hallway. What she was doing wasn't secretive, but it carried an aura of mystery and excitement like Dr. Frankenstein before flipping the switch to reanimate his monster. She wanted to be alone and undisturbed.

With the hallway silent and empty, Tas grabbed her tea with both hands, sending its warmth through her arms, and read the century-old words.

. • • • .

The tired springs of his bed creaked as he sat up and swung his legs to the floor. It had taken a few weeks to travel from Germany and his body was still tired as it struggled to adapt to the new environment. His employer warned him of the heat when he accepted the position, but not until that morning when sweat ran down his back did he understand. He could only imagine how hot it would be if the houses weren't so well insulated. The room was a vibrant blue with ornate decorations swirling along the high ceilings. Beautiful golden sunlight brightened the colors to that of a fairy tale that paled greatly compared to the vast emptiness of desert beyond the window.

Back home in Berlin, his wife and daughter were without him. There was money to be made in Kolmanskop, money that could make their lives better when he returned, and money that, he hoped, would make it worth how dearly he missed them.

He walked with heavy feet down the long hall where earlier others had pressed faint footprints into the thin layer of sand covering the wooden floor. In the common area sat a couple of men making breakfast after the daily delivery of milk, cheese, and ice had arrived. Outside the large arching window on the far side of the room, the sand-removal crews swept the streets, an endless and thankless job.

After twenty years of working exhausting factory jobs, he was no stranger to a tough day's work. Yet he knew mining in such conditions would be a significant challenge. If it wasn't, the wages wouldn't have been so attractive.

"Hi. I'm Heinrich from Berlin," he said, reaching out his hand.

Both men looked younger than himself. The stout dark-haired man on the left stood first. "Hi there. I'm Otto. This here's my brother, Fritz. We're from Dresden."

Fritz stood with a lean frame but shook hands with a firm grip.

Heinrich slid out a chair to join them at the table. "How long have you two been here?"

"Fritz and I got here about four months ago. You just got in, right?" Otto appeared quite comfortable speaking for both he and his brother.

"I did. I start today."

"Oi. You've got yourself a busy day. You know to report to the center for your assignment, yeah?"

"Yeah, but where do I go exactly?"

Otto turned in his chair to better orient himself. "You want to walk a bit up that way there toward the train station. It's a few minutes before that. New people will be there to register and receive their assignments. After that it's on to breaking your back."

Fritz nodded in agreement.

"Where are you two assigned?" Heinrich asked.

Otto poured a glass of milk and set it down in front of Heinrich. "So, Fritz and I have been together since getting here. We're both over in the alluvial fields."

Heinrich dabbed his forehead free of sweat. "How do you handle being in the sun every day?"

Fritz pulled a hat from the back of his chair and dropped it on the table before shrugging his shoulders.

Otto laughed. "That's about it right there. There's honestly no handling it. You'll see. Cover up as best you can so you don't get burned to hell."

"Good to know," Heinrich said. "So what's it like here? The town, I mean."

Otto and Fritz nodded together with expressions of approval.

"It's pretty nice outside of the damn heat and wind," Otto said. "We have stuff here that we don't even have back home. They bring in new performers every week down at the entertainment hall. We got bowling and regular concerts. And I'll tell ya, we have the best butcher shop I've ever been to."

The way Otto described it, the town didn't sound half bad. It didn't sound bad at all.

"Not to mention this." Otto stood from his chair and reached toward the wall. He flicked a switch and lights above their table turned on. "We have electricity. Everywhere."

Heinrich watched Otto turn the lights off and on again. "So this town makes as much money as everybody says?"

Otto laughed again and inspired a quiet chuckle from Fritz. "More. Just wait until you see it all." Otto pinched his fingers and thumb together and blew them away with a kiss.

Heinrich finished his drink and stood to look out the window. The town was alive, bustling with activity. He couldn't have been farther from home but he looked out into a little Germany within the desert.

"You best get on your way," Otto said. "Don't want to be the last guy there."

"Yeah. Thanks," Heinrich said, putting his boots on near the door.

"Best of luck."

As he stepped outside, the wind whipped down the road stronger than he had ever felt. He had hoped it would bring a cooling relief but instead it stung his skin with grains of sand like thousands of tiny pinpricks. He shielded his eyes and walked north toward the train station.

It was the contrast that amazed him. Women walked in and out of shops while kids ran along to school and men came to or from work or the pub. It was a small, lavish town but in the middle of isolation and desert. Even his wildest imagination didn't paint the town so grand.

As he neared the primary office, a small group of men gathered around another, dressed too nicely for the heat, standing atop a crate. Heinrich joined the crowd and glanced around at the growing group who looked much like himself, bewildered by their new environment and awaiting direction.

The man standing above the crowd wiped his forehead with a handkerchief and returned it to his pocket before calling for their attention. With his arms raised high above his head, he shouted, "Gather round! Gather round!"

The slight chatter of the men fell silent and their eyes focused on the man in front of them. His presence demanded attention as he stood powerfully with the panorama of Kolmanskop behind him.

"Welcome to Kolmanskop, the richest town on this here planet Earth. I am Helmut Kohler, the supervisor of these mines and on behalf of myself, CDM, I'd like to thank you for your dedication in joining us here." The crowd erupted with applause and cheers.

"I trust you've found we've spared no expense in constructing this great town. I take great pride in our work here and as a result, I run a tight ship. Safety is a top concern and there is no room for endangering behavior. Not on my watch. Follow the rules and we all live rich and prosperous lives."

The crowd cheered again at the prospect. Heinrich thought of returning home after his contract with enough money to retire and spend time with his family. He applauded at the fantasy and fluttered with an energy to get started.

"You will all work hard," Kohler continued. "You will all work tirelessly. But most importantly, you will all work faithfully." He pounded his fist into his palm to emphasize each point. "There will be no theft of diamonds. Everything found here belongs to not only Kolmanskop and me but Deutschland. Stealing from these mines is stealing from our homeland and I will absolutely not tolerate such actions. Not in the slightest!

"In exchange for your efforts, you will have every amenity made available to you. This may be the desert, but as you have undoubtedly noticed, we have fresh water delivered by rail each morning. We create our own ice to combat this godforsaken heat. You will have entertainment, the finest foods, and goods. I may be demanding, but I am fair. Does that sound fair to you?"

Again, the men roared and applauded. A palpable excitement within the crowd as if the world was within their grasps.

Kohler drew their attention one last time. "Now, if you're all ready to get started, and I imagine you are, head inside here and you will be given your assignments and everything else you'll need. I want to thank you all. Now, let's get to work!" He clapped his hands, and the crowd followed suit, applauding his welcome and the opportunity before them.

Heinrich was thankful Kohler directed them to wait inside an insulated building. Standing idly in the sun during his introduction was hot enough.

Inside the administrative building were more colorful walls and quality woodwork and construction. Flags of German South West Africa hung overhead while posters and signage promoted CDM (Consolidated Diamond Mining of South West Africa, Ltd.), which oversaw all the work in Kolmanskop and other mines in the region.

A sharp voice caught his attention. "Next!"

Heinrich approached the counter. "Yes, I'm Heinrich Engel from Berlin." His tall stature forced him to look down at the man behind the counter. He tapped his fingers upon the wood and waited while his record was located.

"Yes, I see you here. You'll be working in the new underground, first shift Monday through Saturday. Your foreman, Walter Lange, may change this as needed but unless otherwise instructed, that will be your expectation." The man slid a paper across the desk. "This form contains the information that you'll need and confirms your assignment. Any questions?"

Heinrich took the paper and glanced over it before folding it into his pocket. "Yes. Do I go there immediately? And can you point me in the direction of the underground?"

The man behind the counter appeared to be as thin as his patience. "Immediately. Yes. And you will find a map on that wall." He sighed and pointed toward a map with a motion he had done hundreds of times before.

"And last thing," the man said, sliding a small chain and pendant across the counter. "This is your tag, number 3341. Keep this on you at all times while working and going about town. The number is tied to your records during your employment."

Heinrich grabbed the chain and hung it around his neck. He looked down at the small, bronze disk engraved with his number and the CDM initials before tucking it inside his shirt. "Thank you."

"Mm-hmm," the man said. "Next!"

Heinrich reviewed the map before stepping out into the growing heat. With energized strides, he walked into the wind toward the mine. A small group of men gathered near its entrance, again, forming a semicircle around one man Heinrich assumed was Walter Lange. When he joined the group, Heinrich introduced himself to the stocky foreman.

"Great to meet you, Mr. Engel," Walter said. "I think we can get started now."

The chatter amongst the men died down, and they all took a step closer, tightening their group.

"Welcome, men. I am Walter Lange, the foreman of the underground mines here." Walter spoke with a rough voice that matched his strong build and hardened face with days' worth of stubble. "Before we get you into the mines, you'll need equipment and a walk-through of our safety rules and operation. So come with me and we'll get going."

The roads that were swept clear of sand earlier that morning were covered again. They walked against the wind toward a long, narrow stone building. Walter allowed the others to enter first then closed the door behind him when he entered.

"Before every shift, you'll punch your cards here and grab your gear. Any equipment you take is associated with your tag number until you return it at the end of each shift. Each man will need a hat, pickax, and pry. Lanterns are provided in the mine itself."

Two men stood behind the long counter. They gathered the gear for each miner and noted their inventory. Every man in the group, fifteen in all, collected their equipment and punched into the clock.

Heinrich felt the weight of each tool in his hands. The pry bar was of solid steel, the smooth coolness of which was welcomed in his sweaty grip. The pickax had a handle of weathered wood but was also of solid construction. Its head appeared to have been smithed with great care. With each tool he held, the reality of what awaited him grew heavier.

"You will return your equipment at the end of each shift after you've clocked out. Questions?"

Walter waited within the silence a few moments before he tipped his hat to the men behind the counter and led the group out of the building.

The wide-eyed men gawked at their new, desolate surroundings as the foreman guided them farther through town. The town's architect had gone to great lengths to construct a luxurious neighborhood that represented the greatest Germany had to offer. But the lavish buildings organized into convenient blocks couldn't fully mask the bleakness of the desert.

"Now, before you all start getting wise, over there is the hospital." Walter never broke stride as he pointed to the towering building. "You'll be accompanied there after each shift for a precautionary X-ray screening. Follow the rules and you won't have to worry about it."

They neared the mouth of the mine and Walter stopped and turned to the men. He placed his fists on his hips and said, "This town offers only the best of everything. The best equipment. The best amenities. And yes, the best workers. My job is to make sure we return that generosity by working hard, safely, and uncovering every last diamond there is down there."

Behind Walter was a constant stream of men pushing and pulling carts through the mine's entrance. During a brief break in the movement, Walter walked the men into the mouth for their final instructions.

"This sheet here is your homework, men. Our code of signals." He pointed to a large poster secured to a wooden beam next to a heavy metal bell with a weighted clapper that extended well below its mouth. "Again, safety is key, but it requires communication. These signals are how you'll communicate in and out of the mine." Pointing toward Heinrich, he said, "Take a look. How many times will the operator signal before sending you all down into the mine?"

Heinrich scanned the poster displaying all the bell combinations each with their own meaning and action. "Three bells, sir."

"Three bells," Walter reiterated. "That means whenever you're down there working and you hear a series of three bells rung, you know a group of miners are being lowered down. And when you've finished your shift and you're coming back up..." Walter trailed off.

"Two bells, sir," Heinrich again answered.

"Two bells will ring to signal that men are being brought out of the mine. You are all required to know these signals as well as your own mother's face."

The lift was nothing more than a waist-high steel box on a track. The front portion latched shut, not particularly safe for somebody as tall as Heinrich or Walter who could still easily lose their balance and teeter over the edge. With a metallic screech, Walter opened the lift, and the men piled on in groups.

"On your way, men. For the darker it gets, the brighter the diamonds will shine. Time to become rich!" Walter slammed the lift shut and latched it closed. He reached for the bell's clapper that dangled near his shoulder and gave it three strong rings.

The lift jolted into motion and Heinrich heard the chimes echoing into the darkness. They descended at the nerve-racking pace of a roller coaster making its initial climb, one clink at a time, down a moderate grade toward the faint light below—a small collection of oil lamps. The heat immediately subsided as the mine's shade and depth provided a cooler temperature. However, the heat was traded for the odor of damp earth and sweat.

They descended deeper into a chorus of men and shattering earth. Each labored grunt was immediately followed by the impact of an ax into rock. Shadows flickered around the walls and as Heinrich reached the bottom, shadows and dirt disguised the men who were there to greet them.

His brighter future started there in the blackest depths of Kolmanskop.

. • • • .

I had never seen diamonds with my own eyes before. I had stopped to marvel at the first few I found. Covered and encrusted in dirt, they were still special to hold. There was a temptation to take them, but as I made my way to the hospital after my shift, I found myself far more worried that one had fallen into a pocket or my boot without my knowing.

My back is now sore and my hands are blistered but my optimism for a better life for my family is even greater. After a year or two in these mines, I can return home and finally give my daughter all she deserves. Though even one year will feel like a lifetime.

Tas clasped her hands behind her head and leaned back in her chair. A sense of satisfaction and wonderment washed over her. The notebook had fed her insatiable curiosity, but how was such an incredible firsthand account of the mine not included in the show in Berlin?

Tools and equipment were one thing; clothes and accessories were another. They all required empathy for the era and work to have an impact. A personal journal, though, could make an immediate connection with any visitor. It was like the difference between a picture of a tree and one with a person standing under it. People would be drawn much more to the photo with the person. Their attention would not only be grabbed but also held for a far deeper experience. The journal could create the connection she always hoped to elicit with each show.

Sam walked by her office with his bag slung over his shoulder, face buried in his phone. She had lost track of time. Most days she would grab her bag and head home, too, but that night she would stay and continue feeding her interest.

The light from her phone caught her attention as she stood to stretch and she switched on the screen to see a text from Dean.

"Hey. Sorry I lost my phone at work. Want to grab a drink?"

Any other night she would. Sam had been feeding her desire to drink, but she relented. "Ha ha typical. Can't tonight, though. I'm working late. Maybe when I finish up." She tossed her phone in her bag—out of sight out of mind.

The lights in the administrative wing dimmed but there was plenty of evening ahead of her. She grabbed an apple from her bag and paced around her office to stretch her legs. There were so many questions that raced through her mind and her thoughts wandered in countless directions. She would email Jon hoping he could clear up much of her uncertainty. In the meantime, she would continue working her way through the journal.

Back at her desk, Tas rubbed her eyes and translated the next entry.

Adjusting to the work and schedule has taken more time than I expected. Otto assures me that I will get used to it, and I suspect that I will, but it's been a challenge so far. I don't know how he and his brother work all day while retaining energy and interest to go to the pub at night. Most of the time, I must confess, I am coming here to my room when they are going out for drinks, but tonight I made an exception and joined them for a couple of rounds. I had hoped a night out with new friends could make me feel less homesick.

. • • • .

Heinrich walked into the dimly lit pub. Raucous chatter spread throughout the smoke-filled room with an indecipherable wall of conversations. He had agreed to meet Otto and Fritz, but as he scanned the room for them, he wished they had gone together. Was there anything worse than self-consciously standing near the entrance looking for somebody? At the long, wooden bar was an opening where he could order and continue his search.

The bartender walked toward Heinrich wearing stylish suspenders and hat. Heinrich lifted a finger to ask for a pint and the bartender nodded and grabbed a glass.

The electric lights buzzed and flickered. As he continued scanning the room, the number of families struck him. Kolmanskop provided a life for not only the miners but their wives and children. He could have brought his wife and daughter as well, but they agreed it was best if he went on his own. For as much as he missed them, especially with seeing a few happy couples spending their night together, he still believed that was the right decision.

Otto grabbed his attention with an exaggerated wave. Heinrich grabbed his beer and walked toward the center of the pub where Otto and Fritz sat with a third man.

"Heinrich!" Otto said as he and Fritz lifted their glasses in greeting.

The other man, with skin like worn, faded leather, took a long drag of his cigarette. "I've seen you around here before. In the underground, yeah?" The man's voice was rough and direct.

"Yeah. Heinrich," he said, shaking the man's hand.

"Sounds about right," the man answered after another drag. "Anytime I see a new face, I know they're in the underground. Babies in the womb. The real work, the man's work, is done above ground."

He blew out thick plumes of smoke that still wreaked of liquor. His dark hair and beard were both unkempt and his face draped over strong cheekbones. Heinrich stood at least a whole head taller but couldn't ignore the uneasiness that came with the man's presence.

"I didn't get your name," Heinrich said.

The man coughed into his hand, a deep, raspy sound. "That's 'cause there's no point in knowing it."

Heinrich looked over to see Fritz swirling the last of his beer around in its glass and Otto, who tried mediating the tension. "Karl's been here quite a few years. He mostly does digging over on the western edge of town."

Karl tugged on his beard before taking another smoke. "Came here before the war, left, and came back after it. I've worked all over this hellhole. Been here long enough to know this town's going to shit." He slammed a fist down onto the table hard enough to bounce Fritz's empty glass. "It's going to shit!"

Fritz looked at his brother and spun his finger in the air; it was time for another round and a convenient exit.

The uneasiness hung as heavy over them as the smoke. Otto, as usual, tried lightening the mood. "Hit the sauce a little hard tonight, have we, Karl? How about you carry on somewhere else?"

"But the night's just getting good."

"It's good over there, too." Otto pointed away from their table.

Karl smashed the butt of his cigarette against the table. "How cute. You're sticking up for your father figure here, yeah?" He leaned in toward them both, the smoke and booze forming a toxic odor that clung to him. "I may not be as large as this son of a bitch, but the Lord gave me two things: a big brain and a big cock and I know how to use them." An ominous grin appeared from below his wiry mustache. "I'm not stupid. I see what's happening here. This town's drying up like a little old lady. That mine they're digging—you're digging—that's the last hope. They're bringing in all these big dumb brutes like yourself to burrow into the ground and look for a reason to keep this shit town alive. But it won't work. I've been here long enough to know I've mined this town damn near free of her diamonds and there's nothing underground that can bring her back. They think that mine will bring it all back to life, but it'll be the death of it. This place is dying. It's going to shit." He slammed his palms onto the table and stood from his chair. "It's going to shit!"

"All right, ya drunk, get the fuck out of here!" Otto stood and stared Karl down with a pointed glare.

"Or what? You going to sick this big motherfucker on me?" Karl threw his arm forward to shove Heinrich from his stool.

Heinrich stood and shoved Karl with both hands against his chest sending him back into the table behind him. "He told you to get out of here. Just go!"

"I'll go, all right," Karl said. He chugged the last bit of his beer and threw the glass to the floor, shattering it into thousands of shards. The bar fell silent and turned their attention to the commotion.

"I'll go right upside your fucking face." Karl lunged toward Heinrich with his fist cocked and ready to uncoil. But Otto jumped between them and wrapped Karl in a bear hug and pinned his arms to his sides.

"Get the fuck out of here, Karl, you drunk bastard," Otto yelled. He shoved Karl from behind toward the door.

When Karl regained his balance, he turned back. "Oh, I'm getting out of here. When my contract's up, I'm heading south where the real fucking money's at while you're all up here rotting away for nothing."

Karl hocked back a throat full of snot and spit on the floor. "I'll see you all in hell." He threw open the door and stormed off into the night.

The atmosphere returned quickly within the pub as if the grave exit took all the tension with it. Fritz sat down at the table and slid the three beers around.

"Good timing," said Heinrich as he finished his first.

Otto continued joking as if unfazed by Karl. "This is what you miss when you don't come out with us."

But Heinrich couldn't laugh off or shake the interaction.

"Did he mean anything about the town and it drying up?"

"Karl? No. He's just an angry old drunk," Otto answered. "When you're outside, what do you see? You see more buildings under construction. More people arriving by the train full. You're in that mine uncovering how many diamonds? So, what do you think?"

Otto was right. Everywhere Heinrich looked there were signs of prosperity and growth. His family would be fine. He would be fine.

"Speaking of," Otto added, "I'm being reassigned to the mines with you."

"Yeah? How about you?" Heinrich asked Fritz.

Fritz shook his head and returned to his beer.

"We're not too happy about being split up, but he'll be fine. Who knows, it could be only a matter of time until we're all down there," Otto, the unwavering optimist said. "How's the work down there, anyway?"

Heinrich considered his response. "I can't compare it to the alluvial work, but it can be pretty tough. Foreman Lange is fair as long as you follow all the rules."

Otto and Fritz smirked. "Doesn't matter where you're at," Otto said. "That's the foreman's job to be on your ass about the rules."

After a couple more rounds, the pub died down, and they decided to call it a night. The sky appeared endless while the bright full moon dwarfed the infinite stars. With the sun down, the cool breeze was luring Heinrich to a deep sleep—his favorite part of a night out drinking.

. • • • .

Tas stood up to leave her office and walk to the garden window, her footsteps casting faint echoes down the empty hall. The glass fogged with her breath as she looked up at the sky. The stars were mostly tucked behind clouds, but the almost full moon appeared in a clearing, reflecting off of the remaining rain puddles along the walkways. For a moment, she could picture herself in Kolmanskop walking the sandy roads home under the cool night sky.

Heinrich's words were a century old but as captivating as any she had ever read. In her middle school history classes, she found her love for the stories of the past, a love that the journal revitalized and made new all over again. The remote desolation of Kolmanskop fascinated her in an entirely different way.

It was time she learned more about the journal and the man who sent it.

Hi Jon,

Thank you for mailing the journal over. I've had a chance to look through it and am quite fascinated. I would love to learn more about it. Why wasn't it included in the exhibit in Berlin? How did you come to own it? Anything that you can share would be great. Thank you!

Tas Fredericks

Reading through the journal was an incredible journey, but it created a lot more questions. She wasn't even sure how to verify such a piece and request it to be included in a touring show. But she would have to wait for those answers.

Her least favorite part.

- 8 -
THE BUTTERFLIES

Sydney's eyes eased open and focused on the painting on the bedroom wall. The canvas print was of a large distressed clock atop a monochromatic abstract background. It reminded her of the time she and Mike bought it after moving into their apartment. They had driven up and down the furniture strip in town trying to find the right couch and love seat, and around shop number five, she had spotted it. It drew her eyes immediately. She liked that it was abstract but still contained an element that made sense; it was balanced. She made a mental note of it as they walked toward the couches.

By that point, they had their routine down. Mike would drop himself into the middle of the sofa and assume his gaming position, leaning back with his legs stretched as far as they'd reach. Sydney sat on an end, leaning along the armrest and stretching until her feet were kept warm behind his back. That was the only way to test a couch, they thought.

"Are you sure your feet aren't dead?" Mike asked with the warm, charming smile that softened his strong jawline. "I swear, I can feel how cold they are through your shoes!"

Sydney kicked him and laughed. "Shut up!"

They had lain on about thirty sofas that day, but there was something special about that one. Sydney leaned over from the armrest and snuggled next to Mike, a happiness bubbling inside of her.

"Did we find the one?" she asked.

"I don't know about you, but I sure have." He looked at Sydney and kissed the top of her head.

She melted further into him. His cheesy lines made her think of all the dumb romantic comedies she watched that she believed weren't real until Mike came along.

"And I guess the couch is good, too." He smirked in a way that was so uniquely his Sydney thought he should patent the expression.

A husky salesman approached them with his tucked-in button-down doing everything in its power to keep his gut contained. "Now, y'all folks look awfully comfortable there."

Sydney sat up, the intimacy ruined by the outsider. "Well, we've been out all day, so I can't tell if we're actually shopping or just resting at this point."

The salesman burst out in a full, hearty laugh. He leaned back and hooked his thumbs behind his belt buckle as if to help support himself from toppling backward. "Hey, resting on a sofa *is* shopping. Sure, you gotta find one that looks nice and all that jazz, I get that. But at the end of the day, you have to find a sofa you fit. I don't care how nice a sofa is, if I can't lie down, put the race on, and let these puppies rest after standing all day, I don't want it."

Her eyes met Mike's and their shared smile said everything she was thinking. Mike stood to discuss options. "We'd be looking for a full set: the sofa, love seat, ottoman. You know, the whole package."

"Mm-hmm. I hear that. One stop shop," the salesman said.

"More like ten-stop shopping in our case." Sydney giggled at her own joke.

"Tell ya what," the salesman continued. "If you want this full set today, I'll see what I can do about the price, maybe knock ten percent off for ya. Y'all seem sweet."

"I don't know," Mike said. "We'd also need it delivered, and that's probably another, what, couple hundred?"

"Well, our delivery rate is eighty-nine dollars flat assuming you live here in the triangle."

"Yeah, we live a few minutes from here. So we'd be good there. But how about the ten percent and free delivery if we buy today?"

The salesman hiked up his pants and looked over Mike and Sydney. He stroked his graying goatee and hummed a little tune to himself. "I think I can make that happen for you. Let's head over here and we can get you squared away."

Mike turned to Sydney with a smile. His eyes were bright and excited. Sydney applauded his work with silent golf claps as he turned to follow the salesman to his desk.

Sydney stayed behind on the sofa for a moment before getting up to wander around the store. She found herself back near the front staring up at the abstract clock canvas. That, too, she decided, would be delivered for free.

She approached Mike and the salesman. "Hey, babe, what do you think of that picture of the clock over there?"

Mike leaned over the desk for a better view. "Seems pretty cool. Do you like it?"

"I do," she said. "I saw it when we walked in and I still really like it."

"How much for the painting?" Mike asked the salesman.

Sydney answered first. "Oh, the sign says $149."

Mike nodded and added it to their order.

"If that'll fit in your car now, you can just grab it from the wall and take it with you," the salesman added.

Sydney replayed coming home that day and asking Mike to hold the canvas against every wall while she deliberated the perfect spot. After the extensive search, she decided the bedroom wall was exactly that.

That morning, though, she connected more with the erosion of time captured in the painting than the perfect time it represented. She rolled over to find Mike's side of the bed still empty.

It had been gradual at first, almost indistinguishable how Mike's remarks had shifted from supportive to opposing and his openness had closed not only around him but her life as well. Sometimes she would try a new recipe and if he didn't like it he'd laugh it off and make himself a sandwich. But over time, that had changed. She'd make him a specific meal only to have to throw out the food entirely and make something else for them both. There was a time when he would look forward to joining her for a work event or a random party at Tas's place, but that had deteriorated as well until she had to push to keep a life outside of him. She wasn't surprised he had thrown going out to Trophy in her face, but it was like having her blood taken: the needle never surprised her, but it stung all the same.

She still believed in him and, more importantly, still believed in them. They'd become settled, she thought. That happens after some time. But if she picked her spots and worked around him, he would still meet her halfway. She wasn't ready to accept it all as the new normal, but she was ready to acknowledge the trajectory her life, their life, had taken.

Like a timid mouse stepping out into open space, Sydney peeked into the living room where she found Mike on the couch under their wool blanket. The small collection of beers on the coffee table implied he had passed out, not fallen asleep. He had never been the type to shy away from one more beer but it had become more frequent and she was worried given his condition. Was he doing more harm than good to himself?

She moved back into the bedroom where she prepped for work. It'd be a casual day, jeans, and ponytail. She didn't have the energy or the care to do anything else. Technology had done a lot to the culture and society, but one thing she appreciated on such mornings was its lax dress code in the office.

Her shower ran long that morning. It's where she thought best. The rushing water soothed her and the rising steam let her breathe in until her lungs stretched. She'd watched other relationships spiral down the same path before. Surely, though, her relationship was the exception. It had the foundation and the time to carry on. She never felt threatened physically, and that's where she'd say she'd draw the line.

But Mike was right—it was her idea to go out. She was the one driving when the accident happened. He had every right to feel the way he did. Maybe if she had accepted that instead of going to bed, cold and distant, he wouldn't have spent the night drinking himself to sleep.

If she truly cared for him, she would have stayed awake to make sure he took proper care of himself. If she truly cared for him, she would have taken care of him herself. If she truly cared for him, she would have apologized with genuine compassion. Instead, she left him alone. Again.

If she truly cared.

The mirror squealed as she uncovered her reflection from behind a coating of steam. Her eyes lacked their usual bright sparkle and her shoulders were tense and hunched with soreness. When she heard Mike stir on the couch, the muscles in her neck stiffened. To make things right, she'd need to apologize.

Everything about her screamed meek when she stood in the doorway to the living room. "Hey, baby. How're you doing?"

He rolled onto his back and covered his face with his arm.

"Babe? You all right?" Her voice sounded weak and shallow. Her strength diffused from her with every moment she stared at him in that condition.

Mike's voice was raw when he succinctly replied, "Yes. Now go away."

His words cut her down further. "I was hoping I could talk to you before going in to work. I wanted to say..."

He waited no longer before snapping back. "Go away!" Flinging his arm from his face, he stared at her, so his expression and tone combined for full effect.

"Okay. I just wanted to apologize and see if you were okay." Did he hear the tears forming when she spoke? How could she be so cold the night before and so hurt the morning after? The pain and listlessness had become all too common and, again, she justified it by burning herself at the stake.

"And I just want you to go away so I can sleep. Christ, Syd!" he hissed with venom.

Her mind raced back to high school all over again. The harsh years of insecurity defined her and created the patchwork of a person she'd become. Being one of the poor kids in class made her an easy target for bullying that never stopped until graduation. Over the years since, she had developed more strength and independence, but that morning, and mornings like it, she couldn't help but wonder if that newfound confidence was nothing more than the scar tissue of her lifelong anxieties. She never outgrew that shy, timid girl. She remembered walking through the empty hallways hugging along the lockers because the middle was too open and vulnerable. It was the same exposed feeling that drained her, standing in the doorway as Mike demanded she leave.

She obliged and carried herself out the door while her mind kept her back in the apartment by herself in bed. How she wished she could ball up with her pillow and a book, protected enough to build herself up again while nobody was watching.

A quick flip through her high school yearbook would reveal her many after-school activities. She played cello in the orchestra, clarinet in the marching band, and appeared in the back row of the school's Tech Club photo. That's where she felt safest, blended into the background. The less she stood out, the quieter her days would be. Finding peace in the classroom was important because her home offered little of it.

From childhood through her teenage years, her best friend was her mother, Maria. They shared the same love for reading and would often share their books. The nights when Maria placed the teapot in the middle of their dinner table with two cups, a small selection of tea bags, and the jar of honey to talk about their latest book were some of her happiest memories. But those nights were bittersweet. She loved them, but all too often they served as an apology. While her mother loved to read, her father loved to drink and yell at whatever game was on TV. Only later in life did she fill in the gaps where her mother bore the brunt of his anger to protect her from it.

She'd still relive the day after she turned eighteen. She hosted her party at the local bowling alley's weekend blacklight event. There would be pizza, arcade games, boys, and a night that was no longer restricted by the curfews of a learner's permit. That night also meant she could finally buy her own pack of cigarettes.

On her way to the bowling alley, the car windows were down, and she was enjoying her first legal smoke when the ash fell from the cigarette and burned itself into the cloth seat. The car may have been a Ford as old as her but "It runs and it's paid off," her dad would say as he expected it to be cared for like it was a brand new Mercedes.

"You have to respect the things you buy. If you respect them, you take care of them. If you don't take care of them, they fall apart. If they fall apart, you have to replace them and we don't have the money to keep replacing shit around here." Her dad's voice rose from the depths of her subconscious and she cowered at the thought of him finding the charred hole.

When she got home that night, she told her mom. Even though her father was down the street at his favorite dive, she whispered her confession as her tears fell in even greater silence. Part remorse, part fear, her eyes said everything. Her mother held her, assured her everything would be okay, and gave her a birthday present. Underneath the repurposed newspaper comics was the new hardcover release of *Harry Potter and the Order of the Phoenix.*

The next night, while her mother suspiciously wore long sleeves in August, they discussed *The Kite Runner*.

It wasn't until college when she found her voice. As always, nobody saw her without a book but at last, she saw her intelligence as a strength. While others worked part-time jobs to help offset tuition, she was grateful for her scholarship. It allowed her to focus on herself more than ever before. The mornings became her time to jog and the weekends her time for friends. Day by day, she stitched more of her childhood wounds closed.

Mike came along when she wore her brightest smile. She'd seen him around at a couple of parties often wearing ironic statement tees and getting too competitive at the beer pong table. *A typical jock.* When she had bumped into him in the library where he sat all but buried behind a collection of books detailing tech entrepreneurship, her opinion changed. The sports persona was his ticket through college, a role he played, but she came to learn his goals reached beyond the court. Once removed from the moments around others when he had to be *on*, she found him sweet and well read. Replace her childhood tea with a couple of cheap lagers at a dive bar, and her heart fluttered when they'd lose an evening talking about their favorite series and authors. She fell in love with the layers beneath his façade.

But sometimes when a role is played too long, the line between it and reality blurs. The cheap beer, tank tops, and frat houses were replaced by cocktails, tailored suits, and speakeasies. Mike would tell her how important it was that he make a good impression around the office. He was making connections with executives and seniors who would help him angle for his next promotion. His goals became less about innovation and achievement and more about salary and perks. It wasn't long before his nights out impeded their morning runs and they'd changed their early alarms to allow for maximum sleep.

Every relationship struggles with peaks and valleys, but she still supported the man she loved. The safety when wrapped in his arms was still there. Her heart still raced when he'd stare into her eyes and smile.

She still felt the butterflies.

But as the apartment door closed behind her, she resented the parts they had to play and how different they were from reality. She resented having to pretend the butterflies of their relationship were as plentiful and vibrant as ever when she had to admit they were dying and all but extinct.

- 9 -
THE SHINE

Sleep can elude a distracted mind. Tas couldn't stop replaying visions of Kolmanskop in her head, and after only a couple of hours of sleep, she was stirred awake by the clanking of steel and stone in her dreams.

It was an early start to her day when she entered the museum. Only the cleaning crews moseyed around the halls. The soft whooshing of the floor buffers vanished as the door to the office wing clicked shut behind her.

She set her to-go bag on her desk, a breakfast sandwich and banana, along with her tall mocha. The journal and exhibit would provide enough excitement to power her through the morning, though eventually the poor night's sleep would catch up to her. Having the extra bit of caffeine would be her saving grace once lunchtime rolled around. She opened her laptop, took a drink, and dove into some research.

Her first stop was the Deutsches Historisches Museum website. Under their archives was the mining exhibit's information.

"Typical," she said, scrolling through a wall of dry data dumps.

The page contained no mention of Kolmanskop but Tas suspected they hadn't included all the information. She decided to email the museum.

Hello,

My name is Tas Fredericks, a museum curator in the US. I have recently acquired the Mining Evolution exhibit that was on display there in the summer of last year and I was hoping to chat with your curator or somebody who could help me answer a couple of questions concerning its contents. Specifically, I am looking to learn more about a particular journal I received from a Jon Martin that appears to have been written in Kolmanskop. He mentioned that he had tried adding it to the exhibit there but was unable to. I'd be interested to learn more.

I'd appreciate any help. Thank you.

Tas browsed through more photos of Kolmanskop. They were captivating. When she found shots of the long halls of the school with shattered glass littering the cracked wooden floors, she became fixated on the lives of the children. She pictured kids running through the halls from class to class, a chorus of their voices filling the rooms. What were their lives like in such a unique environment?

As exquisite as the pictures were, Tas was searching for the town's history well before it had been rebranded as a photographer's dream. The oldest details she found documented the alluvial mining efforts and the large percentage of diamonds the town supplied to the world. There were pictures of men crawling on their stomachs over the sand grabbing loose diamonds, but there was no mention or pictures of the underground mine Heinrich had described.

Before she knew it, the museum outside of her office was bustling with people. The sounds of children echoed through the rooms: an oddly heartwarming hybrid of laughing, shouting, and the occasional tantrum.

Before she could justify digging further into Kolmanskop, she needed to do some actual work for the exhibit. Only a few days had passed, but there was an underlying stress festering. She needed to make progress not only for herself but to appease Sam.

A knock on her door grabbed her attention.

Speak of the devil.

Sam opened the door and skipped all the pleasantries. "Will you be joining this meeting? We're waiting and you're beyond fashionable at this point."

"Oh shit," she said, jumping up and rushing out the door.

Her laptop remained open on a picture of Kolmanskop's school. The arched windows in the corridor had been long without glass. A doorway in the distance was half-filled with sand and nearly unsurpassable. Time had passed by the school, but once again, sounds of children filled its room as playful laughter spread throughout the museum and into her silent office.

Once the meeting ran long, it was easy for Tas to overlook being late. When it came to a merciful end, she was the first to leave and hide away in her office. Some meetings killed productivity for their duration; others killed it for an entire day.

She had just survived the latter.

Back in her office, she reached for the chocolate she kept in her drawer—a little sweetness to offset her sour mood. She grabbed her phone to text Dean as she worked through her midday snack. "Hey! How's it going? Up for a drink later?"

When she woke up her laptop, the photo of the school welcomed her back. It was the kicker ensuring she'd be doing no work that afternoon. She opened the journal, took another bite of chocolate, and returned to Heinrich's words.

> *It has taken time, as I both expected and was told, but I'm settling into a routine here at last. The work has not become any easier, but I have adjusted. The human being's ability to adapt is fascinating. I have learned my way around the town and mines and have become quite skilled at the bowling alley. I have written my wife regularly and my daughter has started her new school year. All is well. Or so it was.*
>
> *The brightest skies always lead to the darkest storms.*

. • • • .

Otto lifted his hat to wipe the dripping sweat from his forehead, leaving a smear of dirt and dust in its place. "It's slightly cooler down here but I can't get used to this stench."

Heinrich set the head of his pickax at his feet and also took a breather. "And you never will."

Far below the sun-beaten sands wove the endless reaches of the mines. Laboring men, grunting and coughing up phlegm with every swing and strike, filled every tunnel stemming from the primary vein. It all amounted to an overwhelming odor that hung heavy and thick like a putrid layer of fog.

Screams echoed throughout as workers smashed their hands and feet under falling earth or became locked in a hunched position, unable to straighten their backs. Those wounds would heal. Others wouldn't.

The rapid influx of miners meant little, if any, time for training. Some had mishandled the use of explosives and lost fingers and hands adding a fiery and metallic smell of gunpowder and burned flesh to the mix. Foreman Lange prided himself on safety, but the mines became anything but.

Despite the incoming waves of men and round-the-clock work that signaled great value in the mines, the supply of diamonds was drying up. Karl's words haunted Heinrich still.

Every couple of weeks, Foreman Lange instructed the crews to blast their way into a new direction that promised enough riches to restore their faith. But with every ill-placed explosion leading to little reward, the mine's morale took a similar blow.

Each new extension became more erratic than the last. Foreman Lange reeked of a desperation no longer hidden beneath his gruff exterior. He pushed the men to work harder, longer hours as they rushed from one blast to the next. Tremors and bursts of heat from each explosion became dangerously frequent. There were diamonds to be found, safety be damned.

"The diamonds are all around us, but we must work harder to get them," Lange would shout. "The problem is not the diamonds but our effort." He preached that mantra which served as his own reassurance. It was undoubtedly the same tune he played when reporting to Kohler.

Otto continued while he and Heinrich took their break. "Did you hear about the gymnasts coming to the hall this weekend? Can you believe that?"

Heinrich couldn't tell if Otto's excitement was genuine or sarcastic but he had heard. Chatter of upcoming entertainers buzzed around the town like gossip. Yet he didn't share in the excitement. Entertainers made their goodwill trek to his little slice of hell for a week then returned home. They'd never experience the true Kolmanskop in that time. They'd joke about the heat and wind as if they were novelties only to complain about their misery of being in the town once they left. It's not like he loved it either, but it was the life he and the others had chosen.

No, he wasn't excited. He was homesick.

"Yeah, I heard that a few days ago at the lanes."

"Are you going? It should be quite a sight to see," Otto said.

He knew Otto's expression well. The slight gleam in his eye and how his hand wiped over his mouth—he was asking about the gymnasts, not the gymnastics. "I'd rather go bowling. But it sounds like you'll enjoy it quite well."

Heinrich had rested long enough and threw his ax over his shoulder.

"Yep," Otto said, following Heinrich's lead. "Back to searching for that needle."

That's when the ground rumbled and the lights flickered with the latest blast. A thunderous tremor shook beneath their feet showering them with dirt and stone shaken free from overhead.

Where there's thunder, there's lightning.

The nearby wooden supports splintered with a series of piercing cracks. Heinrich turned to see his crew frozen. They watched in disbelief. A dam that spiders must burst and a mine that splinters must fall.

From the depths of the tunnel came urgent cries. "Run!"

A small stampede of men rushed toward him, chased by a rolling wave of dust and smoke. The confining walls shook as the collapsing earth dominoed behind them.

Heinrich and Otto took off without another thought toward the primary tunnel and its exit. The shaking grew violent, and the walls ran with pouring streams of loosened dirt. It was as if hell had opened to pull down everything around them. The sharp cracking of a nearby beam was followed by the tumbling of the boulder it had supported. The wall collapsed with the force of a flood and tackled Otto to the ground.

"Otto!" Heinrich rushed over and reached for Otto's arm but the raging current knocked him away, threatening to bury his closest friend. "Get up!" he shouted, but Otto remained unconscious and pinned beneath the rubble. He fought to dig him free with a futile desperation. The rocks rained onto Otto quicker than Heinrich could wipe them free, and in a moment, they had covered him to his waist. Heinrich could do nothing but watch as Otto's life was pressed out of his body, one blood-filled puff of air at a time as the earth collapsed onto him, consuming him whole.

There was nothing he could do.

Heinrich raced with the remaining crew as quickly as the swaying lights allowed. The whole tunnel shook, jolting the dark shadows from side to side as the collapse continued at his heels. Near the primary junction of the mine is when the lift's bell echoed an audible trail of breadcrumbs toward safety. Hordes of frantic miners converged toward the ringing, a sound Heinrich hoped would not be the last they'd hear.

A man near the front of the crowd was shouting, "Everybody, slow down. Remain calm!"

"We're dying down here!" another shouted back.

Heinrich's mind raced amidst the chaos.

How widespread was the collapse? Were any others left behind?

A frantic shove from behind returned his focus. "Out of the way," the man screamed as he rushed farther ahead.

The man wedged his way through the growing crowd with an uncontrolled ferocity. When an animal is backed into a corner its natural instincts of survival drives it. When men are trapped in a collapsing mine they, too, fight for their survival. The man who rushed by was swarmed by four others who seemed unwilling to sacrifice their lives for his. The scuffle was brief, ending when one man threw his hoof-like fist into the first one's jaw.

Each trip the lift had taken was overcrowded. It strained to bear the extra weight. Heinrich fought his way onto the next cart and slowly ascended toward the light as if he had just escaped the grasping hands of the Devil himself.

When Heinrich rushed out into the open air, the sun was no longer an inconvenience but a welcomed burn. His adrenaline was spent and the weight of the collapse settled on his shoulders.

Once those capable of escaping had left the mine, Foreman Lange ran through the shift chart. His voice shook, and for the first time, his steady control faltered. He called out every name as if pleading for a response, but four had fallen silent.

Some men shared flasks and cigarettes to still their nerves. Others surrounded Lange and demanded action. Heinrich fell to the sand and dropped his head in his hands. The picture of Otto's bloodied body had been burned into his mind. He scratched at his knee and beat his fist against the side of his head. "I could have done more."

His tears fell from both grief and guilt. The scene replayed behind his heavy eyes, versions where he had dug Otto free or fought harder against the collapse. Hindsight and imagination created opportunities that weren't necessarily there. The weight and guilt of survival had almost made it worse to have escaped.

But when a tight, unfamiliar voice called his name, he knew that wasn't true.

Fritz stood behind him, mouth wide and gasping for air. His eyes were glassy and filled with frightened concern. "Where's Otto?"

. • • • .

I can't even recall what I said to Fritz when he ran over. There was nothing I could say to console him. There are no words. I wasn't able to save Otto and can't save Fritz from that reality. I can't imagine he'll stay in Kolmanskop much longer and I have to begin questioning the same thing. There's simply no amount of money for my family—my daughter—that could replace having a father.

"Holy shit," Tas said to herself.

The collapse didn't seem real. There was nothing for her to compare it to. She took for granted the times she leisurely strolled through touristy caves on well-lit pathways and bridges. Nothing could possibly compare to the dread of being involved in a collapse. It must have been like drowning, a death you can see but cannot escape. A few stray tears streamed down her face at the very thought.

Was she reading the fall of the wealthiest city? With the shrinking deposits and growing negligence, she wondered how long the town could sustain itself.

"The problem is not the diamonds but our effort."

Before turning to the next entry, Tas hesitated. She mourned the deaths and was unsure if she was ready to move on to the next entry. But she was certain of one thing: the journal would be the prominent feature in the show to ensure the story of those men lived on.

Finally, almost of its own free will, the page turned over with a dry creek as if awakening from its long slumber.

. • • • .

Heinrich sat at the edge of his bed, elbows pressed to his knees, hands supporting his chin. His body ached with the weight of each day when he gingerly stood to stretch. He wanted to scream in protest of another day, but this day would be different.

Fritz had been moving around in Otto's old room collecting anything he could carry home. It had only been a few days after the collapse when Otto was buried in the growing cemetery outside of Lüderitz and Fritz filed to leave Kolmanskop. In the weeks after, he worked sporadic hours and spent the rest of the time either in his room or at the pub. That morning Heinrich supported himself against the doorframe as Fritz sat on the bed rubbing his shirt over the dial of Otto's wristwatch.

Heinrich cleared his throat then asked, "Today's the day, huh?"

Fritz turned and nodded with somber eyes. It was difficult to read him on his best days and downright impossible that morning. He was returning home with only a few of his brother's items and a memory of his jovial spirit. He would be welcomed back not to hugs of joy but of grief and loss. No, he would not be returning to a home at all. Fritz was leaving a small secluded town trapped within a vast desert for a bustling city where he'd be no less secluded or lost.

"Take care, Fritz." Heinrich didn't know what else to say. There were no words to replace the loss. Hell, he still wasn't certain Fritz didn't consider him responsible. He hadn't yet let the guilt go, himself. *I could have done more. I'm a coward,* he'd often think.

The mines had reopened again, and the men rode the lift down into the mouth that nearly swallowed them. The ringing bells made their descent feel ominous like a funeral procession. Foreman Lange decided against digging back into the directions they'd already explored. Instead, he beamed with excitement as he directed the men to move farther south.

The deposits were immediately more plentiful, and the work was more strategic than the weeks before the collapse. Each move was made with intent, no longer hasty and careless. The slower pace didn't rest the body though. Its actions were simply more methodical—a concentration of force.

The wind was particularly vengeful that morning. It trailed the street cleaners returning every grain they had swept away. There was a weight bearing down on Kolmanskop like a small town that braced for a long winter. The mood had shifted and darkened. The days of lavish luxury seemed behind them. Heinrich still walked streets lined with buildings designed by the best German architects and was entertained by exotic acts imported every week, but the glamor had dulled. Many of the miners moved to South Africa leaving Kolmanskop to feel anemic and beyond its prime.

Otto's bed had remained empty. There was no word on Fritz being replaced. From that night onward, Heinrich would pace the quiet halls of his home alone. The pub, once filled to capacity every night, was closing earlier as the droves of men thinned. Taking a walk through town in the morning, he saw fewer deliveries awaiting residents. Even the train schedules fell victim to the trend and became less frequent.

Kolmanskop had lost its shine.

Heinrich knew that despite the number of diamonds the new mine was producing, it wouldn't be enough to sustain the town much less return it to its former glory. His latest letter to his wife alluded to that same notion—that his endeavor to enrich their lives had fallen short of his intention. He had waited too long to make the move and was late to the rush.

Maybe it was for the best. Heinrich missed his family with a pain so deep it often hurt worse than the physical toll of the work. The house had already become uncomfortably quiet. He had essentially been living alone since Otto's death and the mood had become frigid and overwhelming. If only he had moved when he first had the idea, he would have earned more than he'd ever intended. But he labored over the idea, noncommittal to the sacrifices it required.

He earned more from his time in the mines than he would have made back home, and unlike others, he still had a family to welcome him with open arms and warming hearts. It wouldn't be the retire-in-the-countryside payload he had dreamt and, of course, sold to his wife, but he would return healthy and with money to enjoy a few things that were otherwise well beyond their means.

Sugar was sweet no matter the amount.

He braced himself against the winds and walked toward the mines, yet his shoulders were no longer tensed. He would leave Kolmanskop. His goal was to create a better life for his family and that's what he'd done. He was ready to go home. There were no obligations for him to go down with the ship. After his shift that day, he would file his request with Foreman Lange. The peace of the decision washed over him, relaxing his muscles and conscience.

He'd be returning home.

. • • • .

Lange told me he understood and that I could return home next month which would be perfect timing. I'll get to celebrate my little girl turning eight years old. He needs me here to assist with a new mine just outside of town. Once that is running, I am free to be with my family.

Fritz is now gone and soon so will I, leaving behind this house and the hell that's consuming it.

Tas turned to the next page, but only blank sheets remained. They were all stained and torn, some even ripped out entirely. It all begged one question that nagged her incessantly. What happened between then and now?

Her desire for more information was ravenous yet familiar. When she first learned of the Dyatlov Pass Expedition her world became consumed with the tale. In what felt like seconds, she had numerous articles bookmarked about the expedition and various conspiracies surrounding the deaths of the hikers. She had driven to the bookstore to buy a copy of *Dead Mountain: The Untold True Story of the Dyatlov Pass Incident* and read it in the on-site cafe with a hot chocolate by her side. The pictures of the hikers captivated her for minutes at a time while a slow, rumbling angst toiled around her stomach. The pictures captured the final moments of the kids' lives, and while she knew the fate that awaited them, their bright eyes and enthusiastic smiles did not. That unsettled her more than anything.

Replace the desolate Ural mountains with an equally harsh Namibian desert and her restlessness was no different.

Tas needed answers.

There were thousands of articles and websites dedicated to Kolmanskop, but she couldn't find any mention of the mines or their collapse. She searched for Heinrich and Otto and found nothing. She searched if any diamonds were recently discovered in the town and, again, nothing. It was as if Kolmanskop's entire online presence was curated by its PR rep.

Was the notebook a fabrication? Why couldn't she find any results corroborating any of the details Heinrich had written? She leaned back in her chair and dropped her arms into her lap with a sigh.

"In for a dime, in for a dollar," she told herself, as she placed her hands back onto her keyboard.

Kolmanskop secrets and history.

Enter.

To her disappointment, but not to her surprise, many of the results led to already-visited sites. She skipped through several pages before finding a few articles that went in different directions like mentioning Kolmanskop in lists of most-haunted places. The articles alluded to the hardships of mining life and the inevitable deaths that occurred. A lot of it seemed farfetched until she read a particular post.

> *Step away from the guided tours and you'll find the history the town keeps buried. They won't tell you about the abrupt evacuation that brought the end to Kolmanskop. They won't tell you about the mines just south of town. And they certainly won't tell you about the men who entered them only to never return home. Tourists clamor to Kolmanskop, the ghost town, but never stop to think about the ghosts themselves.*

She never knew how much truth was behind anything on the internet but the post piqued her attention. It was the closest she'd come to corroborating the journal's stories. But a full-fledged evacuation? How could that be hidden from the town's history? Everything she had read alluded to the surplus of diamonds dwindling until everybody left. That seemed far more plausible than a mysterious town-wide evacuation.

That singular post was it. No other article or forum she found mentioned the underground mines or the evacuation. It was disheartening but maybe she was searching for a mystery where there wasn't one. After all, she knew nothing about Jon or the true origins of the journal. Were the hundreds of pages about Kolmanskop the truth, or was he the one spinning a story?

A slight skepticism grew as she placed the journal in her desk and collected her things. Texts from Dean and Sydney awaited her, and she arranged to meet them for a drink.

Hopefully, a night away from Kolmanskop would help her mind settle.

- 10 -
THE HOOK

The sun had almost set and the parking lot was nearly full when Tas arrived. With no spots in the main lot, she drove down the side of the building and found space on the neighboring graveled street. Outside the brewery, a queue of customers waited at the food truck while others swarmed to the picnic tables like moths to a flame. A group of guys were playing a game of cornhole at the far end of the lot with their beers and dogs by their sides.

Dogs made every brewery better.

Fewer people were inside: a couple at the bar, a few playing darts, and only a handful of others scattered around the open, warehouse-like room. After grabbing a beer, Tas walked toward the back where Sydney sat on the couches.

"Hey, Syd. Sorry. Were you waiting long?" Tas asked.

"No. I got here like five minutes ago. You're good."

Sydney's eyes lacked their usual energy making her look tired, almost hollow. As Tas settled into the black, faux-leather cushions, she couldn't ignore the uneasy energy.

"Oh, hope it's cool, but I also invited Dean," Tas said.

Sydney paused midsip for a moment. Her reaction was subtle and foreign despite her familiar response. "Yeah, totally."

Something was definitely off.

"So what's going on?" Tas asked. "How have things been since the accident?"

Sydney clasped both hands around her glass like it was a cup of hot tea before taking a drink. "Yeah, I've been good. I've needed some ibuprofen for aches or whatever but that's been about it."

After a quiet pause, she continued. "Mike, though, he's having a hard time. Well, we're having a hard time, I guess."

That's when Tas made the connection to Sydney's unfamiliar expression. It seemed she was expecting a girls' night out for drinks. Tas cringed with guilt for not knowing that before inviting Dean.

Sydney continued. "Mike's been drinking. Which, I mean, is normal but I guess it's been more than usual." She twisted her hair around her first two fingers over and over again. "We've been fighting more because of it."

"I'm so sorry to hear that, Syd," Tas said, reaching out and touching her hand.

Sydney took a deep breath before letting it out in an exhausted sigh. "Yesterday, I tried apologizing for the accident since he's been holding that against me and he just snapped and yelled at me until I left for work. And then at work, I have to pretend that everything's okay. That he's okay and that we're okay." Her voice sounded hoarse, and she stared toward the ceiling, tears welling in her eyes.

"But we're not okay, Tas. It hasn't been okay for a while now, I guess. I can remember the times that made me fall for him but those memories never change. Like, once I fell he stopped trying, and it's been wearing me down." She ran her hands over her face before taking another drink.

"If I actually try to step back from it, I can see what's been happening. I mean, you and I don't get to hang out as much, for one. If he wasn't distracted with his PlayStation and drinking, I doubt I could have come out tonight. I don't get to go out with my coworkers at all. It's all this stuff. And it's because of him. He never wants to do anything and if he isn't going somewhere, that usually means I can't either. He's pulling me away from everything."

Tas looked toward Sydney and shook her head, her mind racing.

Sydney wiped the tears from her eyes before they could wash down her cheeks. "I don't feel like I'm happy. And I don't think I've been for a while," she murmured

Tas struggled to find a response. "But, what do you mean? Like you're considering leaving him, or what?"

"I don't know. I haven't thought that far yet."

"Wow, Syd. I had no idea. Have you tried talking to him about it?"

Sydney scoffed at the idea. "He's not the talking type. He's never been." She lowered her head and spun her glass in her hand. "It's all becoming so routine as opposed to, like, a choice to be together. It feels like how every morning I take the same route to work without even thinking about it." Looking up to meet Tas's eyes, she said, "It's the routine of going like we've been running off of muscle memory."

"I totally get that," Tas said. "And, of course, once you start feeling that way it can be tough to sort of reenergize everything."

"Exactly. I feel like I need him to at least make an effort, to do something other than coast through this."

Tas nodded. "He needs to get over himself so you guys can talk about this. These are things he needs to hear."

"You're probably right." Sydney sighed and returned to twisting her hair.

Tas pulled Sydney's hand from its nervous fidgeting and took it in her own. "Well, if you need anything, tell me. You know, I've got you," she said with words as genuine as any she'd ever said.

Tas looked up and noticed Dean standing in line at the bar. "Dean made it. Should we go get another round with him?"

All three ordered their beers and returned to the couches. Tas understood her conversation with Sydney was to remain between them, so they all talked about work, the universal topic. After Sydney and Dean gave their quick updates, Tas emptied her excitement and curiosity. She started with receiving the journal and, in a blur, ran through translating the entries and finding the single post mentioning Kolmanskop's hasty evacuation.

"So everybody just left the town?" Dean asked.

"Apparently," she said. "I don't know how much truth there is in that, though."

"Well, I thought everything on the internet was true," Dean said with a smirk.

Tas returned his smart-ass expression and continued. "It's all fascinating. Like who was Heinrich and what happened in the mines and to the town? That's sort of why I want to visit for the exhibit."

"Visit Namibia?" Sydney choked down her latest drink. "You can't be serious."

"Why not?" It was one of Tas's favorite questions. Old reliable.

"You know there's no way Sam would be okay with that," Dean said.

Tas knew he had a point. "Yeah, that would be tough. But maybe if I emphasized the trip as research for the show..." Even she didn't believe herself.

Dean straightened his expression and met her eyes. "Yeah, but no."

"Regardless," she continued, "imagine touring a ghost town like that, especially after reading so much about it."

"I could totally see that. But with all this research you've done already, wouldn't the tour be redundant?" Sydney asked.

"Fair. But even if I don't learn anything new, I think it'd be incredible to experience it all firsthand."

"Call me if you find any diamonds," Dean said sarcastically.

Tas took another drink and set the glass down. "That's the thing. The last journal entry made it seem like there were still diamonds. What if that's true?"

Dean shook his head. "Diamonds that nobody has found after all these years?"

"People wouldn't find them if they're sticking to the tour." Tas ran her finger down the table and tapped it twice. "Farther south, right outside of town, there were mines, and that's where they'd be."

"Tas, this would be crazy. You're not, Lara Craft." Sydney said.

"Croft, Syd," Dean corrected. "It's Lara Croft."

"Whatever," Tas continued, waving Dean's comment away. "I don't think it'd be that crazy. No, I don't seriously expect to find diamonds hanging out in the sand, but it's been so much fun to learn about. It's not like I would be going in blind if I did visit."

"You don't go into anything blind," Sydney said.

And she was right. Tas loved preparing and researching for her trips. There was a satisfaction in organizing all of her ideas into a single map with links, pictures, and reference locations marked. Kolmanskop would be different, though, considering there were no places nearby, but that wouldn't keep her from reading so much about the town that a trip there would be like a long-awaited return.

The pop-punk music playing through the brewery had been turned off. It was time to finish up and call it a night. They returned their glasses to the bar and made their way outside where the picnic tables had fallen empty, the cornhole boards were packed away, and the food truck had gone. Sydney walked to her rental which sat by itself while Dean and Tas waved and turned toward the side street.

Dean cracked away at his knuckles as they walked. His small steps fell behind Tas until she slowed down to his pace.

"Hey, so you know how I lost my phone the other day?" Dean asked. He didn't look at Tas. His eyes stayed focused on his bending fingers.

"Typical. Yeah."

"Yeah. Classic me." His tone lacked his familiar sense of humor. "But about that... I didn't lose my phone. I was kind of blocking off for the day."

"What do you mean?"

He squeezed his thumbs beneath his fingers but there were no more relieving cracks. "Like, I just turn off from the world. So I have these, like, attacks or something. Well, it usually starts with a crazy dream."

"Dean, chill." Tas stepped closer to him before her phone chimed with a new email, stealing her attention. She shuffled through her bag. When she checked the notification, she stepped back in the direction of her car.

"Shit. Sorry, it's a work thing," she said. "But yeah, is everything okay?"

Dean paused and looked down. When he straightened again, he crammed his hands into his pockets. "Yeah. I'm good."

"I'm really sorry," she said. "But I need to check on this. I'll text you tomorrow, yeah?"

"Sure thing," Dean said, turning away with a sigh.

Tas hurried to sit down in her car and read the reply.

Hi Tas,

That's wonderful to learn that the journal made it to you safely. I was nervous to ship it but after sending only copies of it to Musée d'Orsay in Paris and being dismissed, I thought sending the real thing was my only option. And after being told here that there wasn't enough time to verify its authenticity for the exhibit, it makes sense that you would need the actual item to do just that.

My grandfather, Heinrich, is the one you've read about. The journal belonged to him. Finding it, though, was somewhat bittersweet. My mother had passed from cancer and I was tasked with cleaning out our house, which originally belonged to her mother and Heinrich. While sorting through some boxes, I found the journal along with other old photographs and belongings of my grandparents. I don't know what drew me to open it and read, but after doing so, I was also intrigued to learn more.

My mother had told me stories, so many stories, of my grandfather while growing up and his journal brought many of them to life. But it only captured a small picture of life at the mines. Maybe I can share these stories another time.

Will it be featured in your exhibit? I am glad it has ended up in your curious hands. Let me know if you need anything else from me to verify its contents.

Take care,
Jon

- 11 -
THE LINE

Tas sped off from the brewery with her phone in her lap. There were so many questions, yet she couldn't decide where to begin with her response to Jon. The drive home with the windows cracked again would help her think.

Traffic lights taunted her with their excruciating red as if they knew she was in a hurry. When they relented and led her home, she threw off her shoes, brewed a fresh kettle of tea, and dropped onto the couch. The drive helped organize her thoughts. Tas opened the email on her phone, removed the tea strainer from her cup, and hit reply.

Great to meet you, Jon. I can't believe the luck of just happening upon the journal especially after hearing all the stories growing up. I would love to hear more of them and about life once Heinrich returned home. Do you know what happened after the final entry regarding the new mine south of town? What about the diamonds? Do you believe more remain? And this may sound crazy, but I've read about the town being evacuated. Have you heard anything about that?

And yes, I will be including the journal in my exhibit. Maybe I could use your story of finding the journal as supplemental information to give background? I would need to know a bit more about you to tell the story, but I think it'd be exciting. Thanks so much!

Despite the lure of more stories keeping her curiosity piqued, the combination of soothing tea and the beers from earlier pulled at her eyelids. Before her mind caught a second wind, Tas dragged herself to bed.

The next morning started well before the sound of her alarm. The reply from Jon she had dreamt was nothing more than a dream. She tossed her phone onto the pillow next to her and stretched in all directions.

Her body sank deeper into the mattress that morning. The energy that often swung her legs out from the covers wasn't firing. Without a reply, only her tedious morning routine awaited.

Anticipation was like a drug. Translating the journal and the additional research were stimulants that broke Tas's days from the brick-laden walls of the mundane. She would spice up the monotony with traveling, but otherwise, she cycled from one routine to the next. There was a sense of excitement around the journal, but with the entries translated and the wait time for answers indefinite, the effects had worn off. As the highs crept higher, the lows fell lower like an anticipation hangover.

The lack of motivation followed her to the office when she rolled in late, by her standards, and slouched into her squeaky chair.

Sam knocked on her door, *right on cue*.

Tas dropped her hands to her desk with a sigh and mumbled, "Typical."

Even his entrance could have been scripted. The same double knock before stepping into her office with the same smug expression, perpetually condescending even without speaking.

"I haven't received any updates on the distribution materials. We need that stuff today so it can be ready for the opening." Sam adjusted the knot of his tie before crossing his arms.

"Good morning. Come on in."

Tas's chipper tone did not seem to amuse. Instead, Sam cleared his throat and narrowed his eyes on her.

"Yeah, they're coming along," she said, pulling out a folder of materials from her drawer. "I sent a couple emails out for the final bits. Then we'll be good to go."

Sam's arms dropped to his sides. "Jesus, Tas. I don't normally need to babysit you like this. Why can't we use the base set of information we receive?"

"Every museum uses that, and it's not..."

"Exactly," he interrupted. "Every museum uses it. That will include us. I want this stuff handled today." He adjusted his jacket before turning to leave, slamming the door behind him.

He was right. The materials should have been done. Normally, they would have been. Normally, she wouldn't have been so distracted. Normally, she would have written the materials, organized them, and had them ready, so when he stormed into her office, she would simply say, "They're already done."

But she was so sick of normal.

She stood from her desk and stormed into the hallway behind Sam. When she flung the door open, Sam stopped and turned to face her.

"You know, Sam, we get great feedback on our materials—the materials that I put together. I have been doing this for three years here and would appreciate if you respect that I know what I'm doing and not be so condescending all the time."

She almost covered her mouth with trembling hands. The words shot out of her before she could stop them. Words she had kept to herself hundreds of times.

They stood facing each other in the otherwise empty hallway as if it were an old western standoff. Sam's hands eased into his pockets as he took slow steps toward her. He stopped close enough she smelled the coffee on his breath and he stared down at her with unflinching eyes.

"Ms. Fredericks, I would appreciate your respect as to do your work on time and to never speak to me, your boss, like that ever again."

She hadn't anticipated that reaction. She didn't know what she expected. That was the problem with acting on impulse. It's framed as the exciting indulgence of spontaneity, but not all impulses lead to a beneficial consequence. Sometimes they put you in the very position your normal day was constructed around to avoid. As she stood forcing her eyes not to break from Sam's, that realization ate away at her confidence until she blinked.

"I'm only saying, I do good work and you should trust that by now."

His face remained unchanged, unswayed by her appeal.

Her voice was smaller than she'd hoped. "It'll be ready."

"Thank you. I would hate for you not to have the chance to tell me about your four years of experience next year," Sam said as he walked away.

Tas shut the office door behind her and leaned against it. "Fuck," she sighed more than spoke.

The wall rumbled as Sam slammed his door shut. Her face flushed with embarrassment and shame before she cried.

Guilt coiled around her stomach as she had to admit she wasn't being the reliable person she strove to be. She allowed the journal to distract her from the work that needed to be done. She wasn't only failing Sam and the museum, she was failing herself.

Somehow, when pain is self-inflicted, it cuts deeper.

Normalcy could be fickle, she'd found. The casual everyday routines that became muscle memory only made her crave difference, an impulse to break the monotony. All too often, though, once that routine was jeopardized, she grasped for it as a sense of stability. This was one of those times.

Tas wiped her eyes dry and shifted her focus back to the work she'd been putting off all week. It needed to and would be finished that afternoon.

Hours later, the stress that had settled onto her shoulders began trickling away. The information Sam needed was ready. It wasn't to her liking or to her standards, but that was the position she'd put herself in. By neglecting the work, she lost the right to reshape every line.

Sam would be happy. Well, not happy but appeased. Before leaving for the day, she popped into his office.

"Hey. Everything's ready to go," she said.

Sam shut his laptop and looked up at her from behind his desk. His hands clasped in front of him as he said, "See? It shouldn't be so hard. Thanks for the update."

His tone alone made her cringe: so disinterested and elitist. But as she stood in his doorway she questioned if she had burned her final bridge. It was a thought that weakened her. She needed a sense of reassurance.

"Oh, and about earlier, I wanted to..."

Sam raised his hand, interrupting again. "Have a good night, Ms. Fredericks."

She stared in disbelief for a moment as Sam packed his things into his bag, tight and secure in their places. It was a feeling she so deeply desired. Instead, she drove home where she lay on the couch feeling anything but.

. • • • .

While Sydney prepared dinner, she watched Mike on the couch, a beer in one hand and the remote in the other. He sat in their dark living room, only lit by the flashing scenes on TV that also illuminated his most recent pile of beer cans accumulating on and around the coffee table.

He hadn't said more than a few words to her after she came home from another long day of meetings and frustrating clients at work. She longed for a mindless break on the couch, too but only minutes after walking in, Mike had asked, "When's dinner?"

He needed time from the accident but she needed time from him. A resentment scratched at the back of her mind. *He's home all day on the couch. Why am I the one making dinner?*

She wanted to be supportive and make everything better, but she didn't know if he would let her or give her the chance. Draining the pasta, she asked, "Have you talked to your boss yet about when you're going back to work?"

He flopped his arm onto the couch with an exaggerated sigh. "Ugh, not yet. I'll email him in the morning. Maybe next week."

"I think that'd be great. Getting back into your routine could be nice."

Mike grunted an inaudible reply and turned up the volume on the TV. He was watching a true crime documentary detailing the forensics of solving a cold case. The increasing volume meant he wanted her to stop distracting him from the show.

She returned to the dinner prep as she tossed a couple tomatoes onto the cutting board. The knife tapped as she diced them, tap-tap-tap. Gradually, the TV volume increased until it muffled the dicing even for her. When she finished, she set the bar top with two bowls and sets of silverware and pulled a couple of glasses from the cupboard. She cut a few slices of the warm ciabatta and called Mike over to eat. "Dinner's ready. You want to turn that down while we eat?"

Mike dropped the volume and tossed the remote on the table. He lumbered over to the bar area and sat his beer next to his bowl and took a seat. He poked at the food with his fork, like a picky child, dissecting its ingredients. "What is this?"

"It's salmon pasta salad. I found the recipe online and wanted to try it," she said.

Mike stabbed his fork through a green leaf and lifted it to show her. "Is this kale? I've told you how many times I hate kale."

Sydney dropped her fork, and it clinked against her bowl. "You can't even taste it."

"Then why even have it in here?" He took a big drink from the can and slammed it down onto the counter.

"Because it's in the recipe. Plus, it's good for you. It's nice and fresh." She grabbed her fork again, looked him in the eyes, and took a kale-filled bite.

He smiled at her before taking his bowl, stretching it across the bar, and dumping it into the sink. "Why wouldn't you just make salmon and potatoes? Why do you have to add all this hipster shit to everything?"

"Are you serious?" She threw her hands out and let them fall limp to the counter. A few seconds passed where she considered her next move before she took another bite and stared at him again as she chewed.

What she was doing was risky, and she knew it. Mike loathed being taunted. Her mind replayed a moment in college during a basketball game when he started a fight with a player who had gotten the better of him. Mike first threw the opponent to the ground. Then the benches of both teams cleared when he landed the first punch. He had bloodied the other player, the infamous Allen, before coaches and security pulled him away. He was ejected from the game and suspended several more. That was the first time she'd seen him be as volatile as the reputation that followed him.

Mike had never let the confrontation go, even after college. It seemed Allen served as another log on the fire that fueled his desire for greater wealth and more powerful positions.

Sydney recoiled when she realized she had pushed too far.

Mike grabbed her bowl and threw it into the sink as well, sending the food in heaps out onto the floor and counter. He stood from his chair and walked into the kitchen where he grabbed the ceramic mixing bowl holding the leftovers and sent it crashing into the wall. A cloud of pasta and vegetables shot into the air leaving behind a small dent in the wall where the bowl had shattered.

Terror shot through Sydney. She instinctively moved from her chair to behind it. The cheap wood she clutched onto felt like the smallest semblance of self-defense.

"Don't fucking taunt me," he shouted. "You know I hate that shit and you do it anyway. What's wrong with you?"

She clung to the back of the chair, dragging it with her as she stepped away from him. His face reddened and his jaw clenched as he turned back from the kitchen toward her.
"I'm sorry! I didn't mean it," she cried.

Her arms shook as she squeezed the chair back, stepping backward again. The chair didn't slide with her but tilted onto its back legs. Mike marched his large frame to her and slammed his fists down on the cushioned seat, sending the chair's front legs to the floor and pulling her closer with them.

"Either make something else or go out and buy something." He set his jaw and spoke almost entirely through his teeth.

Sydney shook with fear. Mike could destroy her if the idea ever crossed his mind. She could do nothing against him. The tears that strolled down her cheeks caught her by surprise; she hadn't noticed her eyes welling. She was rendered a timid, stuttering pawn.

"I... I don't have... there's nothing else here that's ready." She looked down at her hands, her knuckles stark white as they wrapped over the back of the chair.

"Then go out. Go get me something I'll actually eat. None of that organic, hipster bullshit."

Sydney froze. Her hands remained clenched onto the chair as if it were the last thread of the life she had known. But in a powerful thrust, Mike ripped it from her hands, drawing her attention back to him. "You hear me?"

"I'm so sorry. Yes, I'll go now."

She scurried to the foyer like a scolded dog. As she opened the door to leave, he yelled out, "And get me another case of beer."

The door slammed behind her, hammering home her mental grocery list. There was no more warmth to their apartment. How could she call a place home when she felt walking through the door placed her behind enemy lines? It was like entering a cave where its predatory creature lurked.

Sydney didn't hurry when running the errands. She relished the fresh air allowing her mind to calm. The mess she'd be returning to seemed more symbolic than a mere cooking misstep. Yet there she was, placing another bandage of fast food and six packs over the shattered pieces of their life together.

Only when she returned home, what welcomed her was something different.

Lights throughout the apartment turned the dark dwelling into a collection of warm rooms. The whooshing of the dishwasher drew her attention to the kitchen, sparkling and clean of any debris. The chairs had been pushed in neatly to the bar and the scent of their summer rain air freshener hung lightly. She placed the bags on the counter and stared, mouth open in disbelief, at their home.

Mike stood from the couch and walked to greet her. He extended his hands, palms up, inviting hers to settle and wrap onto his.

"I'm sorry," he said. "I don't know what's been going on with me. Not just tonight but for a while now. I'll go back to work on Monday and, like you said, I think the routine will be good for me."

Her shoulders dropped as if letting down her defenses.

He continued, "And you can set that beer somewhere else, like on the balcony or something. I don't want it in here tonight. It's been making me awful. Especially to you."

She tensed, almost as a reflex, when Mike wrapped her in his arms. When their chests met, and she felt his raise with a deep, soothing breath, she calmed and melted into him.

"I'm sorry. I need to be better to you," he said, only a step above a whisper. "You're beautiful and amazing and I need to stop taking you for granted."

He kissed the top of her head and held it until its warmth brought a smile to her face.

"Thank you, baby. That means so much."

They took their dinner to the couch where Mike had her favorite series queued up and ready to go.

. • • • .

Tas had a habit of falling asleep on the couch only to wake up hours later to drag herself to bed. With her head comfortably on the pillow and her arm tucked underneath it, she watched the intro scene of her current binge for the fourth or fifth time. She didn't remember. Most of her binges served as background noise as she turned her mind off from thinking and decision-making.

Her eyes would open for a moment only to close again, like ongoing indecision between being awake or asleep. Until her phone buzzed with the latest reply from Jon, which pulled her up from her pillow, capturing her full attention.

Hey again. Yes, I had loved hearing those stories growing up, and the journal brought them and my grandfather to life for me. One story in particular comes to mind. Heinrich had been the top bowler in Kolmanskop for a while. The alley hosted many casual games for everybody, but some weekends saw tournaments where men paid to enter and the winners split the money. Heinrich mentioned in the journal about his interest in bowling but modestly left out his winning of several tournaments. He inspired me to try bowling as well, although I've never been much good.

I believe diamonds still exist in the mines today. My mother had alluded to as much when she would dream aloud about going to the mines and picking up where Heinrich left off—there would be enough diamonds there to support us for both our lives, she told me. We never had the opportunity to go, but I have long dreamt of visiting the town and exploring its mines.

Sadly, Heinrich never returned home and the uncertainty as to why has plagued our family ever since. I have heard stories of collapses, evacuations, and corruption, though I have no idea which, if any, are true. I do believe those answers exist somewhere in Kolmanskop and its mines and I would love to know once and for all.

I'm ecstatic to hear the journal will be a part of your exhibit. Thank you! However, I would prefer that my story not be linked to it out of respect for me and my family. I would prefer his story live on separately from mine and my mother's. I'm sure you understand.

Jon's words danced through her mind. The world that had only recently sucked her into its orbit was growing more vivid. There was an endearing quality to read about Heinrich's bowling achievements and knowing he'd kept them from his journal. That simple behind-the-scenes story cast a brighter, more favorable light on him. There were more stories to fill in the life that existed between the pages of Heinrich's journal and she felt justified in craving more.

What actually happened there?

The lure of discovering diamonds fluttered its wings within her, but that wasn't what drove her furious intrigue. For the same reasons that took her to Sedlec Ossuary, and had her scouring for anything related to Dyatlov's Pass, she was consumed by Kolmanskop. There was a story—a history—left buried beneath the thousands of bones, the Siberian snow, or in that case, the sands of the Namib Desert.

She lived for those stories.

When she'd grow older, retired, and hopefully, with grandchildren of her own, Tas wanted to have a life of experiences to share. Her adventurous curiosity was best explored while she was young before she was too old and all but restricted to guided group tours walking in long lines from one attraction to the next. That's not what she wanted. She wanted experiences not simply accessible via a convenient path beaten down by the thousands of footsteps before hers. No. What she wanted was more unique, more tailored to her interests and personality.

She longed for the remote. Craved the obscure. She wanted to learn the truth behind the journal and the history beneath Kolmanskop. Why did Heinrich never return? Was there any truth to the evacuations? Why were there no records of the underground mines? Something was waiting beneath decades of sand, unexplored and unknown, and she needed to find it.

She opened her travel app to research flights. Not every impulse would lead to an unexpected adventure but she'd never know if she never indulged.

- 12 -
THE SINKER

It may have been Tas's imagination but the next morning looked brighter than normal. She opened the bedroom window and breathed in the freshest air her lungs had ever held. Birds sang their melodies in sync from trees swaying with a gentle ease. She embraced every part of the high that came after indulging her curious impulses.

She sat with her back against the headboard of her bed and opened her laptop.

Hey Jon.

I am so sorry to hear about Heinrich. I can only imagine how tough that must have been for your mother and you. If Heinrich never returned home, I wonder how many others vanished without a word. Something must have happened there. The more I think about it, a collapse wouldn't make sense. Wouldn't the families have been notified? And if there was a quick evacuation, where did the residents go? I don't know how either would explain

Heinrich not returning home without a letter or explanation but I believe something else happened there that would.

This will sound crazy, but I booked a trip to visit in a couple of weeks. I'm landing in Lüderitz the Friday after next. There is something about Kolmanskop, its history, and Heinrich's journal that have consumed me. I think going there will help me fill in the gaps and give me a chance to verify the journal for the exhibit. This should be amazing and I will be sure to fill you in on everything I learn.

It would be a quick trip, only a week. After layovers in New York and Johannesburg, she would land in Windhoek, Namibia. From there, she'd hop on the quick flight to Lüderitz where she'd stay for several days before taking the same trek back. Planning the trip was the exciting and easy part. Breaking the news to Sam would be a different story.

When Sam barged into her office that morning, throwing her door open into the adjacent wall, his fists tightened as he stomped to her desk.

"You've got to be shitting me, Tas."

"I know it's bad timing but—"

Sam slammed his fists onto her desk and leaned in. "Put yourself in my position. What am I to do when the person responsible for a new exhibit wants to take a week off right before it opens? What the hell do you expect?"

"I know, but it's a chance for me to visit a mine from the exhibit and learn about it firsthand. It would be very beneficial to the show," she said, still in her chair and looking up at Sam. "I can't pass it up."

She didn't need to tell him she *could* pass it up. Nobody was making her go.

"Goddammit! It's bad timing and you know it. What could you possibly learn there that you can't learn from the materials we have here? There's no way I can approve this."

Sam was such a stickler. She wasn't sure if she could tell him about the journal. It wasn't part of the original exhibit, so she was certain he'd dismiss it. Worse, he could take it from her and do God knows what with it. On the flip side, he could be interested in touting an authentic piece in an exhibit that no other museum had displayed.

Yeah right.

"Look," she said, with a calm tone. "By going to the desert and visiting an old mining site I will get a much better understanding of the environment. That experience will benefit the show. The construction isn't done until after I return, so this will be an opportunity to improve our ideas and make everything that much more engaging.

"Plus, I kind of already ordered the tickets so the calendar entry wasn't so much a request as, sort of, a heads-up."

Sam lifted himself from her desk and brought his hands to his face. "Un-fucking-believable."

He paused with his face covered. His breathing came in whooshes through the gaps between his hands. She didn't know what expressions or thoughts were being hidden. He stood there as volatile as a rumbling volcano and she had no way of predicting the magnitude of his eruption.

Sam brought his hands in front of him as if he were praying. "I don't know what makes you think this is an acceptable way to behave. You don't just 'let me know' about trips that put the whole exhibit and museum at risk. This is unacceptable."

He leaned back onto her desk. "Pack up your shit. I'll have security see you out. I'm not dealing with your shit another moment."

Storming out of her office, he slammed her door with enough rage Tas expected the windows to shatter.

She sat in shock. When her strength to speak returned, Sam was far out of earshot and even further from a willingness to listen. Her body flushed before her fingertips went cold. Guilt, shame, and anger all battled within her. An overwhelming sense of disappointment pulled her head to the top of what was no longer her desk where she closed her eyes and tried to steady her breathing.

"Excuse me," said the guard as he knocked and opened her door all at once. "I have a box here to help you with your things."

Tas exhausted the little strength she had to lift her head. "Thanks," she said, wiping tears from her eyes.

The guard set the box on her desk and backed away with soft, careful steps. "I can give you a few minutes. I'll be right out here."

She stared at the box. "What am I going to do?"

A few frames stacked at the bottom of the box before she covered them with a mound of miscellaneous notebooks, a few tea lights, pens, and her small chocolate stash. She took the opportunity to do a quick purge of a lot of accumulated stuff that served no value to her in the office much less out of it. As she pulled open her last desk drawer, the journal sat atop a bunch of what could only be viewed as junk as far as she was concerned. She hesitated then tucked it into the box.

As she was escorted out of the building, the professional walk of shame, she remembered the couple of potted plants in her office. They would die in the coming weeks without her there to water them. That was somebody else's problem, but she could relate. She thought she would die without a drink, too.

That evening she drove downtown to meet the others for their weekly trivia night. The two-story parking deck was almost empty; only a handful of cars remained as their owners burned the night oil in their offices. Tas waited for the gate to lift before pulling into her traditional spot, second floor and closest to the staircase.

Shutting off the engine, she sat in her car.

I should cancel the trip.

She dropped her head back to the seat and tapped her hands against the steering wheel. The nervous energy needed an outlet.

Take the trip. Worry about finding a job when you get back.

Should she tell the others about the firing?

Tas pulled down the visor and opened its mirror. She undid her ponytail and pulled her hair back again. If she told the others, they'd pity her. They'd be sympathetic and apologetic and the entire evening would be depressing. That's not what she wanted.

With her hair set, Tas flipped up the visor, grabbed her keys, and walked to the bar.

She approached the little dive spot only recognizable by its group of regulars smoking beneath its black-and-white-striped awning. Inside, it was musty and dark. Most of the walls were wood paneled with a coat of paint that tried to brighten up the room but was too stained with age. Wooden tables were arranged around a worn pool table. The long bar stretched along the right wall with the same two bartenders who were there every week prepping for the incoming crowd. Add in some couches that looked to have been picked up from a spring cleaning curbside decades earlier, a dartboard with one dart, and the barely stocked coolers of random bottles, and she was home for the night.

She ordered a drink and took a seat at the same table as every week before. Most of the regulars were creatures of habit with where they sat and she was no different. But others paid no mind to the consistency. That's why Tas preferred being early so she could settle into her table without any hassle.

Minutes later, the room grew noisier. She noticed Sydney and Mike ordering their drinks at the bar. Out of habit, Tas reached for her phone, the fail-safe to never appear awkward in public. That's when she noticed the latest reply from Jon waiting for her.

You raise some great points. There must be others who never returned. There has to be a reason Heinrich disappeared without a word. Do you think something has been kept hidden all these years?

Your trip sounds incredible and spontaneous. I must say, your passion for all of this has inspired me. It wouldn't be right, though, if I sat back and let you go there alone searching for what happened to my grandfather. I can help with navigating the town and locating the mines. With my intimate knowledge of the town and your adventurous spirit, I feel we can learn the truth behind Kolmanskop.

I booked my flights to Lüderitz for that Friday to join. Let's arrange a place to meet to discuss our plans for visiting Kolmanskop and locating the mines. I do hope you're okay with my joining, but I believe my knowledge will be an invaluable addition to your trip.

Take care and talk soon.
Jon

Her heart raced as she looked around the bar as if others would share in her shock.

What the fuck? We don't even know each other. Who does that?

Tas hated to admit it, but he had a point about his knowledge of the town being valuable. She wasn't exploring another city or navigating a rural countryside on hot, infrequent buses. This trip would be different and far out of her comfort zone. Maybe Jon joining would be a good thing.

No. It was dangerous and creepy. She had to cancel it now.

Right?

What if I tell him I'm not going and go, anyway?

That was a big risk to take. Flights to Lüderitz were tiny, and unlike the name Jon Martin, which returned tons of records, Tas Fredericks was a far easier name to stalk online. How dangerous would it be if he called her bluff and spotted her on the plane?

"Fuck," she said, taking a drink.

She flopped against the back of her chair and looked up at the ceiling.

What should I do?

Having a mutual passion was a good start, but she needed to know much more about Jon to be even somewhat comfortable with him joining. She placed her forearms on the edge of the table and dropped her attention into her reply.

Dean tapped his knuckles on the table causing her to jump. "Whoa, chill. It's just me," he said, raising his hands as he sat.

Tas chuckled at herself, more a release of tension than actual humor. "Yeah, sorry. I was distracted with something."

The dim lighting of the bar did little favors for the bags under Dean's eyes. He looked beat. "Rough day, huh?" she asked.

Dean sighed. "I guess. Didn't sleep well last night." He looked over at the bar where Sydney and Mike were paying for their drinks. "Oh, yeah, let me grab a beer before we get started. I'll grab the answer sheets while I'm at it."

Dean reached the bar as Sydney and Mike joined Tas at the table.

"Hey guys," Tas said. "How's it going?"

Sydney smiled. "We're good."

"We're ready to know some shit tonight," Mike said with a pump of his fist. "Is Dean getting the materials?"

"Once he gets his beer, yeah," Tas answered.

A moment later, Dean dropped the stapled sheets of paper onto the table. "Solid visual round tonight. We have to do a mash-up of movie titles again."

"That's all you, man," Mike said. "But more importantly, what's our team name tonight?"

The team name was always the biggest decision of the night. The crafting of short, witty puns was damn near artistic. It was important to create something unique and creative given the host took joy in chastising those with cliché names. He would either shame new teams into never returning or harden them to come back better prepared.

"Anybody have anything? I haven't thought about it at all today," Tas said.

The table fell silent as they racked their brains, willing themselves to be creative on the spot. What they wanted was a top-notch name, but what they heard next was Sydney affirming their weekly fears.

"Ugh, there she is."

They turned to watch their trivia nemesis enter. The thin girl with short dark hair curled to perfection was all but unbeatable. Not even her purse full of first-place gift certificates quantified her immense knowledge of everything.

"Fucking, Babytown Frolics," Mike said, disgusted. "The guy is useless. It's literally just her answering everything."

"That makes it worse," Sydney said.

Dean tapped the pencil against the table "She was on *Jeopardy*. She's like a pro crashing amateur night."

Mike sat his glass down and wiped his mouth with the back of his hand. "And she doesn't even drink. That dude's so lucky. All he has to do is show up and he drinks for free. Forever."

Tas rounded up the troops and focused their attention on the task at hand, the team name. "How about Fantastic-ish Four?"

There was a collective cringe, but with no better ideas, Dean wrote the name across each answer sheet.

The host turned down the music that filled the bar, a playlist of old-school hip-hop, and tapped the mic before beginning his standard announcements. First, he'd welcome the teams, go over the rules, explain the bonus-beer rounds, and lastly, give his famous piece of advice. "The last rule for the night also applies to life in general. Don't be a dick."

He smirked from behind his beard, took a drink, and started the game.

"Here we go! Round one tonight is called 'Lather, Rinse, but no Repeat.' This will be a round of questions on general hygiene." He followed the introduction with his trademark ridiculing: "I'm sure this would be easy if any of you nerds ever cleaned yourselves."

The host rifled through the first round and the following two before taking the night's first scoring break. Most players crowded around the bar during the intermission. Tas wanted to use the time differently.

"Guys, this may sound crazy, but I booked my next trip."

"Are you serious?" Dean asked, with wide eyes. "Where you off to this time?"

"It's that ghost town in Namibia I told you about. Kolmanskop."

Sydney asked, "With the mines, right?"

"Yeah. You can take tours through the town and explore. Who knows. Maybe I'll find some diamonds while I'm there," she said, with a laugh.

The mention of diamonds grabbed Mike's attention. "What? You're just going to stumble across diamonds? I don't think that's how it works."

"Well, no, not on the tour, per se. But I sort of believe there are still diamonds in the town."

That's one way to put it.

"Eh, I don't know about all that," Mike said, shaking his head.

"Well, luckily, that's not why I'm going. Kolmanskop is the main reason, but there are other things there, too, like islands and gorgeous sand dunes."

"How long are you staying?" Sydney asked.

Tas wrapped both hands around her empty glass. "Just a week. I'm still doing some research. I want to spend time in Lüderitz, which is so isolated, it's like the only town near the mine. But from there, I don't have any definitive plans yet. I might spend a little time in Windhoek as well, but we'll see."

Dean set his phone on the table. "So just a casual Namibian vacation to visit a ghost town, huh?"

"Not just any ghost town, though. Have I shown you pictures of it?" Tas asked.

"I was looking at some," Dean said, tapping his phone. "It looks pretty amazing. But come on, isn't this a bit crazy?"

She'd expected a degree of skepticism about the trip. "I've never done anything like it before. It could be so cool."

"It'll be different. That's for sure. And you're going by yourself?" Sydney asked, twisting the ends of her hair.

Tas hesitated. *What do I tell them?*

"Yeah. By myself."

Sydney's hair wrapped farther around her finger. "Well, when do you leave?"

"In a couple weeks."

"There's no way Sam is cool with this," Dean said.

He wasn't. "Yeah, not so much."

Tas stared uncomfortably at her empty glass, thankful the host returned to the mic putting an end to that part of the conversation.

"All right, y'all, let's do a quick recap and standings check before getting into round four. Just a reminder that first place tonight gets a gift certificate for fifty bucks, second place gets twenty-five, and third place gets to come back next week to try again."

Sydney leaned forward over the table. "Guys, I feel like we're doing well so far."

The host worked through the teams from last to first. "In third place, the Fantastic-ish Four. In second place, Lasagna for One and our current leaders, the Babytown Frolics."

"Typical," Tas said with a sigh.

"Hey, but we're right there," Dean said, his voice upbeat.

The host continued. "Round four is called 'I Went to Trivia, and All I Got Was This Lousy Anal Probe,' a round on the paranormal and extraterrestrial."

"Maybe they'll ask about your ghost town of diamonds," Mike teased.

But they didn't ask. The round was a disaster which is all it took to damn them for the night. Tas attempted to remain optimistic as she got up to turn in their answer sheet and attempt the bonus-beer question.

. • • • .

Once Tas was lost in the crowd, Sydney spoke up. "Guys, I don't know about her trip. Europe is one thing, but Namibia?"

"She travels all the time," Mike said. "I wouldn't worry."

Dean stared at the blank screen of his phone sitting on the table. Behind a simple push of a button, pictures of Kolmanskop would be revealed. He almost understood Tas's fascination. "I mean, it looks pretty awesome, but I'm hesitant about her going alone."

"Exactly," Sydney said, extending her hand toward Dean.

Dean could talk himself into or out of anything. As he swirled his glass around, staring into the swishing beer, his mind played through hundreds of scenarios. Once the beer settled, he finished the glass and dropped it to the table. "We should go with her."

"Oh, fuck that!" Mike slapped the table. "I need a beer." His chair screeched as he stood and walked to the bar, shaking his head.

Sydney turned back to Dean. "You can't be serious."

"I think I am." Doubt crept into his voice as his mind weighed the endless factors. "I mean, I have plenty of overtime built up and could use a break from work. Something different."

Sydney glanced back at Mike. "Something different might be good," she said, twisting her hair. "Maybe something like that would be refreshing."

Dean opened the images of Kolmanskop on his phone to show Sydney. "Have you seen the town? It actually looks badass."

He swiped through the gallery growing more intrigued with each picture. The bright rooms filled with smooth waves of sand were unlike anything he'd ever seen. It wasn't like the other morbid destinations Tas had visited. Kolmanskop was gorgeous first and eerie second.

Dean pulled his eyes from the pictures and looked at Sydney. "I think I'm in if you are."

"No way," Sydney said. "I doubt I can afford it. I'd have to charge it."

"Oh, I know I will. I can't imagine last-minute flights here would be cheap."

A nervous energy ran between them as they seemed to wait for the other to decide for them both. Dean remembered the beach, sitting with Tas watching Mike and Sydney attack their own sandcastle. Tas had told him, "Well, next time I consider going off the grid, you should come along. You could use some excitement."

She was right.

Dean spoke at last. "When will we ever have another chance to go? Tas is the only person we know who does this stuff. We could use the excitement."

Sydney began to speak but paused as if changing her response. "Do you honestly think Tas would be on board with us joining? These trips are like her things."

Dean scrunched his lips. "I don't know. I think she'd be into sharing something like this."

He noticed Tas walking back to their table. "Well, one way to find out."

Tas tossed the pencil onto the table and dropped into her chair. "I knew that answer, too, but didn't write it fast enough."

She looked at both Dean and Sydney as they stayed quiet. "What's going on?"

Dean cleared his throat. "Well, we were talking and wondered if you'd like some company to Kolmanskop."

The dim lighting hid Tas's expression. A silence hung and Dean reached with unsteady hands for his glass but forgot it was empty. "I mean, you do always suggest we stop living vicariously one of these days."

Tas shook her head as if pulling herself from her thoughts. "Yeah, totally, you should. Don't get me wrong, I'd love it if you joined, but of all the places I've rambled about, this is the one you're like 'yeah, we should go'?"

"Those other places had more death than diamonds, though." Sydney smirked. "Honestly, if you were spending the whole time at the mines, I doubt I'd be into it. But seeing the dunes or doing a safari would make the trip so incredible."

Dean couldn't put his finger on it, but he expected Tas to react with more enthusiasm. "If you'd rather go alone, we get that. We thought..."

"No, no. Not at all. I would love it," Tas said, tapping the pencil against her palm. "And what about Mike?"

"What about me?" Mike asked as he sat.

"Well, it sounds like these two want to join me for my little trip. So what about you?" Tas continued to fiddle with the pencil.

Mike looked at Sydney. "Are you serious? Africa? And who's going to pay for that, huh?"

Sydney shrank into her chair. "Babe," she pleaded, with a look that said *not here*.

"Don't 'babe' me. You're acting crazy. You were just telling me how getting back into my routine would be good and last time I checked, my routine never included Africa."

"It's not crazy to want to go do something different and travel with friends," she said. "I thought it'd be something cool for us to do."

"Do what you want." Mike grabbed his beer and turned his shoulder to Sydney.

Trivia continued and served as a suitable distraction from the tension, but they struggled the rest of the night in relative silence. When the host announced the final scores, they groaned as they had fallen to tenth and the Babytown Frolics held onto the top spot.

Better luck next week.

They left the bar and gathered together near their cars in the parking deck.

Tas looked to Dean first then Sydney. "So, you guys actually want to do this?"

Dean buried his hands in his pockets, progressing through each knuckle that would crack. He nodded at Sydney. "Yeah."

Mike made a dismissive sound and rolled his head back.

"Yeah? Then this is going to be awesome," Tas said. "I'll send you my itinerary and hopefully we can get on some of the same flights."

"Sure. That sounds good," Dean said. He rocked back and forth from the balls of his feet. A restlessness stirred.

Tas continued. "Oh, and you'll also need some vaccines, malaria and some other crazy things."

"I like how you just casually threw that in there," Sydney said.

Mike stepped away from the group and headed toward their car.

"I guess he's out?" Dean asked.

"I'll work on him," Sydney said, watching him walk farther down the row.

"Well, he's more than welcome, too," Tas said.

She pulled out her phone and forwarded the flight itineraries to Dean and Sydney along with the list of recommended vaccines. "I'll take care of rooms and stuff, but tell me when you book and if your itineraries are any different. We can spend the first couple days in Lüderitz and Kolmanskop but after that, I'm open to anything else that looks good."

"I'll be fine with whatever you plan." Dean scrolled through the messages from Tas wondering if his momentary excitement had gotten the better of him. Only an hour earlier he was scrolling through stunning pictures, yet as he scrolled through a list of vaccines, his mouth went dry.

What am I doing?

"So we're doing this, yeah?" Tas asked a final time.

"It looks that way," Sydney said.

Dean didn't lift his eyes from his phone. He kept staring at the list and skimming the itineraries.

New York. Johannesburg. Windhoek. New York. Johannesburg. Windhoek.

Each name sank like a stone in his stomach.

Tas nudged him. "You good?"

He looked up to see Tas and Sydney staring at him. He shoved his trembling hands back into his pockets. His whole body shivered with chills, and his palms and forehead became clammy with a nervous sweat. At last, he answered with the only sound he was able to mumble.

"Mm-hmm."

- 13 -
THE RETURN

Dean walked to the edge of the water, standing atop a rock that looked out over the sea. Lake? Ocean? All he knew was there was no land in sight before the waves met the sky. The sun was setting behind him, drowning his growing shadow in the crashing water.

Am I dreaming?

The unfamiliar harbor was empty. Benches waited, haggard and unused, for visitors who'd never come. The rusted lighthouse creaked in the wind, spinning its light for boats that never approached. He walked against the wind with the sun warming his back aware of the out-of-body sensation. Like playing a first-person video game, he was aware of his surroundings, but there was a level of abstraction between the two.

He turned toward a small town. The buildings were dated and worn and the roads were scarce of any activity. In the distance shone a vibrant blue building, a burst of color amidst the dull sandblasted hues everywhere else. The building all but called to him, emitting an energy of importance that drew him to it.

Dean was unaware of his first step into town, but the rest followed as if his feet were guiding him.

The movement happened before it registered in his mind, like the delay between seeing a firework explode and hearing it burst into a colorful flurry. Echoes of church bells reverberated through the air, their tones carrying a great weight as they sang out the time.

He turned a corner and found himself in awe of the radiant blue building that stood before him. The building engulfed a group of people, blurred from view, in its shadow but when he recognized Tas among them, he approached. With her hair tumbling in the wind, she smiled and welcomed him to join. But there was an immediate, heavy tension that hung between the others as an indecipherable argument carried on.

All of their voices quieted when another presence, a stranger, masked behind Dean's subconscious fog entered the group. A long skeletal hand reached out for his and they shook. The long, boney fingers wrapped, almost coiled, around his. Their shake rose and fell multiple times with the last drop ripping away the entire environment. The scenery of the town peeled from his mind like it was unwrapping the next scene.

That's where Dean found himself in another moment he knew well. It was the scene he had replayed dozens of times. Darkness had never been so familiar. The hair on his neck stood straight, and a chill rushed over his body. He didn't want to be there in that moment again.

Hell was being thrust back into his nightmare.

Sweat and dirt covered his face, tightening his skin. He wiped at it while frightened with what he knew awaited him beyond the darkness

"I don't want to be here." His voice scratched like blades against his dried throat. "I don't want to be here."

His stomach boiled with panic, sending its acidic taste into his mouth. It twisted into bowlines and square knots, executing each knot he had learned in the scouts. With his heart beating against his chest, he clenched his hands until the nails dug into his palms.

He shouted, "I don't want to be here again!"

Fists clenched, he beat them into the cool, dirt walls that enclosed him in their lightless world, one fist after the other in a succession of desperation. No matter how hard he swung, the impact that threatened to splinter his knuckles did not pull him from the dream—from his nightmare.

That's when he heard her. Tas's voice was a whisper. "Dean, calm down. We gotta stay quiet."

The fury that fueled him had burned as quickly as it ignited. Falling forward, he braced his arms on the walls and let his forehead drop in between. An exhausted sigh forced its way out, loosening the tension constricting his body. Behind him, the dirt cracked and shuffled under Tas as she approached.

"What do you mean 'again'?"

Tas grabbed his shoulder, and the warmth radiated through his body. The knots in his stomach untangled. The panic flushed from his system. Relief wrapped its arms around him, holding him as the calm ran from his shoulder to his chest and down his legs where his knees wavered under his weight. Nothing around him was real but, in that moment, the peace and soothing warmth of her touch were as real as anything he'd ever known.

With a sharp jolt, Dean awoke in bed. His shirt, the same one he had worn to trivia earlier that night, was drenched with sweat and his wet hair stuck to his forehead. The moon loomed down from the night sky as he looked around his disheveled room. He turned on his bedside lamp and threw the covers from his legs. That's when he found the dense puddle of urine soaked into the sheets.

It took a minute for him to shake the disorienting sleep from his mind and register his surroundings. The bedroom he adamantly kept clean was strewn with clothes and crumpled balls of paper with the drawer of his nightstand thrown into the corner.

How did I get home?

What happened here?

He struggled to piece his night together. The memory of his latest dream faded amidst the chaos leaving behind another crippling anxiety. He scanned the mess for his notebook. The memory vanished when his stomach sank at the realization his notebooks were torn into the ripped piles around him.

Some dreams stood on their own. Others served as chapters in the same book. The latest was the latter: merely a piece to a larger picture, a greater nightmare.

Dean swallowed the lump in his throat and ran his hands over his face. The nightmare wasn't over. Against his will, he knew he'd return to that darkness again.

- 14 -
THE STRANGER

The room fell dark once he closed his laptop, killing its light. The old leather chair creaked with age as he stood and shuffled his feet along the cold wooden floor. From the bay window, moonlight shone onto his bare torso, casting shadows under his collarbone and each pair of ribs. He was a feeble man, one who seemed strained by even the weight of the laptop he carried.

He stared outward over the neighborhood and into the trees of the park. If the wind blew just right, he could see the moon's reflection shimmering along the river behind them. The headlights of a lone car crept down the street and around the bend. He knew that car. It was a small neighborhood; he knew all of its cars and routines.

Turning from the window, he moved with fragile steps toward the stairs. Vertebrae seemed to pop from his back and neck as he looked downward at his long shadow, frail and lanky with the arms of a praying mantis. He formed his free hand into a pincher and watched its shadow snap closed over anything unlucky enough to be within its reach.

The old stairs groaned even as he took them one delicate step at a time. With each step, he became more engulfed in the darkness of the floor above, the moonlight falling farther behind him. He supported himself by running his hand along the banister like dragging one's feet through dirt, sending plumes of dust into the air.

Fully plunged in darkness at the top of the stairs, he looked to his left toward the bedroom he no longer entered. The door remained shut and locked. He had buried the key in the park, wrapped in cloth and placed in a small oak box. Only he knew where to find it, and he wasn't convinced that it still wasn't one person too many. Sometimes he wanted to dig it up and revisit the room he had been suppressing. Other times, he was haunted by its mere existence.

Instead, he made his way down the right side hallway, following the metronome-like ticking of the Black Forest cuckoo clock's pendulum. It was an elaborate wooden design of a beautiful chalet surrounded by numerous trees, flower patches, and birds. The satin finish over its wood grain kept a shine throughout the years. The clock hung on the wall for as long as he could remember. He stared at it, the sound of time passing reminding him of times past.

When the clock struck midnight, he remembered lying in his room after a busy Christmas Eve with his family, eagerly anticipating the wonders that awaited him in the morning. He rolled around in bed trying to find sleep in every obscure position and angle, but it eluded him. When the cuckoo bird popped from its upstairs window and sang its distorted tune, he knew it was Christmas Day at last.

The striking of the clock also took his mind back to his troubled days in school. Never the star student and never one to fit in, he'd come home with failing grades as often as he would bruises and black eyes. When the cuckoo bird chirped at 5:00 p.m., he'd cover himself in his duvet knowing it'd never be large enough to hide him from his father's rage after he stomped up the stairs and into his room.

His father didn't always hit him, shouting, "Be a man and fight back!" No. Sometimes he'd rest his dry, weary hands to berate and belittle, destroying him until he regretted not only his mistakes at school but regretted himself entirely. There was a difference between failing and being a failure and his father always emphasized the latter.

The clock and the time it told rekindled many stories he'd rather forget. Every hour held memories, and after almost forty years, he was bound to have one for any given minute.

He'd never forget the story of 6:53 p.m.

He was making dinner for himself that evening and had thrown a few sausages onto the skillet with mashed potatoes. The kitchen was small and doing both used the only two working burners. In the microwave, he warmed a small bowl of bland pea soup. He had made the fresh batch two days earlier and was reheating his way through the leftovers. The peas were total mush by that point, but it didn't matter. Only a few bites would be eaten, anyway.

The clock upstairs played a short, peaceful chime signaling half past.

He mixed black pepper and butter into his potatoes and lowered the burners to keep his dinner warm. He grabbed the bowl of soup, dropped in a small spoon, and carried it upstairs along with a glass of water. Once at the top of the stairs, he turned left and quietly knocked on the first door in the hallway.

There was no response.

With the slightest force, he knocked again and still there was no response from the other side.

With the glass of water tucked between his arm and chest, he reached down and opened the door. The rusted knob squealed as it pulled the latch bolt inward, allowing the door to fall open.

Silence greeted him.

Orange rays from the setting sun colored the room in stripes. Shadows from the sectional windows stretched along the floor. His eyes traced them as they reached an ancient wooden bed frame. Handmade and carved from both beech and oak, the frame was sturdy and even heavier than it looked. Atop the frame was a plush mattress draped in white sheets and duvet. The large, soft pillows, also covered in white cases, lined the headboard. It was pristine, a sanctuary, if not for what lied within it.

In the middle of the bed rested a small, frail figure all but lost amidst its plush surroundings. The mangle of white hair exaggerated the pale, dry skin of the body. Its eyes were closed, sunken so deep it's as if they had fallen into its skull, and the jaw had dropped open revealing the remaining pieces of a yellow smile. The hands lay on its chest, interlaced at the fingers with blue veins that seemed to glow. The rest was buried beneath the covers, nothing more than a ripple in the sea of white.

"Mother?" He ambled toward her bedside and placed the dinner on the nightstand.

"Mother?" The word barely escaped his lips.

The room remained silent and still. The strained, weak voice of his mother no longer responded, no longer acknowledged his presence. With a quick poke of his finger, he nudged her hands, but there was no reaction. He took a deep breath to steady himself before leaning in toward her face. Could he feel even the slightest breath on his cheek, the slightest warmth to signal life? Seconds, maybe minutes, passed and the only warmth came from the few tears that trickled down his face.

His head collapsed onto her chest, listening for even the faintest beat of her heart. But her body was nothing more than a cavern, dark, empty, and lifeless.

This can't be. She isn't...

From the bedside, he stared at his mother's corpse. He placed a hand against his head to balance its woozy spinning. When the room settled, he decided he'd return the soup bowl to the kitchen. It seemed like the only task he could control.

At the top of the stairs, he noticed the clock and its pendulous rhythm. It was 6:53 p.m.

Taking one stair at a time, he couldn't avoid the family photos along the wall. With each step, he walked farther through their years together until he reached the bottom. No more photographs, no more memories. He'd be alone. He paused on the final step, his mental projector playing every moment he held closest. When he took that final step, he would never be the same.

It had been years since his mother passed but the ticking of that clock and its taunting bird still stoked the memory to life.

He continued down the right side hallway, his feet falling numb to the chills of the floor. At the end loomed a heavy door that seemed to dwarf even the hallway that contained it. With a turn of the cold brass knob and a stern push of his weight, it groaned open.

Moonlight filled the room from the large windows along the far wall. From their view, the shimmering ripples of the water beyond the park were clear. Along the right wall was a bulky, towering desk littered with various papers, coffee mugs, and cigarette ashes. He brushed a pile of letters to the side, making room for his laptop. Right address but wrong name; he left them unopened.

She doesn't live here. She doesn't live anywhere.

From a deep drawer, he pulled out an overstuffed, ripped folder. He eased it open hoping to not tear it any further. Inside, attached to the folder's pocket, was an old Deutsches Historisches Museum name tag: Jon Martin. His fingers cleared the dust from his photo when his face was full and his skin was warm.

The picture took him back to before his mother's death and to his first day on the job.

He could still picture when the photographer lifted her camera. "Ready? One, two, three."

Snap.

"Care to take a look?" she asked.

Jon shook his head, a tad timid on his first day.

"Well, I think it's a good one. Give me a minute and I'll get your badge printed."

She walked away, and he dropped from his confident posture into a slouch against the wood-paneled wall behind him. The first day of anything was always nerve-racking and full of unknowns. In fact, the only thing he knew was the opportunity to be a tour guide at the museum would help him support his ailing mother. After his father left, unwilling to deal with the cancer, Jon was alone in caring for her.

Despite being out of the house for the first time in what felt like ages, his mother's voice still hissed in the back of his mind. "You just want to get away from me like your father and leave me here to rot away, alone."

But he didn't. He wanted to be there to care for her and see her illness through.

The photographer returned. "Looks like you're all ready to go, Jon." She handed him his badge, still warm from the laminator. "Now, let's head over to meet Mia and she'll get you started."

With a smile, he pushed himself from the wall. "Sounds great. Thank you."

Back at his desk, Jon wiped his eyes free of the welling tears. The memory felt like a past life, and in a way it was.

He had stuffed the folder with printed newspaper clippings, various articles, and photos. Everything centered around Kolmanskop. Tucked in the other tab were copies of his grandfather's journal from his time at the mines.

If it was his mother's death that killed the Jon he knew, it was that journal that brought him back to life. It was a purpose that had found him on a day he'd never been so lost.

. • • • .

Jon buried his mother on a gray, overcast day. He had already spent nights without sleep and days without anything more than toast and jam. The death had emptied him, withered him to nothing. There was no service at the church, there was no one who'd attend. Not even his father. Instead, Jon accompanied her coffin alone to the bottom of a hill where trees towered over the headstones that stretched all around in organized rows. The hole was dug, waiting to accept a person who once was but was no longer.

Jon stepped from the vehicle, mindful of the rain puddles along the path. He carried a black umbrella in one hand and a vibrant red rose in the other. The priest joined him near the headstone while the pallbearers set her coffin into place.

"Let us read from King James Psalm twenty-three," said the priest, as he turned to the marked page. "The Lord is my shepherd; I shall not want."

The priest continued through the verse amidst the rain while a heavier storm rumbled in the distance. Jon couldn't bear staring at his mother's coffin, but he believed he deserved the torment and never broke his gaze.

As the priest closed his bible and brought it to his chest, he nodded, signaling the coffin to begin its descent into the earth.

The rose teetered in between Jon's fingers as he hesitated to move toward the grave. With apprehension, he wrapped his fist around the stem, stepped forward, and tossed it onto his mother. It lowered into the darkness, its vibrant shade muted along with the woman he had known all his life.

Long after she was buried, long after the priest and hearse were gone, long after the gray clouds turned black and poured over him, Jon stood under his umbrella staring at the fresh mound of dirt. He felt outside of himself as if he were in the earth with her. His strength to leave washed away with the storm. Wind swirled around him with a violent force, contorting the trees and branches in every direction. The ground beneath him shook with the steady thunder as if the earth was gnawing away at its latest treat. Jon's eyes were blank; his emotions flat. It was as if his body hadn't even registered its shivering. It wasn't until a fiery bolt of lightning lit up the sky when his focus returned from its daze.

Looking around in a controlled panic, he was unable to remember when the others had left him to himself. Against the wet chill, his legs carried his body to the top of the hill and out the ornate iron gates that led to the way home.

Home, or what was left of it.

The following weeks were a blur. He paced between the silent rooms of the house catching whiffs of his mother's lingering scent. Each photo reminded him of her face and her sharpened eyes. How could he move on when he lived his life surrounded by the past?

It had taken that time for Jon to build the nerve to step into his mother's old room. He had to sort through her belongings, organize them, give himself a chance to put her life behind his. Sleep had been evasive since her death, his diet had deteriorated, and any interest in his own well-being might as well have been buried with her.

He couldn't continue in her shadow.

After accepting the harsh reality of her cancer, his mother donated and sold what belongings and clothing she had. He hadn't known to what extent until he opened her closet and saw three white nightgowns hanging by their lonesome. A small box of clothes on the floor was half-open and half-full while others contained knickknacks, pictures, and books. She had loved to read until the sickness took that simple joy from her without mercy.

It didn't take long to move the boxes from the closet to the far side of the room. He would need the extra space to sort through their contents.

A fading light from the setting sun shone into the room capturing the floating dust. The air was stale, dry, and weighted down with the remembrance of her death. If he stood still, the entire room was silent.

Jon returned to the closet for the final box. He moved it with the others then stood to look out the window and wipe his forehead of the beading sweat. That's when a slow, rusted squeal grabbed his attention. He turned toward the door where it and the rest of the room stood still. The sound of the doorknob twisting was unmistakable. He was certain it was only his mind playing tricks, but the chills running along his arms thought otherwise.

Rubbing his hands over his arms, he turned his attention to the top shelf in the closet. He pulled down a couple of shoeboxes filled with more photographs, ones that appeared much older than the others. The grainy shots showed his mother as a child, standing with her parents in the same place he still called home. One picture showed his mother, no older than six or seven years, waving to her father at the train station. She was seeing him off to Kolmanskop unaware she would never have the chance to welcome him home at the same station. The thought stabbed into his mind and forced him to look away.

He had grown up hearing his mother talk about Heinrich and how much she loved him for the sacrifices he made. As a child, she didn't understand but when she grew older, she appreciated the risks he took. The stories she told, and exaggerated, only made Jon idolize the grandfather he never met.

Behind the photographs was a worn cardboard box. It looked to have accumulated its fair share of scratches, blotches, and water stains over the years, decades even. When he slid it from the shelf, the bottom gave way sending everything it once held to the floor in a scattered mess. Piles of papers and envelopes fanned outward throughout the closet, but sitting near the top of the bunch was a weather-worn notebook that caught his attention. Its cover was empty but for a lone word: Kolmanskop.

Jon realized the box contained the pictures, letters, and documents of Heinrich's time in the mines. The stories he had grown up idolizing and replaying in his head were all right there at his feet. He flipped through various job papers detailing his assignments and accommodations. He read the letters Heinrich had written home. For the first time, his grandfather felt alive.

Wrapping everything in his arms, he stepped out of the closet to sit on the floor with his back against the wall. He opened the journal with his lightest touch, caring for the words older than himself. Reading the pages took him back to his childhood when he'd rest his head on balled fists and listen to his mother tell the stories of Heinrich with great excitement and animation.

Jon allowed the world around him to fade, to take him to Kolmanskop where the wind breezed through his hair and the sun warmed his face. Heinrich was there, showing him through the world Jon had imagined thousands of times before.

The journal brought it all to life.

One by one, the pages and stories flew by his focused eyes. He labored between savoring each one or rushing to the next. The words filled in many gaps his mother had left out and worse, went against some tales she had once told to captivate.

What was she keeping from me?

She had never told him of Otto's death. She had never mentioned Karl or the gradual decline of the town. Jon had grown up believing that anyone who was anyone lived and worked in Kolmanskop. What else had she kept from him?

He turned to the final page where Heinrich was all but real. Jon traced his hands over the crinkled sheets and closed his eyes. The darkening room and silence in which he sat carried him away into the world he'd imagined.

There, Jon stood in a doorway, looking into a colorful room with wooden floors beneath his feet and tireless sun outside the windows. A man sat in the bed, hunched over and strained.

"Grandpa?" Jon called.

Heinrich didn't move. He seemed beaten down as if carrying the hard labor of each day in the mines on a frame that had thinned and showed its age.

"Grandpa?" Jon asked, again. "What's wrong?"

Silence.

Heinrich sat with his face buried in his wrinkled and dirtied hands. On the bed next to him were his folded and packed clothes. The desk was organized and collected as well. The room felt hollow, almost lifeless as Heinrich mumbled to himself behind his hands.

"I can't hear you," Jon said. He tried moving closer but remained frozen in the doorway, stuck. As if he were nothing more than a fly on the wall, he was invisible to the man he'd give anything to have notice him.

Heinrich slapped his hands on his legs and groaned as he stood from the bed. When he looked toward the door, his eyes squinted. "Hello?" He cocked his head and reached out while inching toward the door. He was close enough to touch, but then he was gone.

The daydream had been ripped away by the ferocious force that slammed his mother's bedroom door closed. The impact made him jump, throwing the journal from his lap and tearing free its final entry. He kept his eyes locked on the door while running his hands along the floor tossing the journal and other remnants of Heinrich in a nearby box.

The curtains behind his mother's bed blew from a wind no more real than what he had just imagined. When they fell back to the window, they revealed his mother lying motionless.

She looked exactly as he had found her that day. White gown and white hair buried under mountains of covers and sheets. Jon dug his feet into the floor and pushed himself backward against the wall. He rubbed his palms over his eyes, yet when he dropped them to his sides and looked at the bed again, she was still there.

"Mother?"

In broken, fractured movements, his mother sat up in her bed, throwing the plush comforter down to her feet. She ran her tongue over her eroding teeth, smacking her dry, cracked lips. She swung her varicose legs over the edge; too short to reach the floor, they dangled almost playfully.

"I only wanted to protect you." Her voice was peaceful and reassuring, a mother trying to calm her child. "I wasn't lying to you. I swear. I'm not a liar."

She pressed her clenched fingers into the mattress and her head fell forward, hiding her face behind a veil of snow-white hair. Her body heaved as she sobbed. "I'm not a liar. I'm not a liar," she repeated.

"Mom, I'm sorry. You're not a liar. Stop crying. You're scaring me!" Jon's voice was panicked as he hugged his knees into his chest.

Her crying stopped. His mother's body collapsed, motionless and silent behind the blowing curtains that danced around her. When her rotting arm pushed them from her, she revealed a face smeared with death and decay. Her eyes had sunken and disappeared into gaping pits with no life inside.

Her body swelled with a deep breath before erupting with a devilish scream.

"I'm not a liar!" her voice roared with rage, shaking the walls that trapped them both.

Jon grabbed the box and raced to the door, but it wouldn't budge. The lock rusted in place beneath his grip. Each twist and pull grew more frantic and desperate as his mother continued to scream to the heavens. Or to the hells.

"I'm not a liar!"

When the screams quieted, the bare feet of his mother smacked onto the floor behind him. Each decomposing step grew closer until her warm, putrid breath covered the back of his neck. Sweat dripped from his forehead while he pawed pathetically at the unmoving door, trapped and too terrified to face what lurked behind him.

A ragged fingernail poked the base of his neck and crept upward and along his jaw before stopping at the tip of his chin. With an effortless flick, she jerked his head toward her and pressed her lips to his ear.

Her voice now angelic, she whispered, "I'm not a liar, son. I was only protecting you."

Jon heard her smile stretch, tearing and cracking her dead lips. Her tongue ran over them, lapping up the pus before she placed a frozen kiss upon him.

The lock clicked free and he threw the door open with every bit of strength he had. He rushed out of the room and the door slammed shut with such force it sent a burst of air throughout the hall knocking him to the ground.

Spit dribbled down his chin as he gasped for air. He wiped his face on his shirt and crawled to his feet. With both hands clinging to the railing, he struggled down the stairs toward a key ring that hung near the front door. The collection of keys belonged to the various locks in and around the home, but there was only one he needed. With the narrow, anvil-like key in hand, he locked his mother's bedroom door, never to be entered again.

Over the next weeks, Jon watched his physical state deteriorate. He'd always had a thin, lanky build, and once his appetite failed him, his body collapsed in on itself. He couldn't be bothered to take care of himself or to take time away from his study where he fascinated over everything he had grabbed of Heinrich's. Even his work at the museum, which once served as a reprieve, became nothing more than an inconvenient chore.

Until he learned of the upcoming exhibit the museum would host.

With a ravenous hunger, Jon ripped through the mining exhibit's information Mia had given to him searching for details he didn't already know. There was more to the town, more to its mines, he just needed to find it. But the show shed no new light on Kolmanskop. There were no references to the underground mines and no mention of Heinrich, the man who called that world his home.

The next day Jon rushed into Mia's office with Heinrich's journal in hand. "You need to see this. It belongs in the exhibit."

"I'm sorry. What is this?" Mia skimmed the journal before sliding it away toward the edge of her desk. "I can't add things to a touring exhibit like this without reason. Or authentication for that matter." Her dark eyes stared, almost sympathetically, at the frail man who stood before her.

"But it's important," he said, pounding his hand against her desk. "It's my grandfather's journal. He was a miner in Kolmanskop. Diamonds. He mined diamonds."

Jon rubbed a fist against his head. He wasn't making any sense.

"Hey. Is there something wrong, Jon? You don't look great," Mia said, standing from her chair.

He clung to the journal and clenched it to his chest. "It's important," he said again, spittle flying from his clenched teeth.

Mia extended her arm, helping guide him to her door. "I understand. I do. How about I take a look at it and you can go home today?"

"No!" He jerked her arm away. "This is important! People need to remember him."

She backed away to the side of her desk and reached for the phone. Without taking her eyes from the disturbed man in front of her, she dialed for security. "It'll be okay, Jon. Just relax."

He stood still with his arms wrapped around the journal. His head fell crooked, and he stared at the floor.

"Jon. Are you okay?" Mia asked.

His motionless stance became a gradual sway alternating his weight from one foot to the other. His focus remained on the floor.

"Jon?"

His eyes crept upward to focus on Mia. It didn't matter how ill he seemed, how withered and weak he appeared, she looked frightened of him.

With an unexpected quickness, he rushed around the desk toward her. He reached for her hair and pulled her onto her desk, sending papers into the air and her computer to the floor. She clenched her eyes tight and screamed.

Jon dragged her farther onto the desk oblivious to her nails digging into his arm. She let out another terrified scream before two pairs of hands grabbed at his shoulders and threw him into the wall sending frames to the floor to shatter. Mia fell from her desk and cried while security dragged him out of the museum and into a world that never felt like home again.

. • • • .

Months had passed since his last day at the museum but the isolation and loneliness persisted. Jon flipped through more files in his folder before sliding out a folded, aged sheet, the original page he'd torn from the notebook and since kept to himself. The words peeked out from behind the folds as he laid the sheet flat on the desk.

The final words Heinrich had ever written.

When I requested to go home, I believed that counting down the days would have been joyous. I believed that as the date of my return neared, the work would become easier and less strenuous. I couldn't have been more wrong. Each day feels longer. The aches and pains grow worse. I need to leave.

For the past few days, I have been helping with the newest project. It's a new mining system a couple kilometers south of the main town. There's no real road created for it, so I trudge through the sand each morning to collect my gear and from there, trek farther to the mine's entrance along the nearby ridge. So far, the work has been lucrative, but I doubt enough to return Kolmanskop back to its glory.

There's something weird about this mine, though. As we've dug into it we've been finding other paths and tunnels everywhere. It doesn't seem like we're the first ones down there. I think the work has been getting to some men who have all but refused to continue underground and have instead forced a transfer to the alluvial fields. There's an uneasy feeling about all of this.

But it's almost over. I've packed my belongings and am mailing them out today. Then in just two more days I can leave this hell and return home. I can hold my daughter and kiss my wife, fall asleep in a genuine home and not this empty house, and eat a warm home-cooked meal. It's all so close.

The wait is almost too much.

- 15 -
THE HOME

It's amazing how a person can adapt to even the most extreme conditions. Like how men in war learn to exist amidst the constant sound of gunfire and the sky-splitting engines of aircraft overhead. It becomes background noise, the new normal. But what separates those who break under the stress and those who tune it out to anticipate an ambush?

Heinrich tossed his gear over his shoulder and left for the mine. Every step toward the mine consisted of one boot sinking into the sand while the other struggled to break free from its grip. He walked with the other men in silence. Tools clinked and clanked against the pummeling wind as if it was attempting to keep them from the mine.

A low, heavy rumble shook beneath their feet from the latest explosion to blast deeper into the earth. The unexpected force stopped a few of the newest miners in their tracks. Heinrich carried on, unfazed, continuing his strenuous trek forward. He thought the sounds of Kolmanskop had become as familiar to him as those from the streets of Berlin.

Home.

The wind continued to fight them with the fury of a beast. Its power threw waves of sand into the ridge, sending it upward and back down upon them. The mine's entrance was near, but the sandstorm masked it from view.

"Is it always like this?" The fresh-faced miner struggled against the wind, shouting over its commotion.

"Always," Heinrich answered, in stride.

The flurry of sand between them and the mine calmed, the entrance visible just ahead. Other men passed in and out of the mouth, but Heinrich thought they looked different. Their gestures were exaggerated. Their movements were frantic. At last, the wind showed mercy and broke long enough for Heinrich's ears to adjust to the screaming.

"Come on!" Heinrich yelled to the others as he jumped into a sprint.

Chaos spewed from the mine. Streams of blood stretched over the ground before puddling under men clinging to their wounds. Even the roar of the winds fell beneath the anguished screams.

The lift's bell rang with two heavy strikes as more men approached daylight. A tall, burly man carried another from the lift who clenched to his throat. Blood spurted from behind his pale hands and his eyes were all white as if too terrified to ever face the dark again.

"Stay here!" Heinrich jumped onto the cart with two other men. The bell rang again, three deep metallic gongs, as their gradual descent into chaos began. As the light faded behind him, he became surrounded by the maddening screams. When the lift jerked into place at the bottom, he jumped out and ran to the first injured man he saw.

"Can you walk?" Heinrich asked, kneeling and placing a hand on the man's shoulder.

"Help me!" The man lay with the side of his face on the ground and his knees bent under him. His arms squeezed around his stomach as he begged, "God, help me."

Heinrich wrapped the man's arm over his shoulder, but when he stood, the man's anguish became unbearable. When the man straightened to stand, the gash across his torso tore further. His body opened from hip to hip, shredded to the intestines. Blood poured from the wound like a flood of crimson before the man collapsed back to his knees, face in the dirt, lifeless.

Heinrich clenched his own stomach and backed away. His resolve weakened.

Cries for help pulled him from his shock and deeper into the mine. The lights phased in and out, growing dimmer the farther he went. Screaming echoes ricocheted around him as the walls tightened. When the lights plunged the mine into darkness again, he was thrown against the side.

Heinrich struggled against the attacker, too dark to make it out and too dire to care. He reached for the neck, held it at bay, and squeezed. When the assaulting arms slowed and fell, he threw the man off of him and against the far wall. The lights struggled to brighten enough to reveal the other miner.

"Help me," the man cried.

"What the hell's going on?" Heinrich shouted, shaking the man by his shoulders.

"They're at the split. Hundreds of them!"

"Hundreds of men?" Heinrich followed the man's stare toward the split in the main tunnel.

The man choked and coughed blood into his hands. "Not men. Hundreds of... things."

"Things?" The man must have been delirious. "Which side?" Heinrich asked, already standing to make his move.

The man coughed more blood into the air and pointed listlessly. Under his arm were more slashes stretching down his side. A body tattered to shards.

A trail of death led deeper into the mines, but the pained screams told him others needed his help. When Otto died, he ran away. He wouldn't have more deaths on his conscience.

He couldn't.

The tunnel had all but fallen into absolute darkness. Its lights fizzled only enough to cast the frenzied shapes in brief silhouettes while carnivorous screams pulled him closer. Metal clashed and collided, bodies thudded limply against the walls, all sounds he could decipher and place. Then there was a shriek, a piercing, blistering noise that sent terror through his body. The loud, cacophonous ringing in his ears made him consider turning back.

Another explosion blasted through the tunnels. Walls of debris rushed through the mine with a thick, smoky air. The blast destroyed what little life remained of the lights painting the entire mine in complete, suffocating black. The earth shook, and the ceiling began to splinter and cave.

Heinrich wavered, cracking under the moment, and broke. "Help!" He was now another voice, lost and faceless.

Helpless.

Before catching his breath from his hopeless cry, a piercing slash ripped down his back, dropping him to his knees. A pair of long cold arms wrapped around him and threw him effortlessly against the wall with a limp thud of his own. He reached for his wedge, anything for defense, and swung it wildly into the black that hid his attacker. The metal collided with something causing another shriek to electrocute his ears. Its hot breath smelled of decay, a sulfuric burning of flesh.

Heinrich's arm was batted to the side as pairs of claws ripped away at his body. His arms covered his head as the relentless attacks rocked him from side to side. He was trapped. Defenseless. He kicked his legs in panicked attempts to create enough space to stand, but the space only closed in around him with feral, preying screams.

The darkness hid the moment but allowed him to drift to a better one. One of peace deep within his mind. He thought of his wife and his daughter. Their home and its warmth, their smiles and laughter. He thought of the life he missed so dearly and feared he'd never see again.

A set of claws reached for his face and pressed his head against the wall. With a swift, calculated strike, the claw punctured straight between his eyes, burying him and every last thought he had in eternal darkness.

- 16 -
THE PIECES

"Here you go." Hanna handed Dean a bottle of water.

Again, Dean sat in an empty lobby. It was as if time never passed in Dr. Vauras's office. The magazines looked untouched. Hanna wore the same black blouse as before. Then he noticed he sat in the same chair as his last visit.

He took his water and moved one seat over.

There wasn't a specific agenda planned for his appointment. But something gnawed at him since Tas mentioned her trip and when he impulsively invited himself. The whole trip made him uneasy. Was that his fear of the unknown or something rooted far deeper?

He tapped his fingers on his knees. When he became anxious, he would close his eyes and take several deep breaths, a method Dr. Vauras had suggested. It didn't always settle his mind to a halt, but it often slowed him down.

Dr. Vauras's door opened and a short, thin man walked out, throwing his arm into his jacket. The man adjusted the collar, pushed his glasses up, and watched his feet as he walked to the door. He muttered a bashful farewell barely heard over Hanna's speakers and left with little evidence he had ever been there.

Dr. Vauras approached. "Hey Dean. Great to see you again. Come on in."

Dean wanted to avoid more déjà vu, so he sat in the chair opposite where he spent the last appointment. Dr. Vauras eased into her usual seat, back facing the window, which overlooked another pouring rain.

"How's everything going?" she asked.

Where to begin?

"Well, things are fine, I guess," he said, with a crack in his voice.

If things are fine, why am I here?

"I guess that's not entirely true," he continued. "I'm taking a trip in a few days and I'm nervous."

"Traveling can be stressful. Where are you going?" Dr. Vauras laid her arms in her lap, clasping her hands.

"Namibia," Dean said, shocked by his own words.

"Namibia? Wow. That's certainly a unique destination. What's taking you there?"

"A ghost town of all things." Dean cracked his fingers. "The idea started with Tas."

Most things started with Tas.

"Are you two going together?" she asked casually.

Dean worked through the rest of his knuckles, a series of twists and bends to crack the tension from his hands. "Not just us. Syd and maybe Mike, too." He paused and wiped his hands over his chest. "Christ, I don't even know where to start."

A lack of sleep wore on him. Dean squeezed the bottle of water before twisting its cap and chugging half of it. He closed his eyes again and waited for his legs to stop shaking.

"Start with Tas," she suggested. "How did this trip start with her?"

"Okay. Well, she likes visiting these weird places. Like vacation spots but not the normal things most people do."

"Like ghost towns?"

"Yeah. Ghost towns, catacombs, those kinds of things. And at work, she's doing a show about this abandoned mining town in Namibia. So naturally, she wants to go."

"That seems reasonable. She's excited about this ghost town, and did she invite you to come with her?" She leaned back in her chair and brought her hands beneath her chin.

"Not really," Dean said. "Syd and I were nervous about her going alone."

"But she's traveled on her own before, right?"

"Yeah, but not like this."

"Well, how is this different?"

Dean watched Dr. Vauras stare, her casual eyes dissecting him. He twisted his bottle cap on and off again before finishing the water.

"It's only... I don't know. Something's off. It's not the same as her other trips."

"How so, exactly?" Dr. Vauras stayed relaxed in her chair, her hands meeting at their fingertips in front of her.

"Maybe because Namibia seems so far away. I don't know. It feels off. And..."

He paused. He didn't want to talk about the dreams. Doing so made them too real, like he could no longer pretend it was something different or that it never happened.

"And?" Her voice stretched, waiting for Dean to continue.

"And, my dreams. I swear they've been about this place. About this trip."

She leaned forward. "You've dreamt about this trip?"

His leg bounced and his palms clenched with sweat. "I don't know. It was like the same nightmare as before only it wasn't. Tas and I were somewhere super dark and she seemed scared. It could have been anything, I guess, but it felt like I was there before. In the dream, I said 'not again' like I knew I was."

Dean's legs shook and he bit at the skin around his nails.

"Dean. Dean. Hey. Stop for a minute," Dr. Vauras said, leaning forward and touching his arm. "Close your eyes and just breathe."

After a minute, she continued. "Now, let's talk about this dream. Or nightmare, rather. You said it was both the same and different. What do you mean by that?"

"It's like there's one full nightmare that's broken into parts or, like, pieces. When I dreamt it this last time, it was like I was seeing a different part of the full nightmare. It's as if I was living in the dream," he explained, doing his best to continue breathing steadily.

"What made you feel like it was part of the previous nightmare?"

"It sort of looked like the same place as before. It felt dangerous again, like we were scared of something. Which I think is what made me aware of my first nightmare at the same time because it was the same way. Like, I even said something about it in this dream and Tas asked what I meant. It was like the dream was real." He shook his head. "This is making no sense. I'm sorry."

"No need to apologize. I think I follow." Dr. Vauras grabbed her pad and took down a few notes. After finishing, she looked back up at him. "Well, last time we discussed whether you believed these precognitive-like dreams could change or if they were set in stone. If you were able to modify the dream the second time around, and the dream responded accordingly, that would lead me to believe these dreams are fluid."

"But it was still in a dream. The dream is different from actually living it."

"Are you sure? Isn't the crux of your attacks the fact your dreams and your conscious life replicate one another? I don't think they're much different and if one can be changed, why not the other?"

Dean squirmed from her words and the tone they carried. Was she right? He dropped his head back and stared at the ceiling.

She followed her train of thought. "What if the dreams and reality can change in unison? If you can adjust within the dreams, can you not do the same whenever you see the dreams play out?"

He stood from the chair. His eyes drifted to the raging storm outside then back to Dr. Vauras. "That's not how it works."

"Isn't it?"

The question lingered in the air between them. When Dean's hands settled, and he returned to his chair, Dr. Vauras broke their silence. "Tell Tas, whether you can change it or not." She paused until he offered his full attention. "You need to tell her she's in danger."

- 17 -
THE DEPARTURE

The size of RDU airport always humored Tas as she rode by the sign for Terminal 2, which only supported Southwest. Her Uber dropped her off at Terminal 1 where there were a few more airline options. For being in a capital city, the airport was underwhelming. There were few directs to common cities and, as a result, she had grown to hate spending so much time in Atlanta or New York on layovers.

Her current trip would be no exception.

Everybody had different flights from Raleigh, yet they all managed to book the same itinerary from New York onward. Even though she planned to sleep as much of the flights as possible, she was thankful she'd have company. The overnight long haul from New York to Johannesburg would be rough, but all things considered, the flights were manageable.

As long as she could sleep.

At JFK Airport, she waited to board, sitting with her Starbucks as the crowd of people huddled around the gates slowly whittled down. That's when her phone buzzed with a new email.

Hello Tas. I'm Mia, the curator here at Deutsches Historisches Museum. Sorry for taking so long to respond, but I wanted to make sure I did. The journal you're asking about doesn't belong in the exhibit. There used to be a tour guide here named Jon. He was a nice guy, but he had some family trouble, and after that, he was never really the same. He came into my office one day and threw the journal on my desk claiming his grandfather had written it and that it belonged in the exhibit. After I told him we couldn't just add something like that to a touring show, he went kind of crazy. He jumped across my desk and assaulted me until security pulled him off and threw him out. Obviously, he was let go from the museum after that. But for the rest of the time we had the exhibit, he would show up most days with the journal, screaming about his grandfather and how people needed to know about him. It was very unsettling. It got to the point where I asked security to escort me in and out of the office for fear he may have been waiting for me outside.

I don't know how the journal continues finding its way around, but I'll tell you what I told the last museum curator, who clearly didn't listen. Just pitch the damn thing and let it go. God forbid Jon finds out it's actually on display somewhere.

"Attention, flyers. This is the last boarding call for flight SA204 providing service to Johannesburg."

Tas looked up to see Sydney and Mike scanning their boarding passes at the gate.

"Tas, let's go. That's us," Dean said as he walked up to her.

Tas stood in a hurry, fumbling for her bag, and knocked her drink to the floor. "Goddammit! Go on. I have to get this." She knew she sounded far more frustrated than what simply spilling her drink would have caused, but her body was shaking.

What am I doing?

Dean left and walked down the ramp to the plane while Tas scrambled to straighten the mess she had caused. All of them.

I'm with friends. If he's weird, we just leave.

She sighed as she pitched the last of the paper towels. "We can always leave."

Tas hurried through the gate and onto the plane to find Dean in his seat. She stored her luggage overhead and let out an exhausted *pfft* as she sat.

"You okay?" Dean asked. "I'm sure you can order tea or something."

"Yeah, I'm fine," she said. "Just some work shit."

If only.

Work was always an easy misdirection even when she didn't have any work to stress over.

"Sam again?" he asked. "Airplane mode and forget all about him." He grabbed his water and threw back a couple of sleeping pills. "Do you want some?"

"No, thanks. I'm good."

Several rows behind them sat Sydney and Mike. While Mike flipped through the menu, Sydney was adjusting her neck pillow, headphones, and eye mask. She came prepared.

Dean placed his pill bottle in his backpack. "Let me know if you change your mind in the next thirty minutes."

It was a compelling offer. But as her mind raced and her chilly fingers twiddled between themselves, she assumed the pills would only disrupt her system—a system currently in overdrive trying to make sense of what she'd just read.

Was it possible Mia was referencing a different Jon or journal?

Don't be so naïve.

The weeks leading up to the trip, she and Jon had emailed often. She grew more comfortable arranging a place to meet after hearing more about his mother, his passion for Kolmanskop, and other remarkable travel dreams. But as much as the alleged assault terrified her, she couldn't be mad at him for leaving that out. God knows she left out much lighter truths. She never told him she'd been fired either or that the others were joining. She thought it would scare him off.

The internet was where people could be somebody else. Anybody else. And with it being so easy to paint a picture with only the strokes and colors you liked, Tas had to wonder, what else were they hiding.

"So how do you think Syd convinced Mike to join? That couldn't have been easy." Tas turned to see Mike handing a sweatshirt from his carry-on to Sydney.

"No idea." Dean shrugged. "Probably pulled up the current value of diamonds per carat."

The plane accelerated down the runway, thrusting Tas back into her seat. Moments later came the weightlessness of takeoff. Before the cabin lights dimmed, she noticed only a handful of seats on the jumbo jet were empty. She romanticized how it would have been for her and Dean to have the row to themselves. But her mind did a quick about-face and returned to the fear that never lessened whenever she'd travel. She'd be 30,000 feet in the air with only the ocean and inevitable death below. Did her total lack of control make that thought more or less unnerving?

Needing a distraction, Tas reached for her Kindle. She scrolled through her downloaded books, looking for one to eat up a large chunk of the flight. With so much uncertainty swirling in her head, she had all but given up on the idea of sleeping.

Sleep was the furthest thing from her mind, at least 30,000 feet from it.

- 18 -
THE ARRIVAL

The shuttle brought them from the Lüderitz Airport into town and down a long, dirt road to their hotel. The orange and beige building sat perched on the absolute edge of the ocean, overlooking the crashing waves. Given the number of unknowns ahead of her, Tas appreciated checking into a hotel that reminded her of the beach back home.

They checked in at the front desk and looked around the lobby. "Want to meet back here in a couple hours?" Tas asked the group.

Tas and Dean's room was located on the first floor, with a sliding glass door that opened to a narrow balcony and the water close enough to touch. The view was breathtaking in every sense. Across the choppy waters rose a small, uninhabited peninsula, the last land between them and the western world.

Tas stood on the balcony, letting the sound of the waves and gusting wind refresh her. "Can you believe this?"

"This feels like a different planet," Dean said, joining her outside.

He was right. It did.

Tas had never seen terrain like that on the ride into town. The rocky landscape stretched for miles. There was no life. No greenery. Only craters and dry desolation.

"The drive in made me think we were on the moon or something. I've never seen anything like it," she said.

They moved inside from the balcony but kept the curtains drawn for the view. Tas connected to the Wi-Fi and plugged in her phone before hopping into the shower. The hot water provided little relief from her fear of what was to come later.

It'll be fine. We can always leave.

Her thoughts repeated like a mantra whether she believed them or not.

After a couple of hours, everybody met back in the lobby looking like the showers and clean clothes did wonders for their weary spirits.

"So, where to first?" Sydney asked.

"Well," Tas said, running through the options. Although they traveled together, they were on *her* trip following *her* lead. "I'm not super hungry yet, so I thought we could walk through town and up to Shark Island."

"Question. How do you plan on walking to an island?" Mike asked, never short on snark.

Tas shook her head. "It's not an island anymore. It once was, I guess, back before it was a concentration camp."

"You can't be serious. You're taking us to a concentration camp?" He scowled.

Tas always forgot how the things she found interesting were rarely interesting to others. "It's obviously not one anymore but visiting the area will be beautiful. There're memorials, a lighthouse, and you're standing at the edge of the world."

Sydney swept her arm under Mike's and looked up at him. "Come on. You'll at least enjoy walking through town."

Lüderitz was beyond its prime. Closed bars and restaurants dotted its narrow streets while the single-track train station had fallen out of use. But despite the hard times, a beauty permeated through its cracks. Rows of brightly colored buildings stood against the sandy, rocky backdrop of the desert. Tas smiled at their vibrant colors, taking pictures she knew would never truly capture the town's character.

She was beside herself in wonderment. Sandwiched between the Atlantic Ocean and Namib desert, she felt isolated and lost in the best ways possible. Everywhere she looked, the views became more magical, and she daydreamt of life in one of the modern luxury homes on the water.

"Hey guys," Dean said, speaking up over the wind. "I'm feeling a bit off from the flights and stuff. Mind if I head to the water and meet up later?"

"Aw, don't be a baby, man." Mike dismissed him with a wave.

"Yeah, that's cool," Tas answered. "We won't be super long. How about we meet over there at seven thirty?" She pointed toward a towering blue building with a color so bold it seemed to illuminate its entire street. "Let's meet there and we'll grab something to eat nearby. That'll fix you up."

"Sounds good," Dean said. "See you then."

. • • • .

Dean stood and watched as the others made their way north to Shark Island before heading to the coast himself. The sand eventually gave way to the clean, landscaped rock patterns running along a small marina where dozens of boats bobbed and swayed. Along the walkways were gazebos, worn but inviting, providing shade to the benches they covered, positioned to overlook the ocean and the endless world beyond. The water blended into the horizon where the setting sun seemed to extend forever across the sky. Its orange glow trickled across the waves to the end of the dock where he stood. The gusts of wind tousled everything around him. He stood silent and still, captivated by the scale of his surroundings and the realization of how small he was in that moment, in that place.

At the end of the empty pier, he sat and let his feet swing above the water. He pulled his pill bottle from his backpack and dry swallowed a single Xanax. The trip had been overstimulating and he needed a familiar calm. He lay on his back, placed his hands over his chest, and breathed in the peace of the wind and waves.

The sun was falling behind the horizon. Only a thin stream of fiery light burned across the water when his heavy eyes waned to a close.

Time carried away while Dean rested in solitary comfort. But too soon, his eyes shot open when his phone vibrated on the pier beside him.

"Dammit," he said, sitting up to check the time.

He hurried to his feet. When he stood, the anxiety had relented, his head no longer congested and cloudy. With one last look over the ocean, he turned to find the blue building where he was sure everybody was waiting. Then, as if the wind had spiraled around his body and squeezed his lungs empty, it hit him; he knew where he was. He had seen it all before, walked through that remote town toward the same distinct blue building. It was the dread of déjà vu.

A burst of wind struck at his back and forced him into his first steps. His sneakers crunched into the sand as he made his way to meet up with Tas and the others exactly like the last time in his dream. He took short, reluctant steps through town. The peace that came from his rest was gone. His stomach quivered. His shoulders shook. Goose bumps prickled all over his arms as if a chill had washed over him.

His walk through town seemed effortless. As if on autopilot, he navigated the streets like they were his childhood neighborhood. Only the familiarity reminded him of anything but home. He turned onto the final street and, again, stood in awe of the same blue building. Its long, dark shadow covered Tas and the others and stretched across the street ending inches from where he stood.

Dean took a deep breath and stepped into the shadow. "Hey all. Sorry about that. I dozed off, I guess."

"Dude, how're you still tired?" Mike asked. "You slept the most out of all of us on the flights. But whatever. You're here. So time for food, right?"

Tas looked around the streets and checked her watch again. "Yeah, but I'm—we're actually waiting for one more," she said, keeping her eyes low.

Dean looked up and down the barren street; they were alone. Who could they be waiting for?

Sydney cleared her throat. "What do you mean 'somebody else'? Who are you expecting?"

Tas rubbed the back of her neck and took a deep breath. Dean met her eyes and saw remorse and confusion in them. "So this guy, Jon. He works at a museum in Germany that carried the same show I was doing—am doing. His grandfather worked in Kolmanskop and left behind that journal I told you about. He knows a lot about the area and we're both looking for..." She hesitated. "I don't even know what exactly, but we want to fill in the blanks the journal left behind."

"What the shit, Tas?" Mike threw his arms outward. "When were you going to tell us we're meeting some guy?"

"How'd you two meet?" Sydney asked.

"So, we haven't actually met." She looked down again. "He mailed the journal to the museum and we've been emailing since."

"An internet creeper," Mike said as if confirming his own assumptions. "That's fuckin' great."

Tas looked up with tightened eyes. "Look, he's the grandson of the guy who wrote the journal—"

"I'm sure he is," Mike said, folding his arms.

"He just wants to join the Kolmanskop tour. That's it," Tas said.

"Then why's he joining now?"

Dean's nerves burned. Something was wrong. He looked to Tas as she cowered from Mike's frustration. "You couldn't have told us?"

"It'll be fine," she said. "I didn't even know this was the plan until earlier today."

"That doesn't make it better," Mike said, shaking his hands at Tas.

Dean tried to stay calm, wanting to hear Tas out. "Why is he meeting us here, though?"

"I don't know. I thought it'd be better to meet over drinks instead of on the spot."

"On the spot?" Mike exclaimed. "This *is* on the spot."

"Sorry, Tas, but this is kind of shitty." Sydney frowned and kicked her feet in the dirt.

The brightness of the surrounding architecture dimmed with the sullen mood. There was a collective sense that everybody wanted the moment to pass, but there was nothing they could say to move around the topic. You can't simply distract those who feel betrayed, Dean thought. It was like dark, overbearing clouds ruining a day at the beach. Nothing could be said to part them until the blue sky brightened the picturesque day itself and pushed them away. Sometimes patience brought with it sunshine, suntans, and sandcastles. Other times, it was met with a wall of downpour that flooded even the deepest of castle moats.

Dean turned from the group, and that's when he noticed the other lone figure walking along the street.

A tall, lanky man approached wearing dark slacks that looked a size too short and a black button-up shirt, a couple sizes too large. His face hid beneath the shadows of his dark bowler hat. Over his shoulder, he'd slung a small black messenger bag which he pressed to his hip to brace against the wind.

"You gotta be shitting me," Mike mumbled under his breath.

With long, strained strides, the man approached the group and stood near Tas. He took off his hat, revealing pale, sunken cheeks and dark eyes that sat atop large, sleepless bags. When he spoke, he sounded only marginally better than he looked.

"Hello. I believe you are Tas?" He reached out to shake her hand. "I'm Jon. Jon Martin."

"Hey. It's nice to meet, finally," she said, her voice shaky. She pulled her hand back quickly from his.

Dean caught himself holding his breath. The tension shook his nerves down to his foundation.

Tas cleared her throat before getting everybody acquainted. One by one, Jon extended his skeletal hand and introduced himself to Mike and Sydney and, at last, Dean.

Jon's hand somehow felt chilled when it wrapped around Dean's. He spoke with kindness but his demeanor, his appearance, his aura were all unsettling. It felt as though he carried himself with an ominous uncertainty that took hold the moment he shook your hand.

"Tas, you hadn't told me to expect others," Jon said.

"Join the club," Mike mumbled again.

Tas ran a hand over the back of her neck. "Yeah, it was sort of last minute. I hope that's okay."

Jon turned through the group as if surveying them before deciding. "Oh, it's fine." He swung his bag in front of him and hugged it to his chest. "I love sharing these stories with anybody willing to listen."

"Great." Tas's optimism seemed forced. "Then how about we grab a drink? You know, long day of traveling and all," she said with a slight chuckle, trying to loosen the mood.

"About time. I could use a beer or two," Mike said.

"There's a great place down this way," Jon said, as he began walking. "Right around the corner."

With a shrug, Tas and the others followed.

Jon led them to a bright red building with large arched windows glowing with a warm yellow light. The sounds of music and a lively atmosphere bled outside to the quiet street. Jon pulled at the large wooden door and let the group enter before him.

"Welcome," the bartender greeted. "You all ordering food or just drinks tonight?" He wore a smile that managed to cover his entire face with teeth that shined impossibly white. An ironic T-shirt claiming Lüderitz to be a small drinking town with a fishing problem rounded out his cheerful presence.

"Both, please," Tas answered. "Can we get three pitchers of your house draft to start?"

"Coming right up. Grab a seat and I'll get them over to you."

At the table, they ordered a couple of pizzas and worked through their first round. Dean looked around the bar and its odd decorations. The bar itself was covered by a straw hut decorated in various ball caps, T-shirts, and bras. The small buffet wrapped around a wood-burning stove while candles and torches filled whatever open space was left between tables. Somehow the mixture worked to create an upbeat vibe, which was exactly what they needed.

Dean was thankful for the raucous, ambient noise of the bar because it often filled the drawn-out silences at their table. Only after a couple of beers, did the tension lighten and the conversations become less forced. As the evening rolled on, the crowds thinned and the noise became easier to manage.

Jon gestured to the bartender for another round then tossed his bag onto the table. "So other than Tas, what do you all know about Kolmanskop and the mines?"

"Not much," Sydney said.

"I heard we might find diamonds!" Mike topped off his glass from the fresh pitcher.

"Oh dear." Jon shook his head. "Well, there's much to know, but I will attempt to be brief."

Piles of clippings, notes, and pictures poured from his bag. Like a person obsessed, he had circled particular phrases and filled the margins of printouts with scribbled notes. He ran through the history of the mines with an excitement that bordered on contagious.

Dean marveled at his level of detail. "You need to put this in your exhibit," he said to Tas, but she hid behind her glass and looked away with a discreet nod.

"And that all brings me to this," Jon continued. He paused before reaching into his bag and pulling out a folded map. Moving the pitchers and plates to the end of the table, he flattened it and started with his plan. "So we will be part of the first tour tomorrow morning, right?"

"Yep. We're all set," Tas confirmed.

"The tour will take us along this route." Jon's wiry finger traced a small line that connected several small blocks. "Afterward, they will allow us some time to explore on our own before meeting back at the shuttle. That will be our chance to head down here." His finger slithered southbound then plopped down along a small ridge.

"This is where we'll find the entrance to the mine, somewhere along here. But first, we'll want to stop here to grab a few things." A small spray of dust burst from the map as his hand dropped at its next point.

Mike jumped in. "Wait, what things?"

"The mine's entrance won't be out in the open inviting us in. We may have to do a little prodding to find it. With any luck, there'll be a few tools that aren't entirely worn away to assist." Jon ran his finger back to the southern ridge. "Once inside the mine, we will have about six hours to explore before having to return to town for the final shuttle."

"Hold up. Six hours?" Sydney's eyes popped as she dropped her palms onto the table.

"Fuck that," said Mike, with the beginnings of a slur.

"That seems like a long time. Do you think we'll need to be down there that long?" Tas asked.

"You're all welcome to go as you wish, of course," Jon said.

"But six hours for what? What are you hoping to find?" Sydney asked.

"A shit-ton of diamonds, babe." Mike pounded back the last of his beer and followed it with a belch. "I'm gonna hit the head," he said, leaving for the restrooms.

"But seriously," Sydney continued. "What do you expect to find?"

Jon stayed quiet for a moment, contemplating how to answer. "I don't know, exactly. I suppose I hope to find evidence of my grandfather. He never returned home from the mines. I don't know if I expect to find anything tangible, but a sense of closure, an end to his story, would be nice."

"Yeah," Tas said. "And we may not even find the mines, so it might not even matter."

Jon fixed his stare onto her and lowered his brow. "Of course, it matters! Why else would we be here if not for the mines? They're right here," he said, tapping again on the map. "Do you not believe me?"

"No, it's nothing like that at all. I only meant, like, yeah the mines matter but if we can't get in or something..." She trailed off as she looked at Dean and Sydney.

Jon's elevated voice brought out his accent yet Dean was taken back more by the surprising force, the defensive anger, with which he spoke. Like a fuse had ignited with Tas's one, simple comment.

"I think all of this will be easier to clear up after a good night's sleep," Dean said. "We have that early start tomorrow. Should we get going?"

Jon collected his things with a huff, running his eyes between Tas and Dean. They all finished their drinks and waited for Mike outside.

The streets were quiet. A couple of figures stood in the darkness, only discernible by the glowing embers of their cigarettes. With the sun down and the calm breeze coming in from the water, a refreshing air welcomed them into the night.

Jon took the chance to light up a smoke as well.

The front door flung open, disturbing the peace, and Mike exited with a slight stagger to his step. "Y'all were just going to leave me?"

Sydney moved to his side and ran her hand along his back. "We didn't leave. We're still waiting here, aren't we?"

"Okay guys," Tas said, grabbing everybody's attention. "So we're set? Our tour is at nine tomorrow. So we'll meet up in Kolmanskop then, cool?"

"Wonderful," Jon said, blowing out a cloud of smoke. "And I'd like to thank you for the great evening and letting me join." He made one last round of shaking hands before tossing on his cap and heading down the lightless road, trails of smoke following him like a train in the night.

"So, we're really doing this, huh?" Dean asked.

"At least I am," Tas answered.

They watched as the last outline of Jon disappeared into the night, indistinguishable from the dark that consumed him. The glow of his cigarette turned and disappeared around the corner.

"At least I am," she repeated, turning back for the hotel.

- 19 -
THE APPEAL

The next morning, Dean stood at the sliding glass door and looked out at the clear, bright morning before him. A colony of seagulls sat in the water, bobbing up and down with the tides.

Tas examined herself in the mirror, readying herself for the day. "God, I look like shit," she said, tying back her hair. "One day of traveling and drinking and this is what I get in the morning. Ugh, I'm getting old."

"You're only as old as you feel," Dean said, dryly.

"Well, I feel like death." Tas turned to Dean and rubbed her hands over her face.

Death was the last thing he thought she looked like, but he could relate to the sentiment. The frenzy of airports, travel, and the unsettling night with Jon had left his stomach in knots. Even with the beers the night before, sleep teased just beyond his reach. He didn't feel like death but he didn't feel alive either.

Tas's bed was a mess, covered in a bunch of items she was debating packing for the day ahead. Sunscreen, a water bottle, and a few snacks were set aside in a pile. But as she grouped the flashlight, duct tape, and bandages, the uncertainty for the day gripped him tighter.

"Do you think we'll really need that stuff?" he asked.

"I have no idea," she said, tightening the strings of her bag and throwing it around her shoulders. She picked the remaining flashlight off the bed and tossed it to him. "Don't forget this."

He stared at the light and clicked it on and off. "Are you sure you want to do this? We don't even know this guy:"

"It's going to be fine," she said.

"But he's weird, Tas. You have to admit." Dean turned the light off and tossed it on his bed. He stared at Tas, begging to be heard.

"I guess, but he's an older dude hanging around new people. He probably feels weirder than we do."

Dean fidgeted with his hands, cracking his knuckles. "Yeah, maybe." He moved to the side of his bed, handling the items he had been hesitating to pack. "Tas, listen," he said, dropping his bag. "This scares me. I think we're walking into something dangerous."

"What do you mean?"

Stepping around his bed, he stood with her. He didn't want to hide his trembling hands or his fraying nerves. He didn't want to hide anything. "I'm scared for you. I'm scared something is going to happen to you."

She checked her watch and sighed. "It'll be okay. If he gets weird, we'll leave. That simple."

It was anything but simple, he thought.

"That's not the point. I mean, we don't know where we are, where we're going, or who we're with."

She moved closer and placed her hands on his shoulders. "I get that. I do. But there's more to it than that. You don't understand it."

"What don't I understand, Tas?" He rolled his shoulders out from under her hands.

"These kinds of trips. The people who take them. They're not some casual, ordinary tourist. It's like urban explorers. They share this same obscure interest that bonds them even though they often meet knowing little more than their usernames. This isn't much different."

Tas reached for Dean's bag and tossed it to him. "Come on. I don't want to be late."

He clutched the bag close to his shaking body. "And I don't want you to die."

"Okay," she said, with a chuckle. "That's a little extreme; don't you think?" She shook her head and started toward the door.

Dean stepped in her way. "Listen, I dreamt that you do. Did. Whatever." His eyes widened with sincerity and he swallowed the lump in his throat. "Here, in the mines."

It may have been his glassy eyes, but he swore she looked at him with pity. "I have lots of dreams but it's not like they come true." She checked her watch again, huffed, and moved past him for the door.

Dean moved behind her and grabbed her hand as she grabbed the handle. They froze and their eyes met. "But mine do," he said.

Her expression softened. Then with a sigh, she pressed down on the handle and opened the door. "Come on."

"Tas, no," he said. "I'm serious."

"Come on, Dean. You're being neurotic. This is your first major trip and I get it, it's a crazy one. If you want stay here, that's fine. I won't force you to come along. But I'm going." She held the door open and looked back at him. "Well?"

The room darkened. A war raged within him destroying his ability to speak and fight. He stood in the doorway, so small, so far away.

Their stare broke as he dropped his head. "Tas, please," he whispered.

The door swung closed between them. Dean fell against it, weak and defeated, and listened to Tas walk down the hallway without him.

What am I doing?

Dean slid down the door until he knelt on the floor, dropping his head into his sweaty hands. His lungs struggled for air with fits of erratic breathing. He crawled to his backpack on the bed and dug for his Xanax. The bottle shook in his hands, rattling like a maraca he hoped would silence the noise blaring in his head. Another pill down the hatch and he stretched across the bed looking out the glass door.

The lonely peninsula across the channel looked calm and still. A solitary stretch of land withstanding the gradual erosion of its captors, the water and winds. Yet with no control over its volatile environment, it projected peace, solitude, and comfort as if reminding the nature that winds mustn't always howl and waves mustn't always crash.

Dean gasped for a deep breath and exhaled with an acceptance. He couldn't control his tumultuous environment but only how he carried himself through it. If Tas was walking into the chaos he feared, he couldn't let her do it alone.

Jumping to his feet, he rushed from the room.

From the lobby of the hotel, he saw Tas, Sydney, and Mike take their seats on a raggedy, old bus. He threw the hotel's doors open and ran out into the glaring sun. The bus started down the road away from him before its bright red taillights glowed. It rumbled to a stop as a cloud of dirt and sand wafted around it. Dean ran along the side to see the folding doors open. He slid as he reached them and pulled himself up the stairs.

"Welcome aboard." The bus driver didn't let a face of wrinkles and a couple of missing teeth keep him from smiling with all the joy in the world. According to the name on his badge, Merrill wore the same smile even on picture day.

"Sorry, I'm late," Dean said.

"Not a problem. There's no hurry in Africa, friend. Grab a seat." Merrill flashed another gapped smile and closed the door.

Dean looked back into the empty bus. Only Tas, Sydney, and Mike were on board. He had every other seat to himself but there was only one he wanted.

"About time, dude," Mike said.

Dean smiled then sat with Tas. She offered him the window and the old leather seat crunched beneath him when he sat. He looked at the initials and dates scratched into the seatback in front of him, reminding him of the school buses back home. "Sorry about that," he said, quietly.

"It's cool." Tas turned to face him. "I'm sorry, too. But I'm glad you're here."

The bus clunked into gear and started down the road.

"Hope you all can squeeze in okay back there." Merrill laughed at his own joke. The bus filled with his infectious laughter, which was funnier than the joke itself.

"You're all a lucky bunch, you know that? We got this ride to ourselves this morning. Nothing fancy here. Just the bus, four wheels, and me. And a steering wheel, of course. You see these new city buses with air con and internet and all those sorts of things? Nope. Nothing fancy here. Not like that." Merrill craned his neck to look around a corner before turning onto the main road out of town.

"I picked up a group last week, or maybe three weeks back, but can you believe they asked about internet? The internet on this thing?" He slapped his leg several times, cracking himself up at the memory. "This bus may not have the internet, but it'll take you back in time, that's for sure. What's taking you all to Kolmanskop today?"

Tas leaned forward to answer, but Merrill hopped right back into his spiel.

"Probably coming out here to get rich and find some of those diamonds, huh? Yeah, I keep saying I'll find some and finally get to take the misses out."

Mike spoke up, "And buy a bus with Wi-Fi."

Merrill howled at the crack. "That's exactly right! I like this guy."

The bus rumbled to the edge of town and approached a hillside cemetery. "Lots of miners buried over there. Rumor has it the unmarked graves contain several bodies from the heydays of Kolmanskop. But them's just rumors. Want to know what I think?" He paused for a breath and continued before anybody could answer. "I think they're filled with tourists who were unsuccessful in finding diamonds here. Gory stuff, too, I bet. But don't worry. You guys'll be fine." Again, he laughed with himself.

Dean sat only a few rows back from Merrill, but his words seemed to drift miles away. The window fogged from his breath as he watched the cemetery roll by. His head bounced with every bump in the road, but his vision remained forward and unfocused. Once the bus left the small town behind, there was only desolation around him. Nothing but a lunar-like landscape of craters and rock stretched far into the distance.

No color. No brightness. No life.

He closed his eyes and the barren terrain faded. What began as a calm darkness behind his eyes glittered into little flashes of light as the bus tumbled along its route. Each light became brighter, a dim flicker to a blinding strobe, until his eyes shot open.

He found himself within the darkened walls of his nightmares. They followed him halfway around the earth to confine him once more.

"Try it again," Tas said, hidden from view, with a quiet, cautious voice.

"What?" He was dazed, looking around a blackness so deep it was disorienting. "Try what again?" The muscles in his neck constricted and a deep throbbing pain dug into his side.

"The fucking flashlight, Dean. Try it again," Tas snapped, her voice sharp and frantic.

In his hand, he registered a flashlight, and a sudden sense of dread burrowed into his mind. *Please don't be dead.* He smashed the light against his hand and it surged to life with a burning brightness.

Tas stood an arm's length away. Her face was dirty and desperate. Trails of grime and blood smeared over her. She ran her hands across her face making the mess worse and sighed. "Okay. We need to move. That way's fucked, okay? We've got to head this way and try to find a way back up."

Dean couldn't look away from the filth that covered her. Blood stained her top and ran down her arm. The calm she often projected betrayed her when she turned toward a small opening, a tunnel they'd need to crouch to pass through.

"Dean? Dean. What the fuck?" Tas clapped her hands to catch his attention. "I need you here with me."

"What's going on?" His head spun. "Where's Syd and Mike?"

He ran the flashlight along the walls, following long, distorted gashes leading into the path behind Tas. Two thin scrapes anchored a large, deeper scrawl between them. They dug into the walls and jerked sporadically like a heart monitor from a hellish past.

Tas exhaled with an unmistakable frustration. She moved toward him with quick, controlled steps. "You know as well as I do. But we need to move before those..." She flailed her hands, searching for a word. "Before those things find us."

A chill ran down his spine, stiffening each vertebra it passed. His mind drew grotesque, horrific images of anything that could have torn those marks into the walls. "What things?"

"Have you been asleep this whole time? The fucking things that did this to you."

Tas stepped closer and lifted the side of his shirt. The fabric clumped together and pulled at the wound of drying blood it covered. Dean looked down at the three scratches running from the bottom of his ribs to his hip. The shock paired with the blood loss drained him of his color. His head spun into a frenzy and his legs wobbled. He looked at Tas with helpless eyes begging for something stable, something to explain what was happening. Then his face glazed over.

"Dean, stay with me," Tas said, clapping her hands again.

But his head dropped forward, and the flashlight smashed to the ground. Tas reached for his hands. "Dean, I need you to hang in there. I need you to wake up."

Wake up.

Dean jumped from the bus seat in a panic.

"There he is," Mike announced. "Dude, how do you fall asleep everywhere?"

Outside the window was a long, drab, two-story building. There were a few tourists wandering around with their maps and handheld fans. But one tourist stood out from the others: the thin man in black hidden beneath the rim of his hat. Jon. He stood near the stairs that ran to the upper entrance of the building with a backpack at his feet looking down at some loose papers.

Tas sat next to Dean. "We're here. Looks like you conked out pretty hard."

"Tas, you can't do this," he pleaded. "We shouldn't do this."

Merrill stood from his seat and looked back. "I wouldn't stay in here too long. You think it gets hot out there? Sitting in here will be the death of you."

But leaving could be the death of him, too, Dean thought.

"It'll be fine. I promise." Tas grabbed his hand and led him off the bus, thanking Merrill as they left.

The middle of nowhere. Only sand, desert, and destitution.

As the wind tore through the town, stinging his face with the walls of sand it carried, Dean couldn't avoid the sense it was trying to push him away. He watched the handful of other tourists pose for pictures, smiling at the environment as if it were a mere novelty. But something darker loomed beneath the sands. Alive. Breathing. Unwelcoming.

Jon approached them with a tip of his cap and a thin smile. "Welcome to Kolmanskop."

- 20 -
THE TOUR

"Good morning, ladies and gentlemen. Any kids?" The tour guide spoke with a charisma that drew the group's attention. "Nope, just the ladies and gentlemen today it seems. I'm Joseph and I'll be guiding you through Kolmanskop today."

Tas looked around the group, no more than a dozen people. Many had their cameras wrapped around their necks with a black leather bag of additional lenses at their sides. They had come well equipped for the photo opportunity of a lifetime.

Joseph brought his hands together and walked before the group. "Quick reminder that there is no smoking on the tour. And a final disclaimer: these buildings are in disrepair so be careful as we move through them. We make no promises to dig you out from the rubble of a collapse. But we'll do our best to salvage your final shots for a posthumous Instagram."

Joseph was clean-shaven with a youthful energy. He seemed young, probably younger than he actually was, Tas thought.

The tour began from the welcome area and moved toward the outset of town. From building to building, Joseph entertained, or tried to, with stories and quips about life in Kolmanskop. The historical information was little more than background noise to flashing cameras.

They came to a two-story home, emptied of everything but its doors and a rusted bathtub. “This here is the engineer’s house. His front yard was the home of the only tree in the whole town. Story goes, he poked a hole in a water line that ran through his property to keep it alive.”

As they walked down what remained of Millionaire’s Avenue, it was well beyond its wealthiest days. The streets were long covered in sand and the town looked to rest on slopes and dunes. It was hard to picture the bustling, lively days in such an environment. The buildings were a spectacle, but to see the past required a lot of imagination to look beyond the decades of deterioration.

The grand entertainment hall was next on the tour. Its large echoing rooms were bright and clean. The theatre room contained a full stage and upper loft area for remarkable views of the performers. Outside and up the hill from there, the architect’s house stood with similarly bold colors amidst the sand. It was another example that even the grandest towns fell victim to time and Mother Nature.

It must have been a challenge for Joseph to keep the group together. Many wandered in all directions then hustled back before straying too far. As a few stragglers caught up to Joseph at the old hospital, he couldn’t resist more humorous tales. “It’s true that the hospital here carried the first X-ray machine in the southern hemisphere. But it wasn’t just for broken bones, mind you. Some miners had tried spicing up their lunches with a diamond or two. But a cup of castor oil and sometime later, the diamonds would be back where they belonged.”

The group laughed at the implied embarrassment as Joseph continued. “I’m serious.” He stopped to address his tagalong audience. “If you happen across any diamonds here today, think twice before grabbing them. We can plug that old baby right back in."

Out along the train tracks that once served as the town's lifeline, Joseph ripped through another history lesson about the staggering amounts of water and ice the train delivered each day. He showcased a refurbished train car from that time to illustrate how the women piled into the cars with their lavish dresses and numerous bags from a day out shopping.

Joseph dabbed at his forehead with a red handkerchief as the sun crept farther overhead. "Are you all still with me? And drinking plenty of water?"

On cue, Tas and several others grabbed their water bottles, appreciative of the reminder.

"Water's probably not too cold anymore, huh?" Joseph asked. "Well, conveniently, we're at the old ice factory. We can't help you out today but back then, this factory produced ice for the entire town.

"Homes had little primitive refrigerators like this one," he said, moving toward a wooden box that didn't appear much different from a common nightstand. "A block of ice from the factory here would be delivered and placed in the bottom drawer. It would chill the top drawer which contained milk, cheese, and other perishables."

After they left the remains of the factory, Joseph led them back toward the welcome center. "And that brings us to our final stop today: the butchery."

The group oohed and aahed at Joseph's ominous tone while the clicks of cameras fluttered at their last guided opportunity. Joseph closed the door behind them, keeping the floors quite free of sand. Heavy concrete walls created a cold, almost menacing, environment. In the back room stood a massive oven dominating the far wall with its smokestack leading out through the ceiling.

"Story has it," Joseph began, "when men in the town partied late into the night, they'd come in here before going home to raid the ovens for any remaining sausages. I'm not sure why they'd steal from a man known for cutting up meat, though."

Images of a vengeful butcher camping out in the dark shadows of his shop waiting for hungry intruders, knife in hand, crossed Tas's mind. She could picture him, camouflaged in all black, his long legs bent into his chest, waiting on the floor. Only when the light caught his blade, could he be seen. His face tucked beneath a black hat, pulled down covering his eyes. She could sense him, feel him as though his stare had fallen upon her.

The thought shuddered through her as she left the shop, but the weight of fixated eyes still lingered.

The group gathered around Joseph as the tour came to its end. Tas spoke up, almost shouting over the wailing wind. "What about underground mining? Was anything like that done here?"

"No, Kolmanskop worked with alluvial mining and aboveground operations only. The deposits were so plentiful you never had to dig for them to begin with," Joseph answered.

"I've heard stories, though," Tas said. "There were underground mines a little south of the town, right?"

"Well, much farther south, sure. Down into South Africa and all along the Orange River were plenty more mining towns."

Tas clasped her hands and took a couple of steps forward. "Well, South Africa, yeah. But here, in Kolmanskop, there weren't any other mines operating?"

He cleared his throat and looked over the rest of the group before focusing back on Tas. "Well, it's possible you're thinking of Pomona or Elizabeth Bay, which are other towns nearby."

"Yeah. Maybe," she said, dropping her arms to her sides. "Thanks."

"No problem. Kolmanskop has a lot of ghosts, and each one has a story. But if this place was hiding some secret mines, it'd be news to me."

He scanned the crowd one last time, shielding his eyes from the whipping sands, inviting other questions, but nobody else spoke up. "Well then," he said, back on track with his regular script. "You all have been a terrific group today. At this time you're free to walk around and explore the town as you wish. Again, be mindful of the conditions of the buildings. And don't forget when you've finished up, our cafe and gift shop are right over here. So, come by when you're done and we'll get you set for the rest of the day. Thanks, everyone!"

He waved goodbye to the tour, placed his hands in his pockets, and left them to walk through the town on their own. There was an awkward delay as if after being guided for the past hour, the group had forgotten how to wander without an agenda. Jon hadn't forgotten though. The sole purpose of their visit was to wander from guides and scripted stories. Their whole purpose was to head south.

He nodded to Tas, and they began their journey.

They trudged through the shifting sands. Tas strayed from one place to the next taking pictures of the gorgeous and derelict buildings. They walked down the rows of family housing and near the end of town came to the school.

"Jon, we have to go in here," Tas said. The building captivated her, and she led the way inside with excitement.

With patient steps, she walked the quiet halls. The wooden floorboards were broken and warped, covered in broken glass. At the end of the hall, a windowless frame smacked against the wall with the wind. Crack. Crack. The sound pierced through the lonely hallway.

The windows offered views farther south into a bland emptiness. Waves of sand swept down the hills and across the town. Tas knelt at the end of the hall, her back to the window, and imagined the school in its prime.

"Why is there nobody else here?" she asked.

"Doesn't look like the others came down this far," Dean replied. He knelt next to her. "Pretty amazing, though."

"It really is. This whole town blows my mind, but this is something else." Tas looked over at Dean. He stared down the hallway with wide eyes, shaking his head. "Come here," she said, throwing her arm around him. Tas held out her phone and took a photo.

"Oh no," Dean laughed. "You caught me off guard. Try again."

And she did, snapping a series of shots to capture that moment before Jon approached and cleared his throat. "We should go," he said, tapping his fingers against his watch.

Tas and Dean stood to leave, crunching sand and straining wood beneath their feet. Tas stopped to watch the lone window frame whip open and closed a final time before following Jon to leave.

He led them at an arduous pace.

"Aren't we going to check out more buildings?" Sydney asked.

Jon looked back. "We've wasted enough time," he said, without breaking stride.

Sydney looked to Mike. "Okay?"

Mike jogged ahead. "Hey, Jon. Buddy," he said, reaching out for his shoulder.

Jon whipped around at his touch and stood still, a firm gaze burning into Mike. "No, we won't be checking out more buildings. That's not why we're here." Jon spun on his heel and continued onward again.

Mike rolled his shoulders and shouted, "You heard the guide. There is no fucking mine."

Jon, again, stopped and turned around. "I heard the guide. I heard he didn't know the difference between

Kolmanskop and Elizabeth Bay." He spit into the sand. "If it's not in his little script, he doesn't know it. I know there is a mine. So does she!"

Tas's breath caught in her throat as Jon pointed her out, thrusting her into their argument.

Mike didn't wait before shouting back, "Well, what I know is we're in the middle of the goddamn desert in Africa following a man nobody knows to a place the guide said doesn't even exist. You're not telling us where we're going or why and it's fucked up. That's what I know."

Jon let out an exasperated sigh and walked up to Mike. "We're walking south. In a couple kilometers we'll reach what was once the equipment shed. And where the equipment shed is, is the ridge. And along the ridge is the mine. My grandfather knew this. He lived here. And now I know this. Follow if you wish. I had only planned for two anyway."

Jon's stare stayed fixed and unwavering.

Mike pressed both hands into Jon's chest and shoved him back, stumbling and falling into the sand. "What the fuck does that mean? You only planned for two. What'd you plan?"

Sydney yelled and ran to Mike. "Baby, stop!"

"No." He shook his arm free from her grip. "This guy isn't telling us something."

Jon stood and dusted himself off. "You're such an ignorant brute."

"And you're a creepy asshole," Mike shouted back, taking powerful strides toward Jon, balling his fists.

Tas ran between them and placed her hands against Mike's heaving chest. Her heart raced and she was unsure how Mike would react to her standing in his way. "Mike, chill! If you don't want to come along, then don't. But if you do, we'd prefer it if you aren't an asshole the entire time."

Mike rubbed at his chin and laughed. "Yeah, I'm the asshole. He's the psycho who wants to lure us all into the desert to do God knows what. I'll fucking kill him if he tries to touch any of us." His eyes never left Jon who returned his stare.

"Fair," Jon said.

Tas looked at him, surprised by his response. "What?"

"Fair. Now, can we get going?" Jon asked. "We've wasted enough time already." He stood in silence another moment then turned away.

Mike huffed and shook his head. "See? Fucking psycho."

Tas dropped her hands and exhaled. "Come on."

She led the rest after Jon. When she'd imagined walking through the desert, she thought of the sun glaring down, burning her skin and singeing her hair. Trudging over sandy, shifting ground, though, burned the muscles in her legs not unlike hiking through drifting snow. As the wind reshaped their footing like an endless tide, they trekked southward into emptiness.

She had also underestimated the dryness of the air, the heat and its merciless burn. A swig of water provided brief relief before her mouth parched again. The sand ate away at her hands, drying her eyes, so much so, she rubbed at them when she thought she spotted the broken wooden posts and debris of their destination.

"Is that it? Is that the building?" she asked

She stepped over long-forgotten train tracks almost covered entirely by the shifting sands. What stood before her was not built with the same wealth and German architecture as the town behind them. A long, narrow shed fought to remain standing. Its windows shattered, roof collapsed, and its door hung ajar by the mounds of sand holding it in place.

Tas followed Jon through the door with cautious steps. "We definitely need to be careful in here, guys."

Jon walked to the far end of the open space, his arms tracing imaginary counters that no longer stood. He turned and with a childish smile said, "He was here. This is where he went every morning to check in and collect his equipment."

"Yeah? That's wild," Tas said. "He wrote about this place."

They stood in a place the world had forgotten. A place that barely existed. Untouched since the mines had closed decades earlier, only the history accompanied them there.

Tas stepped along planks and boards, unsure of what may lie covered. "Are we looking for anything in particular?"

She watched Jon slide and flip pieces of debris around the edges of the shed. He knelt, his long arms and legs overlapping like a tangle of wires, to flip a section of the roof. The chunk toppled to the side spraying dust and sand throughout the entire space. "We're looking for this." He lifted a haggard spade by its dry-rotted handle flicking a patch of sand to reveal its dulled head. "I know a lot about this area, but what I don't know is if we'll need tools to get into the mine. Or what we may need once we're inside. It's best we go prepared."

After looting the shed further, they met again outside with two spades and a pickax. Jon looped the ax through his bag while Mike and Tas carried the spades. The sun hung behind their backs, casting shadows in one, lone direction.

"The ridge." Jon pointed. "It's about a kilometer from here. The mine's entrance is there, but we may have to dig some to find it."

"Lead the way," Tas said.

Jon turned headlong into the wind, shielding his eyes while Tas stood back with the others. "Listen, you guys have been awesome going along with all this, but if you want to head back now, I totally understand. He and I are at least drawn to the history of this place and his grandfather. It's a lot to ask of someone who doesn't share that."

Mike stuck the spade into the ground. "We're already here, Tas. This speech would've been better back in Raleigh."

"Yeah, Tas," Sydney said. "We've already come this far. And no way am I leaving you alone with that guy."

Tas looked to Dean with empathy and compassion. Her eyes didn't focus solely on his but they looked at his every detail. Like the wrinkles where his crow's feet appeared when he'd smile or laugh. The tiny scar on his chin almost hidden beneath his two-day stubble. She looked at him like she wished to look into his head and see what he was thinking. Why was he so scared?

Dean stared back, his eyes sullen but warm. A subtle smile pulled at the corners of his mouth. "None of us are leaving you here. That includes me."

"I love you guys," she said, with a smile of her own.

And with the light behind them, they walked into uncertainty following Jon and their stretching shadows.

Jon took methodical steps along the ridge, hitting his ax against the rocks and examining every spot. Mike followed, banging his spade against the same rocks, though with less precision. "What the hell are we looking for?"

"Something that isn't rock," Jon answered. "I don't suspect the entrance will be clear and open. Maybe there's wood that frames or blocks it." He spoke almost in rhythm as he swung his ax with each step.

"How do you know it's even here? I don't see anything," Mike said.

"It's here," Jon shot back, in the same cadence. "I've heard stories it's here. I've read from my grandfather it's here. It has to be here. This is the ridge."

Then it happened. The metallic clang of ax on rock skipped a beat. When Jon hit the ridge, the ax bounced back with a greater rebound as it created a low, dull thud. He swung again, another thud sending more sand down over the surface. "Bring me a shovel," he ordered.

First with a slight hesitation then with uncontrolled fervor, Jon dug away at the sand along the ridge. With every swing of the spade, he listened for more thuds, more flat tones that couldn't be created by steel on stone. He dug at the decades of solidified dirt and sand that had blown into place.

At last, he stood back and dropped the spade at his feet next to his ax. Tas moved to his side, and the others joined, forming a long line. Together, they stared at a wall of cracked and dry-rotted wood, a boarded opening kept hidden from the rest of the world. In the middle of nowhere was the entrance to a place that never was.

Jon huffed with exhaustion and placed his hands over his face. "This is it."

"Holy shit," Mike said. "I don't fucking believe it."

Tas dropped her spade to the ground, her mouth open in awe. "No way."

Mike grabbed the ax from the ground and took its strong steel to the aged wood. The barriers shattered and fell in pieces revealing the entrance further with each strike. The shadowed world beyond seemed to creak and groan at its first sunlight since its forced slumber. And as the last of its protection fell to shards, Jon ducked his tall frame into the entrance. With a light in hand, he illuminated the cavern beyond.

One beam of light became two, then three, as the others moved in after him.

Tas watched the lights move around the otherwise pitch-black landing. A cracked bell dangled from a wooden beam off to the side, its clapper gone, lost to the years. Sand covered sections of a rusted, metallic track that stretched downward out of sight. She turned back to see the bright world behind them. Its light shone with an immense, powerful radiance that stopped abruptly where they had entered, helpless, as if the darkness forbade it from reaching any farther.

"So, what now?" she asked.

Jon looked ahead and answered with a straight expression. "We go in, of course."

- 21 -
THE MINES

"Hey, be quiet for a second," Tas said. "Kill your lights."

After descending into the mine, the full force of the darkness enveloped them. The mine cradled them with its deathly reach and coaxed them deep inside, away from the sunlight and the warmth and safety it offered. Few had experienced the unbelievable weight of total darkness, the psychological strain of having your eyes open only to see a sea of black so limitless it's claustrophobic. Tas wanted herself and the others to be part of that group.

"Sorry, that's way too much." Sydney clicked her light on and spun it in her hands.

One by one, the group turned their flashlights back on. The beams searched the cavern like many spotlights tracing the clouds above a city. The walls jutted outward in uneven ridges with wooden support beams bracing them. Dirt and dust hung in the air reminding Tas of driving at night with snow shining in her headlights.

At the base of their descent, old, broken equipment lay scattered around the ground. Bulky metal carts, dented and scratched to hell, protruded from their partial burials. Signs of life that once was but was no more.

"It's tough breathing down here," Sydney said, clearing her throat.

"When I was a kid," Tas said, "my parents' house had a cellar door outside. We almost never used it but when you did, it smelled like this. Thick and musty."

Sydney coughed again. "It's awful."

They continued deeper until the light from the entrance vanished from view. The main tunnel was large enough for the group to walk in pairs while secondary trails had been dug with smaller, erratically formed openings. Each step crunched upon the ground, vibrating little deposits free from the walls and overhead.

"Guys, is this safe? This doesn't feel safe." Sydney hugged close to Mike as her flashlight shivered back and forth. When it settled, it focused on a large mound of earth in front of them. She ran the light from the ground to the ceiling, gashed and hollowed. They were standing at the base of a collapse, blocking their way.

"Jesus!" Tas gasped. "When do you think this happened?"

"I don't even know how you could tell," Dean replied.

Jon walked up to the collapse and ran his hand along the wall of dirt and stone. "I suspect a collapse brought the town to its end. Why else would Heinrich not have returned home?"

"Wait, that's what this is about?" Mike asked. "Your obsession with this place is because your granddad ran out?"

"Mike!" Tas hissed.

"Think about it," Mike continued. "He probably made out with a few diamonds then bounced. That's what I would have done, for sure."

"Mike, shut up," Tas said. "I'm with Jon on this. You didn't read Heinrich's journal. There's no way he ran off from his family."

"Thank you," Jon said, still tracing his hand along the mound.

"Dude, stop," Mike said, to Jon.

"Excuse me?"

"No, look." Mike walked next to Jon along the sloping right side of the collapse. "Holy shit! Guys, check this out." He wiped the small stone in his shirt before holding it out. Between his dirtied fingers he held a small chip of a dull but shiny stone encrusted beneath layers of dirt. "This has got to be a little fucking diamond; right?"

Tas looked closer. "No way." She scanned the blockading mound and the ceiling with her light for any other glittering treasures. "So he was right," she said, to Jon. "The journals, Heinrich said there were more diamonds down here."

Dean wasn't convinced. "That could just be luck. I mean, what are the odds?"

"Quite good, actually," Jon said. "There will be diamonds down here, a surplus, I'm sure. Heinrich said so." He kicked at the collapse. "They'd be back there, though."

Mike tossed the stone in his pocket and readied his shovel. "We can dig through right here and keep going. Hell, there might be more in this pile."

"I don't want to," Sydney said.

"Are you serious?" Mike showed her the diamond again. "Babe, there are diamonds back there."

"I don't want to either, man," Dean added.

Tas took a deep breath and ran her hand along the back of her neck. She felt the onus to decide, the tie-breaking vote. She made it to Namibia, made it to Kolmanskop, and was standing in an unknown mine. The story, the experience she wanted was right there.

But the what-ifs dug into the back of her mind. What if there was more to learn about the mine beyond the collapse? What if Jon was right and more diamonds were inside? She had experienced what she came for but how much else would she miss by turning back?

She had to know.

Tas tucked her flashlight into her back pocket and took her spade in both hands. "Give me a hand with this," she said.

Tas and Mike alternated strikes at the lowest section of the collapse. One slow load at a time, they carved into the rubble. As they dug farther, they created an opening where the fallen debris no longer blocked them from moving ahead.

"We can crawl up over this," Tas said, patting her hand against a waist-high clearing.

"I think going farther is dangerous," Dean said. He pulled out a snack bag of peanut M&Ms and ripped its corner. "If we're going to do this, we need to leave a trail so we don't get mixed up down here."

"Good call," Tas said with a nod. "But do you have any bread in there, Hansel? You're wasting chocolate."

"It won't be wasted if it keeps us from getting lost," Dean argued.

Tas watched him drop the first piece to the ground. A little red pebble cratering into the dirt. She didn't believe in fairy tales or witches but breathed a small sigh of relief at his idea.

"Okay. I'll climb over first and we'll go a little farther. How are we on time?" Tas asked.

Jon checked his watch. "We have time to explore a bit longer still."

"All right. Well, then let's take a quick look." Tas led the way, followed by Sydney and Mike, climbing through the narrow opening. Their bags dragged across the jutting ceiling as they crawled on their hands and knees to the other side.

"Go 'head." Dean gestured to Jon.

The tight space swallowed Jon's lanky frame. His body tucked in on itself like a malformed stick figure as he slid forward, gripping his hands along the rugged base until his fingers stretched over the edge. Tas watched as he inched forward to step out into the open space when his foot caught and he crashed to the ground.

"Oh shit! Are you okay?" Tas hurried to his side.

Jon peddled his arms and legs backward into a wall. "Don't touch me! I'm fine."

"But your hand."

Jon held up his right arm. Blood trailed down from the gash in his palm. His face turned white and his head fell back. He closed his eyes, wrapping his hand in his shirt.

"Dammit." Tas pulled out the bandages from her bag. "Okay, it's not bad. You're okay," she said, easing close enough to help. "Let's just rinse it first. Then I've got a bandage right here."

Jon never opened his eyes as she reached for his arm. He resisted but gave in as she walked him through each step. Tas poured water over the cut and he cringed. Then with the bandage, she wrapped it tightly over the wound and rubbed it in place. "It may be tough to use the ax, but you're good, otherwise."

"Thank you," Jon said. He clenched his lips together and peeked at the bandage, darkened with blood and the red smears running down his forearm. Tas reached down and helped him to his feet.

"It's all good, Dean. Come on," Tas called.

Dean squeezed through the passage and eased onto the other side. When he did, he dropped another candy.

"Check it out," Mike said, showing a couple more diamonds in his hand. "You say there are more back there?"

"I'm certain of it," Jon answered.

Mike pocketed the little stones. "Then screw digging here. Let's go." He took off ahead of the others, following his sole beam of light.

"Mike, wait," Tas called out, stopping him. "We'll go but let's be smart about it and take our time."

They walked in pairs with cautious steps. Before long, the tunnel shrank around them, forcing Jon and Mike into slight crouches as they moved. The digging of the passage looked frantic, burrowing off in zigzags like it had been dug without any light or plan.

"This doesn't seem right," Jon said. "Mines don't have this many interchanges and turns."

"I didn't know what to expect," Tas said.

Jon highlighted several small holes. "Look at these. They're dug differently than this main route we're in."

"And what are those?" Sydney asked, from behind the group.

Tas walked to a small opening with an arched entrance about two feet tall. Its passage stretched well beyond the reach of her light. "Christ, this goes on forever," she said. "Why would they even build these?"

Jon crouched down to see for himself. "And how?"

"Looks like there's more down here," Mike said.

Mike led them farther while Sydney clung to his side. The more he pulled her along, the more her flashlight trembled. Tas walked with Dean as he continued dropping candies every few minutes. "Once I'm out, we need to turn around," he whispered.

Tas nodded. That's when she noticed everybody had fallen quiet. As the passage tightened, their voices softened until nothing more than fragile whispers crept into the unnerving silence.

The constricting passage saw an increase of collapses and spills from the ceiling. Long, jagged scars stretched overhead like veins bearing down upon them. Tas wiped the back of her neck and couldn't tell if the sweat was from the dense air or her nerves running hot.

Every crunch of earth beneath her steps seemed amplified. Each stream of dirt trickling down the walls made her breathing hitch as if it signaled an imminent collapse. The darkness grew heavier, and she knew it was imperative to not let her mind wander. It's what created her nightmares and fueled her imagination. It's what interpreted every sound as the last she'd ever hear. Her mind could scare her on a deeper, cerebral level and make her lose control. She took a deep breath and let it out through pinched lips. Remaining steady and calm is how she'd survive the darkness.

"I was not expecting this," Jon said, coming to a stop.

They stood together where the mine split in two directions. The left tunnel had collapsed and was inaccessible, spilling outward. The right side seemed passable with a little digging, again.

Dean tapped Tas on the shoulder and dropped another candy. Then he turned the bag upside and shook it.

Empty.

"Okay, I think we're far enough," Dean said.

Sydney agreed, unable to contain her anxiousness. "Yeah, I vote we leave."

"Well, hold on," Tas said. "That side is definitely collapsed, but this way looks..."

"Also collapsed," Dean interrupted.

"I was going to say doable. And check this out, it wasn't built like the other tunnels either. There aren't any supports in this one." She shined her light around the arch of the entrance to show its bare construction.

"They probably realized they were useless. Supports didn't help that side at all," Dean said.

Tas wasn't ready to turn back. There was a mystery that pulled her—a sense that something awaited her just beyond the split. "Look, we're out of candy, right? So no more turns.

Straight shot. We go through and when we reach another spot to turn or split, we head back."

Mike didn't wait for anybody to argue or disagree to start digging at the semiloose dirt blocking the right side. "Yeah, I'm not leaving until we find a shit-ton of diamonds."

And his wait wasn't long.

After Mike powered through much of the obstruction, he found a deposit of smooth, irregular stones. "You guys won't fucking believe this!" In his outstretched hand was a fistful of shining jewels: a wealth of diamonds. "I can't believe it. Babe, we're going to be rich!"

He threw his bag to the ground and tossed his tickets to early retirement and luxury inside. Sydney rushed over to help until his bag became bloated like an overstuffed pillowcase of trick-or-treat candy.

"Aren't you guys gonna take any?" he asked.

"I think you've grabbed enough for all of us," Tas answered.

"No way. These are mine."

"Don't be mean," Sydney said, with what Tas noted as her first smile since entering the mine. "You can take them from my share."

Dean kicked his foot through the dirt. "I don't know. It doesn't feel right taking them. We're not even supposed to be here."

"Dude." Mike held out his bag as if it was the only argument he needed.

"He's right," Jon said. "They don't belong to you. Nevertheless, you've taken what you've come here for. So now, if you don't mind, I'd like to go a bit farther still."

Mike stood and tossed his bag onto his back. "Actually, I do mind. You're right. I got what I came for, so now I cast my vote to leave. Why should we let you drag us any farther?"

"Mike, come on," Sydney said, grabbing his arm.

"No. If it's not diamonds, I want to know what this guy is so determined to find down here."

Jon raised his hands, keeping the exchange calm. "Maybe it's closure. Maybe it's to learn what happened to my grandfather. There must be a reason nobody knows about this place."

"Spoiler alert, man." Mike shined his light deeper into the tunnel. "I bet the diamonds in my bag that your grandfather's back there somewhere buried under the rest of that shit."

"Dude!" Dean shouted.

"Don't you dare say that!" Jon shouted the words in an unfamiliar voice—deeper, stern. Hateful.

Tas, again, rushed to stand between them. "Seriously, Mike? You got the diamonds like you wanted, now chill the fuck out. Why does everything have to be such a confrontation with you?"

"I'm only saying, which one do you believe?" Mike asked. "Is his grampa buried down here, or did he run off and never come home?"

"Goddammit, Mike. That's enough!" Tas yelled. Her voice bounced deep into the cavern.

But Mike continued, his focus never leaving Jon. "Yeah. I bet he's back there with a bellyful of diamonds."

Jon stumbled backward until he found himself against the wall. "That's not true. He would never!"

"If you want to go back there so bad let's go back there. You can take that gimp-ass hand of yours and dig him up yourself." Mike beamed with a shit-eating grin. But Sydney left his side to join Dean.

"You're a fucking asshole," Tas said, walking away from Mike as well.

Mike stood on an island—he and his bag of jewels. He raised his hands, surrendering. "Okay, okay. My bad. I take it back. I'm sure his grandfather was an honest man down here."

"Shut up and let's keep going," Tas said.

"But Tas," Dean said, holding up the empty bag of candy.

"Next turn or split or whatever and we head back. Deal? Jon's not the only one who wants to learn more about what happened down here."

Jon pushed himself up from the wall and nodded to Tas. "Thank you."

Tas couldn't ignore boiling tensions within the group as she led them through the passage Mike had cleared. Unlike their previous path, she walked into a cavernous tunnel that stretched into infinite black. Its depth and weight swallowed their lights. But like the earlier tunnel, short paths wove their way around them, branching into every direction like alleyways from a dark, deserted road.

Despite the extra space allowing them to stand, the air grew stale. No breeze. No freshness. An acidic, rotting odor hung and caked the back of her throat.

Dean's face glowed with the light of his phone. "So, the last tour leaves in about three hours. We should head back."

"How have we killed that much time already?" Tas asked.

"It's the darkness," Dean said. "It messes with you."

"Three hours and what though till the last tour?"

Dean checked his phone again. "Like twenty minutes."

"Can we go just a little farther? After those twenty minutes, we turn around and head straight back."

"Tas, really? We're already cutting it way too close."

"But think about it," she started. "We wasted how much time with digging and stuff. On the way back we can breeze right through." She looked around at the others. Their expressions showed they didn't seem to share her enthusiasm. "Plus, you know me. When do I ever risk being late for anything?"

"I know but..." Dean sighed and shook his head. "Fine. Twenty minutes."

Sydney groaned and buried her head into Mike's chest. He kissed the top of her head and wrapped her in his arms.

They walked. Deeper into the emptiness. Deeper into the mouth that could swallow them whole whenever it pleased.

Farther into the mine, the ground became littered with growing stacks and piles of dirt and stone. With each mound they stepped around and climbed over, Tas struggled to fight the growing sense that each served as an escalating warning of what lay ahead.

Sydney gasped. "What the hell are those?"

Scurrying across the ground, several little creatures crawled out from one of the small paths carved into the walls. Their protruding white eyes reflected the shine of her light. "I don't like them. At all," she said.

"How can anything even live down here?" Dean asked.

"Maybe there are little holes or trails that run up to the surface," Tas replied. "No idea."

Sydney snuggled into Mike and peeked out from behind his shoulder. "Do you think they bite? What if they bite?"

Tas shrugged. "They ran over there so let's keep some distance just in case."

The mound where the little lizard-like creatures ran was covered in more of their crawling figures. Their tails, longer than their bodies, waved back and forth as they burrowed their little feet into the dirt. They dug and clawed in a frenzy then in an instant, they scattered. A rock fell from above and smashed into the mound, sending them and debris in every direction.

Tas crept over to the rock that fell. What drew the creatures to that particular pile? She knelt with her flashlight and sifted her hand over what partially stuck out. "There's something here."

The item was lodged in the dirt, almost hardened into place. She wiggled it from side to side to pry it free.

"Oh fuck!"

With a shock and scream, Tas fell back and dropped her light to her side. It rolled out of reach but remained focused on the bone she had pulled free. An arm? A leg? She didn't care to know. Knowing the specifics made no difference. But it was human, and that was more than enough for her.

"Is that..." Dean trailed off as he realized the answer to his own question.

Tas leaned over for her light and glanced into the small tunnel next to her. Inside lay piles of bones. The empty sockets of soiled skulls, punctured between the eyes spidering outward, peered back at her. The small mountains of remains shifted her stomach in a nauseous terror.

That wasn't the Czech bone church or the catacombs of Paris or Palermo where they preserved death, on display in remembrance. The scattered bones in front of her weren't on display at all. They were discarded. Used. Tossed aside. Their deaths weren't honored. They were raw and feral—from a time that'd been sealed away and forgotten.

Tas screamed and jumped to her feet. "Fuck!" She rushed over to Dean. "There're fucking bones. Everywhere. The little things were digging at one there and this hole has tons more."

Dean shined his light into the small opening with Tas close behind. When his light fell onto the pile of death, he covered his mouth, coughing and looking away. Tas stared longer, long enough to see the bones shift. A small piece tumbled over itself to the ground. From underneath, crawled another of the small creatures. Its buggy eyes shined bright but its body somehow remained shadowed.

Tas stood and turned to the rest. "Let's get the hell out of here. Now."

Jon stepped forward. "Wait. Tas, I should show you something, first."

"Are you serious? Now?" Her hands shook, her voice sharp and panicked. "Can it not wait until we're out of here?"

Jon stepped closer. "It's about the journal. I need to show you."

Tas doubled over with an exhausted sigh. "You've got thirty goddamn seconds."

Jon walked away from the group and Tas followed, waving off the others for their privacy. In the mines, even hushed voices carried, but Jon seemed to think the distance was important.

He pulled out a folded sheet of paper and handed it over. "This was the final entry in Heinrich's journal. He was scared."

Tas grabbed it and stared at the folded sheet. "Wait. What do you mean 'final entry'?" She asked, with an edge to her voice. Her suspicion grew with each word.

"I accidentally ripped the page out and forgot to send it along."

She looked at Jon and no longer saw the simple, older man with a shared curiosity for the mines and their history. The man who stood before her was the Jon who had left out the part about being fired, the part about the assault. She stared at the man—the stranger—who waited until the most dire moment to share a critical piece of information.

"And you just now thought it'd be a good time to bring this up? Not in any of the emails? Not before getting on a plane to come here?" She turned away. A raging silence hung between them. "So? I can't read this. What did he say?"

"Well, he said those smaller tunnels we've been seeing everywhere were here when they were digging. Something else down here must have made them. He alluded to it being dangerous.

"There were no more letters to my mother. He never returned home. Now, we come across piles of bones? I think there's something down here. Something that could have killed him and forced the mine to close."

"Fucking killed?" Her voice shot through the cavern. "Are you serious? And you kept this to yourself till now? Right fucking now?" She shook the letter with each word.

"Think about it," he urged. "Something bad enough had to have happened to force the town to evacuate. This mustn't be a coincidence."

Tas crumpled the page and threw it into his chest. "How long have you thought this?"

"Not long. I didn't think—"

"Exactly!" she said. "You didn't think. You never thought to tell me about a final entry in the journal? And you casually leave out your theory that everybody was killed? What the fuck, Jon? Why bring us down here then?"

He moved forward and reached for her shoulder, but Tas jumped back. "Don't you dare fucking touch me."

"We need to find out what happened," he said.

"No, that's what *you* need to find out. We don't need to find out anything." She turned and stormed away. "Stay here if you want, but we're out:"

Dean rushed to meet her. "What happened?"

"Nothing. Let's go."

"But what about him?" Dean looked around her to where Jon stood.

"Fuck him," Tas hissed. "He can stay here if he wants."

They rushed back the way they came, leaving Jon behind. After squeezing through at the split, they moved as quickly as the darkness allowed. The tunnels blurred in their swaying lights while they kept their eyes peeled to the ground ahead of them.

"Where are the fucking M&Ms, Dean? I'm not seeing them." Tas's flashlight jumped ahead of each hurried step.

"They're here somewhere," he said.

But they weren't. Her frenzied eyes couldn't spot the trail. No color. No direction.

"I dropped them everywhere but they're small. I'm looking," Dean said, panting.

Tas slid to a stop and stretched her arms out to catch the others. "Wait." They stood in a squared intersection: four tunnels stretching in four directions, all disappearing into a lifeless black. "Where the fuck are we?" Tas spun around searching for anything that looked familiar. "Dean, where the fuck are we?"

Dean's light shot around their feet, but there were no candies leading them out. "This isn't right. I don't think we were here before."

Sydney doubled over in a panic, her breathing erratic as her face flushed. "Guys, I'm scared."

Tas ran from tunnel to tunnel shining her light into each. "Do you guys remember any of this?"

"We weren't here," Mike said.

"Yeah, this isn't right," Dean agreed.

"I know this isn't right!" Tas stopped for a moment to settle herself.

Those who rush are bound to miss.

Tas took a deep breath until her head stopped spinning. "Let's stop for a minute and think. Let's walk back the way we came and look for our trail from there. Okay?"

"So we're going to leave Jon? What did he say to you?" Dean asked.

Tas huffed and dug her hands into her head. "I don't even know. He's a creep. You guys were right."

"We knew that already," Mike snapped. "But what did he say? What made you rush us into wherever the hell we are right now?"

Her mind flashed to the cracked skulls and piles of bones. She could only assume they belonged to miners whose families had since passed without closure or answers.

"Some stupid idea of his. He said the miners were scared to work down here."

Mike shook his head, moved in front of Tas, and crossed his arms. "No, don't sugarcoat it. I heard him. He said something killed them."

"It's a crackpot theory he has, but he doesn't know that." Her mind raced. She needed air, fresh air.

Mike scoffed and walked back to Sydney.

"But neither do you," Dean said. "Tas, this is serious."

"I know it's serious. We need to calm down for a second so I can think." She slammed her spade into the ground and paced, wearing her tracks deeper into the ground. From her backpack, she grabbed her water and took a drink tasting every grain of dirt that washed down with it.

"Okay," she said, tossing her bag back around her shoulders. "We need to kill our lights, use one at a time and alternate just in case."

"Just in case?" Sydney asked.

Tas paused. Dean stared at his feet. Sydney hid half her face in Mike's chest while he stared toward the ceiling. Nobody wanted to hear the inevitable.

"In case we're down here longer than we planned."

Sydney choked back a cry and covered her face.

Tas reiterated her plan, hoping to project a more optimistic tone. "Listen, we're going to head back the way we came until we find the trail. Okay?"

One thing at a time. Every problem was easier to manage if she broke it down into smaller pieces.

"Fine," Dean said, clicking off his light.

Mike switched his off next.

"Oh God," Sydney cried. Her hand shivered as she reached for the switch.

As if their lights had protected them and kept the darkness at bay, as their four beams fell to one, the tenebrous black tightened around them.

Tas struggled to breathe. She strained to piece together and organize her thoughts. They stood together, steadying their mettle without a single word. It was an infinite silence in an endless void.

And that's when they heard it, a monstrous scream from the darkest corner of hell.

- 22 -
THE SCREAMS

When CDM constructed the mines south of Kolmanskop, they were built to avoid the mistakes of the earlier systems. No more arbitrary digging. The southern mine was strategic with greater attention to organization. However, the cobwebbed passageways that disoriented Tas and the others were not built with the same order and care. They were dug and connected during the centuries prior to and after the town's evacuation.

"What the hell was that?" Sydney clicked her light back on, shining it with both hands into each of the tunnels that fed straight to where they stood.

"Do you think it was Jon?" Dean asked.

Tas shook her head, the only part of her she could move. "Not a chance."

The guttural throat-ripping scream rumbled like the exhaust of a motorcycle from an impossible direction. The single sound surrounded them, trapping them where they stood.

Tas listened, wishing for the ability to throw her hearing farther into each tunnel to patrol for the source of the spine-freezing roar. But she couldn't. She had to rely on the echoing walls that carried the sound as if it were nothing more than a simple breeze.

"What do we do?" Sydney asked.

"We have to stay calm," Tas said. "We're sticking with the plan, going back the way we came, and looking for the trail. But we can't rush and risk missing it again."

Sydney trembled. Tas's light shook over her face, highlighting every ounce of her fear. "But what was that... that... scream?"

There was no comforting answer. No answer at all. Tas shrugged against the growing weight of the unknown that tightened her shoulders. "I don't know. But we have to go now and we gotta stay calm," she reiterated as much to herself as the others.

She led the way with her flashlight. One step. Two steps. They moved with slow progress through the tunnel. Her sole light only emphasized they were alone and far from help. The feet of the others behind her pushed her resolve with every step.

That was Dean. That one's Mike.

She identified each person by the crunching earth beneath their steps. Once, and if, a sound didn't fit the pattern, she'd push her internal panic button.

Where's the damn trail?

The thought repeated through her mind while she searched back and forth across the ground. If she could find one piece—one measly piece of color in the sea of gray—then that could get them started in the right direction. But until that first one, she was aimless.

"Where are you going?" Dean whispered. "Didn't we come from that way?"

Tas looked around the featureless cave. She replayed the chaos of their rush, but her mind distorted it with static and splits. Nothing was clear. What parts did she remember?

Which memories did she create on the spot? "I… I don't know." She looked down the paths before them. "Everything looks the same."

"Wait," Dean said. "Check your phones. If you have a connection, we might be able to use Maps. We roughly know where we entered, so we'd simply have to see where we're at now."

They pulled out their phones, little lightning bugs flashing in the night.

"Nothing," Tas said

Same for Mike and Sydney.

Dean stared at his phone, dragging the app over and over trying for a connection. "Shit!" He slid it back into his pocket. "And the last tour leaves in a few minutes. We're stuck."

"We're not stuck," Tas said with a controlled calm. "First, we get out of here and then we figure out the rest. But up there, outside, we have connections and, worst case, places to crash. But one thing at a time."

Tas appreciated being methodical, taking the problem and breaking it down. Whether it calmed the others or not, it helped her keep focused.

"So, which way then?" Dean asked. "I thought we came from the left."

"I have no idea," Tas said.

Dean stood to orient himself with his memory. "I feel like we turned right into here so I'd say we head back this way:"

"Then, yeah, let's go left," Tas agreed.

One step. Two steps.

She followed her light over the rocky ground and along the winding route. Sweat ran down the side of her face, one bead at a time, before dripping from the tip of her chin.

Three steps. Four steps.

Just find the fucking trail.

She continued listening to the rhythm of the feet behind her, first Dean then Sydney and Mike. Their footsteps were the grip keeping her from spiraling into utter isolation.

Find the fucking trail.

The task looped through her head. A high-stakes Easter egg hunt. Whatever it took to keep her from reliving the scream. The scream. So wretched and distressed as if the muscles in the throat were moments from tearing apart. What could make...?

"Focus," she whispered, to herself. The minute her mind drifted away from the task to the unknown, she was done. They were done. She couldn't afford to waver.

They were twenty steps, thirty, forty, fifty steps into the tunnel and not a sound had echoed their way. Aches tightened in her legs, threatening to pull her concentration from the task, to the pain, and to the unknown.

Where's Jon?

At the edge of her light, she scanned the blank distance for the slightest glow that wasn't her own. What if he was looking for her? Did he know the way out? She bounced between unanswerable questions, their uncertainty dragging her shoulders down further until her focus flooded back.

"Guys," Tas said, straining to keep her excitement controlled and low. "An M&M. We found the trail!"

In the middle of her light gleamed a little green pebble with a shining "M." Nothing so small had ever carried such relief. From where the marker sat, Tas scanned the two directions looking for the next checkpoint. Again, one step at a time, she eased into a decision, waiting for something to pull or push her away. But she rushed ahead when she spotted the next yellow piece of hope.

The others sped behind her.

"Over here!" No longer speaking in excited whispers, Tas declared throughout the mines, "This way!"

"But Tas, hold up." Dean hustled ahead. "I dropped these the whole time. I have no idea in what order. We could be going in either direction."

He was right. But any direction was better than no direction. Right?

"What if we follow this until we see something we remember?" Tas asked. "Then we'll know which way we're going." In her mind, it was that simple, but she was getting ahead of herself. She needed to reset and refocus. Deep breath after deep breath, she worked to slow herself down.

"Until we see something we remember?" Dean asked. "Tas, literally everything down here looks the same."

"Something will stand out. We need one small thing to stand out then we have our answer. And our way out." She nodded and continued her methodical pace.

One step. Two steps. The counting kept her focused on their slow progress and away from the dark and what lurked behind it. When she was in between markers is where she felt most lost and vulnerable, like she was leading them out into open waters. Her mouth ran dry and her breathing hitched. But when another colorful candy appeared in view, she exhaled the tension and reset her count. The process repeated for six markers where they moved in the same rhythm and cadence. But when a sound broke their pattern she froze. Her body stiffened, shooting alerts to every nerve in her body.

"What was that?" Dean whispered.

The sound was dull, followed by something of a dry scrape. It sounded familiar, but Tas struggled to place it. She shined her light straight down, straining herself to focus more intently on the scratching.

But she couldn't pin it down.

Tas inched forward, almost in half-step increments. Half steps. She lost count.

She ran a hand over her face and reset her count. The sound ahead fell silent until her tenth step when it crashed again. She stopped. Fear constricted her muscles and her hand clenched onto the spade she carried, with patches of dry rot clinging to her sweaty palm. The sound continued ripping and dragging as she worked her light farther ahead with an unsteady hand.

The light stretched off into the distance until it revealed Jon. He stood alone with his pickax, chipping away at the collapsed side of the split.

They had gone the wrong way.

Jon dropped his arms, the head of the ax crashing into the ground. He turned to face Tas's light and ran his bandaged hand over his face. "Is that you, Tas?"

He walked toward her. The ax dragged behind him, scarring the ground with each irregular step. "Would you be willing to give me a hand with this, you know, given the condition of mine." His gashed hand shielded a grime-smeared face that looked weathered and worn the closer he trudged. Fresh blood spread under the bandage and ran down his forearm. His pickax scraped and creaked over the ground like a rusted locomotive struggling to life, casting clouds of dirt and dust in behind it.

Each step brought him closer, but Tas froze. Her lungs clung to a breath they refused to release. She could only stare ahead at the lone figure in her light creeping closer.

"Close enough, asshole!" Mike rushed ahead, his spade already midswing. With the form of a slugger, he smashed the steel head into Jon's stomach, doubling him over and collapsing him to all fours.

"Fucking creep!" Mike shouted as he lifted the repurposed bat up and around his shoulders. He lined up his target like a piece of wood he intended to split.

"Stop!" Tas's lungs exhaled, at last, and her voice cracked as she yelled.

But Mike didn't stop. The spade crashed down onto Jon's back and flattened him. With his target battered and without fight, he stepped forward for another attack. He dug the steel tip in between a pair of protruding vertebrae and lined up a paralyzing stomp.

"Dude, that's enough!" Dean rushed and wrapped Mike to keep him from the fatal strike. "Stop!"

But rage can be nuclear.

"Fuck off of me!" Mike threw Dean aside and stomped back to find Tas standing between him and his prey.

"Stop! You're going to kill him," Tas said.

"I know." He tossed Tas out of the way without strain. "That's the fucking idea."

From where she had fallen, Tas stared at the face of a man resigned to death. Jon's eyes were wide and deep, longing for what was to come. It wasn't the face of a man who feared death but one who appeared to welcome it.

Mike planted a foot onto Jon's back and, again, aligned his spade across the back of his neck. Jon squirmed beneath the piercing steel and Tas covered her eyes from the fate she was helpless to prevent. The dreadful anticipation of the inevitable sounds and screams to come shut everything around her out. Her hands tightened over her ears, and she squeezed her eyes as tight as their lids would press.

When an earth-shattering scream erupted, she convulsed with anguish. But the gut-wrenching chords weren't those of a man being torn apart. No. They weren't of a man at all. It was the crippling, monstrous roar. And what she heard next, a raw cry, human and terrified, made her open her eyes, and rush for her light.

Sydney.

Tas scrambled to shine her light where Sydney stood only moments earlier. Hidden under a cloud of dirt, Tas caught only a glimpse of Sydney's legs being dragged out of view and into one of the arched, winding tunnels that wove throughout the mines.

Sydney screamed from inside the narrow space, with each echo adding another layer of horror to the last. The chorus crescendoed then fell until every last cry faded to an agonizing, deathly silence.

- 23 -
THE FAULT

"Don't take pictures of things," Sydney's mother had always told her. "Take pictures of moments."

Mike stared down at Jon with vile in his eyes after tossing Dean and Tas out of his way. Sydney couldn't believe what was happening. Any of it. Not where they were, how they got there, and definitely not what she was seeing. Everything slowed down as she struggled to capture the moment, no matter how much she wanted it to end.

As she stared, motionless, at the madness, she hadn't noticed the slight shuffling sneaking from behind. When it stopped, the disorienting shriek pierced through the mine. The force of the scream blew her hair out in front of her face and made her ears rumble. Before she could turn around, the long reach of it—of something—took her by her waist and pulled her to the ground. By the time she managed to yell, a cry almost lost amidst the chaos, she was already being pulled out of sight.

The claw that latched onto her hair like a vise dragged her through the dark, narrow tunnel with an ease that told her she was insignificant. The ground ripped from beneath her.

Every rock and jagged edge of earth protruding from the path bludgeoned her helpless body, wrenching her from side to side. Her shoulder shattered against an immovable boulder leaving her nauseated and lightheaded. Shock waves of pain jolted from the break with every bounce of her limp arm. As if lost at sea, she was at the mercy of the petulant waves that controlled her.

The frenzied dragging continued without restraint. The pathway bent and twisted, tying her stomach in knots. A sudden explosion of pain, violent and crippling, flashed through her head, blinding her with bolts of lightning. Then just as quickly, her entire body slacked, and the world disappeared.

. • • • .

Mike dashed to the tunnel that swallowed Sydney's cries for help. "Syd!" He slid to his knees and searched the winding passage as deep as his light would shine. "What the fuck was that?" He jumped to his feet and stomped toward Tas.

The flashlight dangled from his wrist and Tas watched it shine over the tracks Sydney's body left behind. "I don't know." Tears welled in her eyes, and her heart pounded against her chest, desperate to punch itself free.

"I have to find her," Mike said.

Tas knelt at the same opening and its depth was as disheartening as it was endless. "Maybe we can find another way."

Mike stood over her, shoulders squared and firm. "What do you mean 'we'? If it wasn't for your fucking idea to come here, this wouldn't have happened. None of this would!"

"That's not fair." Tas stood to meet Mike's burning stare.

"No, what's not fair is because of you and your weird ideas." Mike jabbed a finger into her forehead. "Sydney is missing, taken by God knows what."

His chest puffed with heavy, forceful breaths. Tas returned her eyes to his to find a volcanic rage within them.

"Mike, I'm so sorry." She looked away as if the cold grip of guilt pulled her eyes to the ground. Did she cause this?

Jon coughed from the distance. "You can't save her," he said with a beaten, choking voice. "I don't hear her anymore. Do you?"

Mike threw his head back and took a deep breath. He burst into a sprint and with all the force of his erupting rage, he drove his foot into Jon's ribs. "Fuck you!"

The savage kick sent Jon writhing in pain, retching up blood and mucus. He choked and gargled on the mix, struggling to breathe with ribs that Mike had undoubtedly cracked.

"Say something now." Mike kicked Jon's shoulders to roll him around in the dirt. He stopped and looked down at him. "Fuck this," he spat, with a final kick.

Mike grabbed Jon's bag from the ground and turned to Tas. "Come on," he said, throwing her the bag and taking off in a direction he hoped led to Sydney.

Tas considered the man curled in a fetal position, helpless and empty-handed. Did a man, even that man, deserve to be abandoned without light or even water? With a voice too small to hear, she whispered her apology and gestured to Dean for them to follow.

As they hurried, flashlights jumping with every step, Jon's strained groans faded to painful whispers then to nothing. Tas's heart continued its assault as a cold sweat broke out over her body. Whatever happened to Sydney, she felt responsible. The realization dragged her down as she fell behind the others.

Whatever happened to any of them was on her.

She doubled over, hands on her knees and out of breath. No, she didn't force them to come with her, but everybody was there *because* of her. Everybody. Whether direct or passive, guilt can feel like cement in your legs and tar in your lungs. Her ribs felt shattered, her head seemed to split. She bore their pain like stigmata.

The cold sweat dried in a moment of flashing heat. Her stomach convulsed and tensed, and she vomited at her feet. The pressure forced her tears to fall. They streamed down her face and mixed with the snot and bile before she wiped herself clean with her shirt. The holds in her mind were cracking under the severity of the situation.

It wasn't the moment of reprieve she wanted but it was the one she needed. Like a boiler overheating and ready to blow, the body will flip its own release to salvage itself. The damage from the pressure remains, yet it survives to address the strain later. Tas stood and knew her repairs would need to wait.

From ahead Mike shouted, "Over here!"

Tracks like those where Sydney was taken streaked across the ground. They stretched through the cavern before vanishing into another narrow opening.

"We're following this," Mike said. Without Sydney's cries, they had no other option.

They crawled into the passage, constricted by the walls squeezing at their shoulders. Their bags dragged across the top, raining down trails of dust and dirt with each sluggish crawl. The space narrowed further and their pace slowed behind Mike as he struggled to push through the pinch.

"Shit," he said, coming to a stop. "There's blood up here."

Like lines dividing lanes of a road, Sydney's blood dotted and smeared her tracks down the middle of the passage. But the splatter wasn't all she had left behind. Just ahead, the tunnel opened into another large cavern where her bag sat, ripped open, and its contents scattered.

She had to be close.

"Syd!" Mike yelled. No response other than his echoes disappearing into the dark.

Time was precious, and the seconds ticked ominously away while they looked around the lifeless chamber. Mike yelled again then followed the tracks farther. Their pace quickened, Mike leading the way, and Tas following Dean. Mike continued calling for Sydney.

They all did.

Desperation burned at her nerves, frantic and accelerated. Tas rushed ahead with the others, dismissing the menacing claw marks etched along the walls. When their voices peaked, their shouts became drowned out by the hellish scream surrounding them again.

Dean clenched his eyes from the mind-strobing howl. He stopped dead in his tracks, covering his ears. Tas slid to a stop behind him, short of crashing into him. Her light focused on him and she watched as an obscured figure darted from the right edge of its glow and pummeled him into the wall. It slashed its branch-like arms and jagged claws into him, with feral, devilish screams. Dean crashed to the ground, crying for help and curling himself against the attacks. His body tumbled and rocked with each strike cutting and slashing into him.

Tas yelled for him, crying his name, willing herself to do something, anything, to help. But the fear had crippled her.

Mike rushed from the darkness toward Dean with his shovel already cocked for another vicious swing. The creature turned its pale, elongated face and bulging cue ball eyes toward him right before the impact. The thing roared in pain and fell from Dean.

From all fours, it dug its claws into the ground and fired another shriek before pouncing to its feet and tearing after Mike.

Mike turned to a sprint and rushed into the darkness chased by that thing, the creature that hunted them. Tas went blank. Should she run after them? Should she run away? Everything was a blur. A million nameless options flew through her mind, impossible to grasp and impossible to act. She wanted to do something, anything other than stand there.

Helpless.

- 24 -
THE MOMENTS

We spend our lives suppressing baser instincts and rounding the harsh edges of our primitive pasts. We've evolved beyond the basic needs of survival. Only in extreme moments, where time to think doesn't exist, are we forced to act instinctively. And not until attacking a creature, evolved over millennia for pure survival, did Mike realize how quickly his instincts could shift from fight to flight.

The adrenaline searing through his body burned the muscles in his sprinting legs. His lungs ached, grasping for enough air to power him through the fear. He only understood why he was running, not to where or from what. Over his shoulder, he glanced at the contorting creature with its glowing, round eyes pursuing him. It unleashed another blistering scream before closing the distance in mere strides and swiping at his legs.

Mike collapsed forward, landing on a pile of rocks that cracked into his chest. He dug his hands into the ground and kicked his feet, desperate to reach the spade that fell out of reach. But before he could wrap his hands around his only semblance of defense, claws ripped into the back of his legs.

They stabbed and crawled their way up to his back, pinning him down.

The beast flipped him to his back, tossing him with a feral strength. It roared into the darkness then crashed its unbridled rage down upon him. Mike squirmed under the beast but couldn't shake free as it slashed at him from all directions tearing into his shielding arms. With each strike came its incessant shrieks threatening to shatter his eardrums.

Mike was pinned down. The warm, putrid saliva dripping from the creature's screams burned into the gashes in his arms.

It took strength he didn't know he had to thrust his hips upward and create space to maneuver. He'd hoped enough space to survive. The spade wasn't far, and he scrambled backward, digging his elbows and hands into the ground, flailing his legs, straining as he squeezed them free. When his hands landed against the spade's wooden shaft, he grabbed it and threw himself to his feet.

He rushed to attack, but the claws gripped into his chest and threw him back. Warm trails of blood ran from the punctures. Mike gritted his teeth, pushed himself forward, and swung into the darkness with a vengeful roar of his own.

The impact was brutal and stung his hands as it reverberated to the handle of the spade. He swung over and over again with a savage desperation until the ghoulish mantis fell back against the earth.

That was his chance.

He lined up his next strike and rammed the spade into the creature's torso. Blood poured from the gaping wound as he forced the blade deeper until its metal vanished beneath the pale, dangling flesh and flooding crimson. As its sinew stretched and muscles ripped, the creature unleashed a series of agonized screams, piercingly high and distorted.

Mike screamed with every bit of his ferocity and rammed the spade deeper still, pinning the creature to the wall. It flailed and writhed, dangling mere inches from the ground. The life in its glowing eyes dimmed as its blood drained from its body. Grabbing the bloodied spade with both hands, he worked it from side to side until the final muscles and ligaments holding the creature together severed. Its legs crumpled to the ground into the growing pool of blood. Its torso fell slack and slid along the metal blade until it toppled over its edge, falling in a lifeless heap with the dull thud of dead weight. He pulled the spade from the wall, but its wood splintered into pieces, suffering the same fate it inflicted.

Mike's body shook from the brutal exertion. The fiery adrenaline that fueled him extinguished, dropping him to his knees. A mixture of congealing blood and mucus covered his arms while his legs fared little better judging by his shredded jeans.

The receptors that had blocked his pain triggered back to life. His shoulder burned and screamed with a bulge pushing out from beneath the skin. Sharp, piercing bolts shot from his ribs, stabbing him as he worked to catch his breath. His chin dropped to his chest, rising and falling with short, unfulfilling breaths. He sucked in all the air he could, closed his eyes, and pulled the arm of his dislocated shoulder outward. He cringed and whimpered with the immense pain waiting for the socket to drop back into place. The grinding made him nauseous, yet when his shoulder caught, he fell to his back and exhaled the breath he'd been holding.

Sweat covered his face. Even in the darkness, the world spun like a devilish ride that refused to let him go. He fumbled for the water from his backpack, chugged what remained, and labored to his feet.

"I gotta move," he said.

His balance wobbled as his head continued to spin. With his good arm, he stabilized himself against the wall and waited for his world to settle and his focus to return.

When his legs were steady enough to support him, he picked a direction and moved.

The darkness beckoned him farther, calling him deeper into the passages that held him captive. Jagged trails of claw marks scarred the walls, following him, reminding him with every glance of the death that lurked within the shadows.

Through the twisting bends he walked. Strenuous and silenced, he cradled his arm and choked back the throbbing pain. He didn't know how far he'd gone, but he needed a breather. With his good arm against the side, he lowered himself until he was sitting with his back against the wall.

He scanned his light around the long corridor-like tunnel. Arched openings had been dug into the earth like doorways leading to rounded, empty rooms. The longer he stared at the scarred walls and ragged entrances, the more debilitated he became. Was he in the middle of the hive? He pulled himself to his feet and moved again, not wanting to wait around to find out how much danger surrounded him.

With each room he passed, Mike shined his light inside. He'd creep to the edge of the entrance, ease his light with shaking hands, and search the space as fear held onto his breath. He didn't know what he'd do if a creature awaited him, ready to attack, but he found more reassurance in searching than walking blindly ahead.

The corridor extended until it split in a T. Mike looked left at another endless black passage lined with more archways.

Sighing, he turned to the right.

He shook his head and rubbed at his eyes. The passage contained more rooms that disappeared into the darkness beyond his light. But something else caught his attention, filled him with a renewed energy. Hanging high above at the end of the tunnel was a light. Its glow didn't scan and wave nor was it warm and focused like his flashlight. It was motionless and still, shining down to the ground with pale, cool rays.

"Oh, thank Christ," he whispered, to himself.

Mike ran his hand over his dirt-smeared face and rushed ahead to the light of the outside world.

. • • • .

The darkness smothered Sydney as she strained to open her eyes. A throbbing pain radiated over her, making her wish for the reprieve of unconsciousness again. Dirt dug into the side of her face and she scratched her nails into the ground. She slid herself around in the dirt, over patches of warm dampness, reaching for any sign of familiarity. But with the mask of black hiding everything from view, plunging her into desolate silence, she knew she was lost and alone.

Her digging hands fell flat, and she whimpered. "Help me." She was alive but at what cost? Tears fell and soaked into the earth with her silent cries.

But something broke the silence. In the distance, the ground cracked. She held her breath and waited for the dry sound to echo again. And it did. One after the other, each sound grew louder, closer. With a racing heart, she pushed herself in an indecipherable direction. It felt too dangerous to remain still.

As she spun, she saw it, a bobbing beam of light. A flashlight. She'd been hearing footsteps.

"Help," she cried. "Help me!"

The feet slid to a stop, and the light scanned with a methodical attention.

"I'm in here," she whimpered. "Help."

The light shined in front of her, and a figure stood behind its glow.

"Syd! Oh my God!" Mike rushed to her, sliding to his knees. "Baby!" He closed his hands around her face, holding her as if it were the first time. "I'm here."

Sydney cried tears of pain, suffering, joy, relief. She cried, pulling herself further into his arms.

"Are you hurt?" he asked.

She nodded, clinging to him tighter than she knew she could.

"Baby, it's gonna be okay. I'm getting us out of here," he said, turning his light onto him. "Look at me."

Sydney pulled herself from his chest and looked up at Mike's beaten and bloodied face. But despite the horrors covering him, his eyes showed his undeniable belief that everything would be okay.

"You're hurt," she said, running her fingertips along his cheek.

"It's nothing."

Mike blew out a calming breath then wrapped Sydney over his good shoulder and lifted her to stand.

Her throbbing pain erupted into fierce burning. She screamed out and Mike laid her back to the ground. "It's my leg," she said, gasping with pained breaths. "I think it's broken."

She reached down and touched a puffy, swollen knee pushing against her jeans.

"Shit," he said. He scooped her into his arms and attempted to stand, Prince Charming carrying her to safety. But his body strained, and he screamed his own anguish and collapsed to the ground.

Mike huffed for air and she cried with frustration. The safety and reassurance that warmed her when he raced to her side were gone. Time felt delicate as if each moment pushed them further from their escape and closer to danger. The anticipation and fear swelled inside of her and her cries grew to hysterics.

"What if they come back?" she asked. "We have to get out."

"We will, but we gotta be quiet," he urged. "I think they're attracted to sound."

Scooping his arms under her again, he gritted his teeth and fought his way to standing. The pain that trembled through his body transferred to hers. Each shake added to her uncertainty, her nervousness. Her head swiveled, eyes scanning the room as much as his sole light allowed. The creatures could return at any moment, she thought.

"Stay still," Mike said, hoisting her upward to attempt a better grip.

But she couldn't. Against her greatest efforts, her body shook and rocked like a rowboat caught in a storm. The urgency crashed over her. Her anxiety flashed in waves. She had to move. Stillness was beyond her control.

As Mike steadied himself, he turned to the archway that led to safety. Their safety. But they were too late.

A pair of demons, with rigid, stuttered movements, crept around the corner and into the room. Clawed hands dug into the ground. Clubbed feet stomped behind them. Their skin wasn't pale but white, glowing with pulsing veins that looked to sit on the surface like vines slithering over their bodies. Their faces stretched, almost melted, from large foreheads to wavy, narrow chins extending over their chests. Oblivious to the light, they lingered in the doorway, rising and falling with their breaths.

Sydney squirmed in Mike's arms, fear driving her nails into him like the creatures themselves. He groaned at her shifting weight and his knee bent back. Again, they crashed with broken bodies to the ground. And in their wave of tortured cries the creatures attacked.

Sydney was surrounded in a blur of swiping claws and ravenous screams. She rushed to pull herself away, clawing into the dirt, unable to see behind welling eyes and streaking glimpses of light.

"Mike!" she screamed into the void.

Sydney pressed into a wall at the edge of the room. The edge of escape. Cold, bone-like claws traced her face with a fragile care like the beasts savored teasing their prey. She cowered from their glowing eyes and looked around to the light on the other side of the room where Mike hunched beneath its shadow.

A claw latched onto her face and shoved her back into the wall. Rage boiled within her and when she faced her hunters, it erupted into a terrible scream of pain. A scream of defiance. Her dry throat scratched and bled, ripping with every bit of desperation pouring out of her. "Fuck you!"

The claws ripped into her flesh, effortless strikes tearing across her stomach. Her cries of anguish grew louder, more tortured. "Fuck you!"

Each cry was met with another strike. One across her arm. Another plunged into her chest. The creatures screamed in return with an overpowering cruelty. Their jaws unhinged, revealing a monstrous and cavernous black.

With another gashing slice, Sydney crumpled to her side. Her face smacked into the ground, throwing a cloud of dirt over her. She stared through the falling dust at Mike. The broad shoulders that once looked strong enough to carry the world had fallen and shrunk. The confidence in his posture, his aura, had been reduced to that of a scared boy clutching to wounds of his own.

Her screams were no longer of words or pleas but inaudible, primitive cries. The creatures attacked her as relentlessly as she yelled, a defenseless and lopsided brawl. She didn't fight. She didn't struggle. Each gash dug into her with the ease of a pin cushion. She accepted each attack but refused to break her longing stare from Mike.

She pictured them buying the couch and their first night together where she fell asleep in his arms. Her mind jumped to every time he reached for her hand and every time he said, "I love you" first.

A cold, uncontrolled anger pushed the warmth of their past out of her. With a power that surprised even her, she continued to scream.

She breathed in his memory as she thought of them snuggled together, wrapping her arms around him. When he'd squeeze her into his side, she felt safe and at home. She was at peace. Her screams weren't for the memories they made but for the ones they'd never have a chance to create.

She imagined their wedding with Tas by her side, Mike in front of her reading his vows. Her eyes would fill and overflow with the purest love she'd ever known. Tears of joy, not those of pain and remorse streaking her face in that moment.

But she would never see that wedding. She'd never hear his vows. She'd never again get to tell him he was her world. No matter their valleys, their patches of miscommunication, they had always found their way back to each other. The work is what made it beautiful.

With her final roar of defiance, she lifted herself and lunged at the creatures. With one last strike, quick and precise, a claw slashed across her neck. Two small tears straddling a large gash, the blood washed down and covered her.

The wall dug into her back when she fell, pushing out a gasp on impact. A spray of blood shot from her mouth. The colors of the world drained, plunging her into a palette of grays. But her stare drifted to Mike, almost of its own will. With his hands clasped over his mouth, he watched with tear-filled eyes.

"Go," she whispered.

She inhaled her final breath and belted out her dying cry. The cold grasp of a claw wrapped over her head, forcing it against the wall. She clenched her eyes, dropping her world of grays into black. The beast traced her face as if visualizing every texture and savoring every bit of her pain. Then with a quick thrust, its claw punctured deep between her eyes.

No more screams. No more cries for help. Only the grotesque sounds of the claw digging itself out of Sydney's skull.

The creatures roared, stretching their jaws to reveal teeth like devilishly chiseled rocks. And when their screams peaked, they wrapped their jaws onto Sydney's still-warm corpse. They gnawed at her arm, latched around her neck, tearing her flesh from bones. With fresh waves of blood pouring from their mouths, they feasted and screamed in between mutilating bites.

But masked beneath their roars, Mike slid his way to the edge of the room.

"Go," she had said.

And with one strained step at a time, he did just that.

- 25 -
THE FALL

Tas tried to think of the time when she was most scared. Her mind raced to when she was a teenager, standing atop a wooden bridge stretching far above a tranquil river. Her friends swam below, avoiding the overbearing North Carolina humidity.

They encouraged her to take the leap. "Jump! Come on!"

Tas's dripping toes clung to the edge of the railing as she looked down with quick, unsteady breaths.

She jumped.

In reality, she knew the fall wasn't more than twenty-five feet, but every time she relived the memory, it grew. It felt like she fell for a full minute. She screamed until she ran out of breath, inhaled, and screamed again. Before crashing into the water, she straightened her flailing limbs and clenched her nose closed until the muscle along her thumb ached.

The cutting sensation of the water shocked her. As she sank, the pressure squeezed her head tighter until her toes, still ghost white, touched the rocky bottom. With a desperate sense of urgency, she kicked upward and pushed for the surface.

When her head met the air, there was no enjoyment of the rush. The fear and impact had left her body shaking beneath the cloudy water. She swam to the wooded shore, wrapped herself in her black-and-white-striped towel, and watched her friends from the safety of the dry, grassy hill. She could count on one hand how many times she'd gone swimming since that day with a finger or two to spare.

The movie of her imagination wasted little time before transporting her from the sun-caked riverbank to the damp, fall day in Prague.

At an antique table by herself, three other chairs pushed to the wall, she sat in a room with a manufactured sense of foreboding. The walls were lined with grandiose gold frames of Victorian-era portraits. Dust collected on every surface and cobwebs stretched between the dark corners. On cue with the scratchy record playing somewhere in the shadows, the oil painting of the mansion's owner crashed to the floor.

The lights flashed, and the planchette on the Ouija board in front of her spun and jerked around. It flew to highlight the word "No," jerked away, then pulled itself back again. The loud surround-sound system rumbled the room with heart-pounding bass before everything stopped and the room plunged into darkness.

When Tas entered that haunted house, she expected the cliché foggy hallways with teenagers in grocery-store masks shouting "Boo!" before running away. She expected blinding strobe lights and the generic *Sounds of Halloween* album blaring through crackling speakers. But the haunted house she walked into alone was nothing of the sort.

The room was black until a heavy door scraped open behind her. She jolted up from her chair, knocking it backward to the floor. A silhouette of a large, lurking man crept into the room. She traced the grain of the round table as she moved in tiny increments to keep it between her and the hidden figure.

It's only a person, some kid, she thought.

The shape moved into the shadows to her left, and once she no longer saw it, she darted along the right side of the table to the open door.

Semitransparent strips hung from its frame, glowing with a green tint. She pushed through, and before her eyes had a chance to focus on her next move, a man twice her size took her by the throat and slammed her against the wall. He shouted from behind a grotesque, skin-like mask with an augmented voice

They can't hurt you, she thought. It's all fake. Through the screams and horror-movie environment, she remained rational.

Until she ran into the morgue.

Cold fluorescent lights flickered overhead and dark ambient music layered with anguished screams pumped through the entire room. In the middle of the mess of stretchers and gurneys stood a woman in white, her back turned and shoulders hunched over.

For a moment, Tas paused, surveying her options and best route through the mess of dissection tables and medical equipment. When she decided to move, the lights strobed in a disorienting succession. The woman in white turned to show her face, smeared with blood and decay, and screamed with murderous conviction. Blasting over the noise was a door at the edge of the room, booted open by another mountainous man. He loomed in the doorway wearing a blood-soaked lab coat. After allowing a moment for his presence to be known, he swung a chainsaw out from behind his back, revved it to life, and charged at her in a straight line.

She ran.

The rational thoughts she clung to minutes earlier were no more. She no longer thought of it as a sick game. She broke. Through the poorly lit hallways, the damp, sewer-like rooms, she found a small cubby dug into a corner. It was her best chance to hide.

Broken dolls littered the floor and the glassy blue eyes of a severed head with blond pigtails stared up at her as she hugged her knees to her chest. Tas listened for the chainsaw with a pounding heart and a helpless sense of being trapped. If the raging engine and its grinding teeth turned toward her, she'd have no way out.

She scrambled to think. *What was the fucking safe word?*

The roaring engine grew to a debilitating pitch then turned and faded down the other hallway. Tas sprang to her feet and ran through the rest of the haunted house as quickly as possible, reaching the final stairs to exit and taking them two or three at a time.

Afterward, the hostess returned her jacket and bag. "Come back later for our extreme haunt," she encouraged.

Tas would do no such thing. Instead she walked to the bar. "Dark and stormy, please."

Looking back, she knew she had never been in any true, life-threatening danger.

"Tas!"

Until she was.

Dean's shouting voice pulled her back to the mine. He slouched against the wall, covered in blood and clinging to his side.

"Shit! Are you okay?" She rushed over and knelt beside him. "Let me see."

Tas pulled his hands from his side revealing his shirt, ripped and bloodied. With apprehension, she lifted it to see the cut up close. Its three slashes stretched down from his ribs a few excruciating inches. Dean kept his eyes on her when he asked, "How's it look?"

"I can't tell. Hang on." She spun the cap off her bottle and poured water over the cuts. Dean hissed through clenched teeth, but the clean look revealed slashes that were deep but manageable. "I don't have any more bandages to cover it, though."

"That's fine," he said, pulling his shirt back down and applying more pressure. "We need to find Mike. And my light."

Tas searched nearby and found the light lying among some rocks. She tried the switch a few times but nothing. "Dead."

"Shit," he said, standing with a pained groan. "Just yours, I guess. We should move."

But time seemed to be against them as the ravenous screams of the creatures launched through the caverns before they took a step. Had they been moving, though, what they heard next would have frozen them. It was Sydney, crying out, sending shocks of terror through Tas.

"We have to go now," Tas urged, taking off toward the screams.

The chilling echoes swept like a breeze through the passages building to a ringing decibel. A single light only let them move so fast, navigating their way past the broken spade where the screams fell quiet. Tas feared the worst.

With the mines silent, she couldn't avoid the sense of the walls closing in around them. The back of her eyes throbbed with an ever-growing tension and the pulse clamped around her head. The stress was debilitating, and she needed to slow down.

Her focus was cracking.

"What are you doing?" Dean asked. "It sounded like they're right up ahead."

She dropped to her knees. "I can't. I have to breathe or something."

"Tas, come on. We heard them."

"But I don't hear them anymore," she snapped, returning her stare back to him. "I need to sit and think."

Dean looked back into the darkness and sighed. He moved next to her and sat.

Moments of emptiness passed between them. Thousands of thoughts rushed through her mind, but she didn't think of anything in particular. She let the storm stir on its own, keeping her distance. As the mental winds slowed, her racing heart did the same.

"Check these out," she said, shining her light around the tunnel walls. "They're like little rooms or something."

The intrigue pulled her to her feet and into one of the arched entrances. She ran her hands along the scarred walls, letting her fingers dig into the chaotic slashes. "What the hell?" she mumbled to herself.

"What are these?" The sound of Dean's voice made her jump. "People didn't live here, right? Like the miners?"

"No way," she said. "Not here. Can you imagine?"

Tas moved from room to room with a quiet, uneasy curiosity. Could somebody live in such isolation? Such darkness? "There's a town in Australia that's like entirely underground, but it's nothing like this. No way did miners live down here. That would've been torture. This has to be something else."

She looked to Dean as if he would have the answer to make sense of where they were. "I mean, how long could a person even live like this?" she asked.

But when another scream shot from the quiet reaches of the mines, it reminded her of the other things, devilish and alive, that posed much greater unknowns than the claustrophobic rooms.

"That sounded like Mike," Dean said. "That's Mike!" The tension built in his voice as the scream became more clear. He went pale, a look of pleading in his eyes, his need for direction palpable. "What is happening?" he asked, in a defeated whisper.

"Come on." She grabbed his hand and pulled him with her out from under the hellish archways.

As they rushed through the passages and twisting bends, it disturbed her how she once searched for a trail of colored candies and was now searching for drying splotches of blood for guidance. Each little puddle led her to where she didn't want to go, but she didn't have a choice. Every drop and smear added a brick to her weighing conscience. Her guilt and remorse ate at her, gnawing through her resolve. But she still had Dean, and she refused to quit on him.

Would this have happened had she gone to the mines alone? How strong would she be without the others? How much of her drive was her own will and how much was guilt? Or shame? If she had gone alone, would she have fought through everything the same way?

Focus, she thought, in a scolding tone. The mines teased her, pulling her in different directions knowing they could break her whenever they pleased.

Then, as if the blood-soaked man and his chainsaw shattered her sense of reality all over again, she turned into a room and her light landed on Sydney.

"Don't look!" Dean rushed to hide her from the maimed, lifeless body, but he was too late.

The Polaroid was developing behind her closed eyes. A pale, blood-drenched body, gnawed and ripped apart, lay disfigured like a mutilated contortionist. The image seared into her mind, imprinted in an instant. She clutched onto Dean with a grip that said she couldn't stand without him.

And she couldn't.

"Sydney," she cried. "Oh God. What happened?" She tried turning from Dean to look again, but he cradled her head back into his chest. "I did this, didn't I?" she asked, from behind tears.

Dean held her tighter. His silence was better than him hesitating to reassure her. He eased the light from her hand and kept it facing the ground. They stood in the middle of the focused beam, the death hidden outside its glow.

"We gotta go, Tas. We gotta find Mike."

She pushed her hands into his chest. "We can't just leave her." Her voice came out weak, but her words were sharp, almost venomous. "What if she's not dead?"

Dean fought again to keep her from looking. "She's... I mean, we need to move. There's nothing we can do. But we can still help Mike. The sooner we get out of here, the sooner we can get somebody who can do something."

Empty words with even less conviction. But she didn't need to believe them to understand their purpose.

"Give me the light," she said.

"No. I don't want you to look," he pleaded.

With both hands, she pulled the light away. "I need to see her on my terms, not some fucking surprise. Like whoops, here's your dead fucking friend."

The decision to turn and face her fear and guilt head-on crushed her, but she had to do it. Not at the wounds or the death, but she wanted to see her friend, a person she knew and loved. To stare was torture, but it was pain she believed she deserved. It was the least she owed Sydney.

She shouldn't suffer alone, she thought.

Another scream from Mike shattered the moment with the reality that still held them captive. Every muscle in her body screamed its opposition, but Tas sprinted off again leaving Dean a few steps behind to catch up. Waiting wasn't an option.

With panic and intensity, she screamed for Mike. "Where are you? Are you okay?"

She ran against the pain, following the stretching tunnels with her gut. There was no way Mike had time for her to deliberate over which way to go. Besides, any sense of direction was pulled away from her when they found Sydney.

Sydney.

Mike's voice rang out, louder than before. "Tas!"

"Mike!" The passage split up ahead. "Where are you?"

He didn't scream a direction to bring her closer but a demand to send her farther away. "Run!"

His cry made her hesitate long enough for Dean to run up by her side. "Let's go," he said.

"But he needs us. What if..."

And for a final time, Mike cried out. "Run!"

Dean grabbed Tas by the arm and ran away from Mike's voice. The sense of being hunted overwhelmed her. A predator masked from view pursued them with a ruthless ferocity. They were outnumbered and out of their element.

With each stride, Dean clenched his side with a grimace. Tas wanted to rest, give Dean a chance to heal, but his wounds were better than the alternative of being caught. Sydney's desecrated body flashed before her eyes as a crippling reminder.

The winding routes grew more disorienting and their pace slowed. Adrenaline isn't unlike a powerful firecracker. It explodes with an immediate fury but leaves behind damage to everything in its wake. Her lungs burned and her body threatened to shut down. When they reached a massive chamber that domed far overhead, they took the minute she needed.

The air was thick with a wretched odor that hung like a fog with no breeze to carry it along. The entire cavern felt stale with endless plumes of dust and dirt clouding their light. They looked around from the middle of the large room and froze when they saw a group of creatures, their pale bodies clumped together, burrowing their claws into the wall. They dug in unison, like rowers, coordinated and efficient, their limbs intertwined, blending together as one. There could have been six just as easily as twelve of them there.

Tas jumped back into Dean and shot the light away from the horde. It fell onto a series of three passages that fed into the room. Two of the paths were alive, filled with monsters lumbering and crawling toward them. Tas looked back to where they entered. The hunting pair of creatures had followed them all that way.

It was the center of their hell.

They inched away toward the only clear tunnel. Each step was a labored, conscious effort to press the balls of their feet as lightly as possible into the ground. If a step cracked loud enough to hear over the ominous growls and scratching of the beasts, her heart stopped until she believed it was safe to move again.

Or as safe as she could be.

She looked at the creatures, tearing deeper into the earth. They don't notice the light, she thought. Their malformed bodies staggered around the room showing no indication they sensed her presence.

When she turned and put the creatures at her back, she saw Dean a few steps ahead. The light from his cell phone looked no more powerful than if he had been carrying a fading tea light. The glow highlighted where his next step would fall but what Dean couldn't see behind him, Tas did.

"Dean." Her voice hitched, but it was too late. Her instincts had taken over without thinking. The creature lurking right behind Dean turned its attention to her. Its protruding eyes faced her as it dug its first steps into the ground toward her solitary word.

The stretched face that stared her down was an arm's length away. She quivered and squeezed her hand over her mouth. The thing rose from all fours and towered before her. A rotten odor radiated from its decrepit body. Its head jerked from side to side and its neck craned around with murky strings of saliva dripping from its mouth. Every part of her tensed. The tears that welled trickled over her hand that clenched her jaw so tightly it grew sore.

When the glowing eyes seemed to glance away, she eased into her first step. But the crunching dirt betrayed her. The creature returned its stare, unhinged its jaw, and belted a vile scream. It attacked with slashing claws, one digging across her chest and knocking her to the ground. The pain had yet to register when Dean was there, pulling at her arm, and dragging her until she climbed to her feet to run.

Hunted again, they ran down the winding passage. The roars echoed at their heels.

Then their world fell black.

Tas's light had cut out surrounding them in a directionless void. With their next stride, it glared back to life. A moment later the light faltered again.

"Tas!" Dean screamed as if she were choosing to turn it off.

She slammed the light against her hip and it returned. Up ahead, the tunnel split, curving off into two directions out of sight. "Left," she shouted.

When they rounded the turn, her light died once more and plunged them back into darkness. The ground fell out from beneath them. She crashed to her side and rolled down a long, steep slope, smashing into rocks and debris along the way. When the ground leveled, they tumbled with momentum into a wall with a loud, audible crack.

It was like they had been sucked into a black hole. Everything was quiet but for the streaks of dirt falling against her shoulder. The stream grew until rocks and chunks of stone fell nearby. Tas hit the light against the ground and its beam shot back to life.

They had fallen into a tunnel lined with frail wooden beams. It seemed Dean had crashed into one, leaving it cracked and splintered behind him. Small chunks of earth continued to fall. She shined the light to the top of the slope where their hunters gathered, waiting for the slightest sound to attack. When Dean leaned forward, the post behind him snapped and gave way. The cracking of the wood and shaking of the mine sent the creatures into a rabid sprint down the slope and toward them.

The walls rumbled, and the ground shook. Chunks of earth fell from the ceiling. More beams snapped and their piercing cracks brought Tas to her feet. She pulled Dean with her and they sprinted away, boulders and mounds falling behind them. The collapse thundered, threatening to crush them beneath it. The life-threatening roars and collapsing walls grew to a deafening height that pushed them deeper into the mines. The flashlight showed mercy as they ran, illuminating the long, narrow tunnel that was eager to pummel them in its ruins. Only when the sounds quieted and the earth settled did they slow.

The creatures that pursued them had disappeared behind the collapse. Their screams muffled until they, too, fell silent. The rumbling ground steadied and the shattering earth stuck together with the smallest sense of relief.

At the edge of the rubble, Tas stood with Dean. Small clusters of dirt tumbled down to their feet as the entire mine settled.

Tas huffed and puffed, doubling over. "Jesus. Are you okay?"

"Yeah. I guess so," Dean replied, short of breath, as well.

Their light died again and plunged them into another suffocating darkness.

"Goddammit. Give me that," Dean said. Tas fumbled around in the dark to make the exchange.

He hit the light. Nothing. He tried again. Still nothing. The light rattled and shook before Dean tried it again.

It worked.

They stared around the small space in uncertain silence.

Dean cracked his knuckles then ran his hand over his forehead, replacing the dripping sweat with smeared blood and dirt. He wavered and took shaky steps to the edge of the room where he beat his fist into the dirt.

"Not here," he said. "I can't do this again." His eyes struggled to stay open and his head shook as if refusing to believe what was happening.

Something was wrong.

Tas approached with gentle steps and placed her hand on his shoulder. "What do you mean 'again'?"

- 26 -
THE OUTSIDE

Mike looked up at the faint glow. The sounds of Sydney's body being ripped apart followed him down the tunnel and to the steep slope that stood between him and escape. He looked back and considered a life without Sydney. It wasn't what he wanted, but he preferred that to remaining trapped in the mines another second. He propped his bag into a better position with its tattered straps and started his crawling ascent out of the mines.

The light breeze brushed against his face. It was a subtle touch that stung, reminding him of the gashes he'd endured. His eyes blurred and watered as they adjusted to the soft moonlight. He blinked and wiped away the haze and the world fell into focus.

To be outside in fresh air felt foreign but the place he found himself was familiar. He was peeking out from a broken section of a long wooden hall in the school. The labyrinth of mines bent and twisted their way beneath the town, an unknown subterranean world below the feet of everyday tourists.

At the far end of the hall hunched a rigid body as pale as the moon. When it stood, it stretched a writhing snake between its clawed hands before clenching its jaw around the body. It pulled at both ends, tearing the snake in two. The creature gnawed and snarled while the snake twitched its final systemic jolts.

Mike turned to look down the other end, out the vacant doorway and into the world beyond. But the town was alive. Not with people reeking of sweat and sunscreen viewing the town through their phones, but alive with more pale-bodied creatures, hunkered to the ground and prowling across the sands.

He placed his palms on the wooden floor and lifted himself with a quiet caution. The narrow opening snagged at his body, but he pulled himself through. He rose from his knees, never taking his eyes from the still-feasting creature. When he stood, he grabbed the straps of his bag and pulled it against his back. Then he heard it.

The straps that clung with their last threads to his bag had given way, sending it and everything it carried to the floor. The crash was like shotgun blast that scattered the diamonds down the hall. His breath caught despite his mouth falling open. The creature dropped the remains of the snake and turned toward the noise. They stared at each other, but much like one-way mirrors, Mike could see it while the other merely sensed the presence.

In a quick spurt, Mike bolted toward the door but as his feet teased the threshold of the open world, long, menacing arms wrapped around him. The creature threw him to the ground and pounced. It slashed with a maniacal frenzy at his back and the wounds that had dried ran with fresh blood once more.

Facedown, Mike squirmed along the aged wood toward the door and its illusion of safety. If only he could get out into open space. He stretched his arms and dug his fingertips into the sand just beyond the doorway. In a flash, the beast dragged Mike back into the hall. Splinters dug into his arms and his nails ripped from their beds, leaving the raw flesh to burn in the cool air.

Pain tore through him as sharp and relentless as the claws that inflicted it. He had no momentum, no defense, no options. His body came to a stop and the warm puddle of his own blood grew out from under him.

The sky looked endless, dotted with shimmering stars, alive and bright. It was a sky he'd never seen in the city with an air as fresh as any he'd ever known. He wished to savor it with a final breath, but his crushed lungs revolted, forcing a blood-splattered cough instead.

Claws latched into his back and swept him down into the mines, a regretful descent back into hell.

A pile of limp flesh, he tumbled and folded down the rocky terrain. An explosion of heat burst from his shoulder but that paled compared to his leg. His body crashed to a stop with his leg twisted beneath his weight. The snap was piercing in both volume and pain. A wave of nausea rushed through him and he turned his head in time to vomit.

There was to be no reprieve. The scorching pain began to fade, dulling and numbing with a chill that crept in from his fingers. In the mines, broken and trapped again, total hopelessness didn't set in until the light overhead eclipsed shut while he was dragged away.

The creatures pulled him back into the chamber where Sydney's corpse lay mangled. If he had any fight left, the sight of her drained him of it, depleted into an acceptance of the fate that awaited him.

In a separate rounded room, creatures gathered around. They fixated on him with their bulbous eyes while swaying from side to side. When a set of heavy, lumbering steps entered the room, their focus turned to the doorway. Ducking beneath the entry was a towering monster, stomping its hooves into the ground, dragging a pickax behind each step. It entered with a roar that sent the others to the edges of the room. Mike should have squirmed away, should have fought to escape, but he lay there and watched the devilish beast stand before him.

It grew and shrank with its heaving chest. With a deep, possessive growl, it scanned the room, keeping the others at bay. When it returned its alien stare to Mike, it wrapped its clawed hands around the ax. Mike reached for the light that still dangled from his wrist and clicked it off. He shut his eyes to hide further from hell and the cold steel punctured through his stomach, pinning him to the ground.

His head toppled to its side and his arms splayed outward. The ax ripped out from him and plunged through him again, twisting further into his gut and spinning like a winch. Pairs of claws reached into the wound, shredding him even more and pulling at his intestines, gutting him while his heart still beat.

When he heard his name yelled, it sounded miles away.

The claws tearing his flesh paused as their attention shifted.

"Mike? Where are you?"

The creatures scattered, shuffling and pushing back out into the mines toward Tas's shouting voice. Mike was helpless, pinned to the ground and choking on his own blood. A memory of Sydney played in his mind. Her hair blew in the summer breeze. Her eyes and smile glowed in the sun. It was a beautiful day at the beach. But her eyes would never again shine. Her smile would never again radiate in the sun. She was gone, feasted upon like a delicacy, and soon he would be, too.

But Tas still had a chance. She had some fight left.

"Run!" Mike coughed his mouth free of blood and mustered a final cry. "Run!"

- 27 -
THE CHORUS

"We die here, Tas." Dean's eyes were empty. His skin pale.

Like anytime death is mentioned, there was a delay between the words and when they registered. We all know that one day we'll die but we tend to see that day far in the future when we're wrinkled and gray, dying peacefully in our sleep. Truth is, we can go at any point and that part's harder to accept.

When death's harsh reality hits, it's a shock that cannot be processed right away. Tas stared at Dean with a blank expression, not even a blink. Shadows hung heavy over his cheekbones and he slouched against the wall, short of breath. A gaunt expression for a man who'd been beaten and dragged through hell.

"I've dreamt this," he said. "All of this. From those marks on the walls to this." He lifted his shirt and winced as its fabric pulled at his wounds. "I've dreamt this."

Tas shook her head. "I don't know. Could it be a coincidence?"

Dean laughed and clenched his side. "It's not a damn coincidence." He pulled his shirt back down. "I have these dreams that do something to me, like panic attacks or something. It doesn't matter if they're good or bad, but I write them down when I wake up to remember them because, eventually, they come true."

Tas ran her hands over her face. Lumps of dirt and dried blood flaked away. "You're serious."

"Very," he said. "That day at Trophy after you came home from Helsinki. The family with their baby, the guys playing video games, and then the homeless man asking for bus fare. It was more than déjà vu."

"It was a dream," she said, with a softened voice, finishing his thought. "Why didn't you tell me sooner if you knew this would happen?"

"I didn't know *this* would happen; the dreams come in pieces. I don't understand it but I wish I could change it."

She tugged at her hair and huffed. "You could have changed it by not letting us come here."

"I tried telling you. I just—"

"You just what? Didn't care?" she interrupted. The pain boiled over into anger. "Didn't care that Syd and Mike would be killed and that, apparently, we'd die, too?"

He pushed himself from the wall and took a step toward Tas. "That's not fair! That's not it at all."

Tas turned away, resetting herself. Did she want to ask her next question? *How do we die?* Shaking the question from her mind, she let out a big sigh. Dean was the last person she wanted to argue with. She needed him.

"I'm sorry. You're right," she said, turning back to face him. She pointed to the collapse behind them. "But that way's fucked so we gotta head through there and find a way back up."

Opposite the collapse was a tall, narrow opening. Too dark and winding to see where it led, it was the only option they had.

Dean opened his mouth, but Tas replied before he could protest the decision. "No. If I die, it won't be while sitting here and waiting for it. Look around. What other choice do we have?"

Whatever awaited them on the other end of the passage was a mystery. But she knew not to waste time planning for the unknowns. If you want to make God laugh, tell him your plans. She imagined death was no different. Everybody dies, whether they planned it or not.

She dropped her bag to the ground and took stock of their resources. "Looks like Jon was more prepared." She sorted through a small roll of duct tape, a couple of flares, matches, water, and a Swiss Army knife. "We're getting out of here." She looked up at Dean and traded him the knife for the flashlight. "You ready?" she asked with a stabilizing breath.

"As I'll ever be."

Carrying the bag at her side, Tas stepped sideways into the tight passage. It squeezed her between its rocky walls, threatening to never let go. Her face rubbed against the jutting stone as she pulled her dragging feet one step at a time. Dean grunted behind her, fighting to keep close. The ceiling sloped down and forced her neck to crane. Her heavy breaths shot clouds of dirt over her face. She'd dig her hands into the walls and pull her shoulders ahead then fight by angling her feet to slide them back under her.

If the mine wanted to take her, it had her deep within its jaws.

But the ceiling opened upward, and the passage led her to a clear room. Tas caught herself from falling to the ground as she pulled herself free.

She could stand.

She could breathe.

She could take her next step toward escape.

A quick survey of the room showed only one way out. With strong, definitive steps, her instinct led them through the winding tunnels. Any route with even the slightest upward grade, she took. Her focus was on reaching the surface. The darkness no longer affected her. The thick air no longer weighed down her lungs.

They would not die there.

Crunching dirt beneath her steps followed by Dean's formed another rhythm she followed. But when an out-of-place noise broke their cadence, she stopped, looking back to Dean with her finger over her shushing lips.

The room stood still. While her heart raced, a slow, demonic scratching moved behind them. She eased the light back to find the source, but it found her first.

A creature dashed from the edge of her light and wrapped her in its chilling grip. It flailed her around and slammed her into the wall, knocking the air from her lungs. The impact sent her light to the ground in a crash that immersed the room in complete darkness.

There was no air for her to scream. Her eyes watered. Each frantic breath grabbed less and less oxygen. She wrapped her arms over her face and braced for the attacks.

The light returned.

The creature raised its claws over its deformed head, ready to strike as Dean rushed from behind and plunged the knife deep into its back. With an agonized scream, it spun in a violent blur, shaking the knife loose. It swiped at Dean as it spun, knocking him to the ground and the light out of his reach. He crawled away from the irregular steps of the creature until his back found the edge of the room.

"Find the knife," Dean shouted as he threw handfuls of dirt and stones. A futile deterrent.

Tas braced herself against her knees, pleading for air. Dean needed her but she couldn't move. She took short, frantic breaths until she settled, and her lungs filled with merciful oxygen. Her head stopped spinning, and the nausea subsided.

The knife.

She rushed to the light and searched the ground for the blade. A sole glint of a reflection would give it away. But her attention was split. One eye stayed on Dean, squirming along the wall and throwing anything in his reach.

The distance between hunter and prey narrowed. Dean slid himself up the wall to stand. "Come on, Tas!"

A monstrous scream, like an eruption of nails and glass, shot chills down her spine. Tas turned as the creature arched back its claws and thrust them deep into the wall on each side of Dean, trapping him and centering him in its sights. Dean's face crunched as he whimpered.

Tas returned to her frenzied search and found the blade stabbed into the ground. "Found it!" She clenched the handle, pulled it from the dirt, and turned to return the blade back into demonic flesh.

Dean cried out. A blood-curdling scream that took her strength away. The creature dug its claws into his sides, puncturing deep below his ribs, and lifted him from the ground. Dean's hands slapped at the creature's face as his blood painted its pale arms red, almost black.

"Tas." His voice gargled on more blood before it dripped to his chin.

The creature lifted Dean higher with a jerk that ripped further at his sides. Dean's hands no longer fought, and the beast pulled its claws free, dropping him to the ground with a disgusting thud. Its jaw opened and snapped shut, strings of drool shooting into the air.

Tas shook free of the paralyzing terror and ran to stab the knife deep into the creature's back.

Over and over.

Stab and twist.

Stab and twist.

She avoided the rampant claws that swung at her. The creature screamed with jerking motions like a bull raging to dislodge the matador's sword but its fight was fading. Tas pulled the knife out again, focused on a fatal strike, and plunged the blade into its neck and out the other side. A final twist, a projecting stream of blood, and an insufferable scream. The creature collapsed at her feet writhing in pain. Its blood-soaked body twitched, harmless claws jerked into the air, and with a final shrill cry, its misshapen head fell to the ground.

"Oh, Jesus Christ," Tas said, with an exhale as she, too, fell to the ground. The rage had burned away, leaving her empty, powerless, exhausted.

"Tas." Dean coughed and choked on his word.

A new wave of energy filled her. One problem was solved, but another arose. She needed to help Dean.

"Don't get up. Just sit," she ordered. She crawled over to him and saw the nauseating amount of blood that flooded from his body. "Fuck." She shook her head. "Give me your shirt."

As his shirt lifted over his wounds, their fatal extent became clear. Tas wrapped the shirt around him and covered it with the duct tape until the roll was empty. Her hands trembled despite the warm blood that gushed out and covered them. "We're getting you out of here."

She pulled the knife from the neck of the creature, wiped its blade, and pocketed it, then moved back to Dean, wrapped his arm around her shoulder, and pressed on. "Come on, Dean. Hang in there," she said.

Their steadfast pace had trickled to an uncoordinated three-legged hobble. Her head throbbed and legs burned but she couldn't quit. Not on Dean.

Over the years, she'd lost track of how long they'd been friends. When she moved away for college most of her friends fell out of touch. But the distance somehow brought her and

Dean closer. They would chat every day and visit as much as possible. She never expressed how much she appreciated him making such an effort at a time she felt lost. Even the most seasoned sailor finds comfort in the company of a distant lighthouse reminding them of land and stability.

Their three-legged walk degraded to a two-legged drag, and she thought of the lighthouses along the North Carolina coast. Spending summer nights sitting on the beach around a firepit with beers and a playlist.

Maybe I will, he had told her.

She could still see Dean as she encouraged him to join for her next adventure. But there they were. Lost underground, surrounded by earth and death, and hunted from behind a veil of darkness. "I'm so sorry," she whispered.

Dean's head dropped forward, and he coughed more blood to the ground.

"Hey," she said, trying to catch his attention. "Do you remember the time we went to the Bodie Lighthouse?"

His weak laughter morphed into another strained cough. "Just us getting kicked out from mini golf."

"Oh my God, because we kept yelling 'suck it' after every shot!"

"That was a wholesome place, Tas," Dean said with a sad weakness to his words.

Although she smiled, the distraction was brief and forced, somehow making the following silence worse.

Her makeshift bandages around his torso were darkening with blood while his body shivered and paled. The memory picked his head up, if only for a moment, before its weight became an unsupportable burden again. Dean's feet dragged behind him as if blocks of ice weighed them down. His balance faltered, and he collapsed, taking them both to the ground.

"I need a minute," he said. With painful effort, he shifted into a seated position against a wall and downed the rest of his water.

Did he have a minute to spare? She was beyond exhaustion, running on the remnants of fumes that had dissipated long ago. To be honest, she also needed the minute.

Tas sat beside him, handed him her water, and scanned the room with her light. Tall, narrow slits ran vertically along the walls of the circular room as if it were a gear. In its center stood a pit, molded from mud that reminded her of the ones they'd built on the beaches back home.

"Do you see that?" she asked.

Dean whispered as she stood to investigate. "Ash and bones."

Her light shined into the pit. "Yeah. Looks like it." She turned back to him with a confused expression. "How'd you know?"

With his voice low, he confessed, "I know this room."

"Was this part of your dreams?"

He nodded, somber and silent. He wiped his mouth with a hand and sniffled. "We have to go there," he said, pointing to the large archway on the far side of the room. "But," he hesitated, "they're waiting for us."

Tas moved back to his side. "What do you mean?"

"Light a flare and toss it down there."

"But we only have two."

"Tas, please," he said, each word more strained than the last.

With a flick of the lighter, the fuse of the flare lit. The room illuminated in a hellish red glow. Tas looked at Dean once more then threw the flare into the archway. It hit the ground and bounced farther into the passage.

The rumblings and snarls began.

A horde of creatures flocked to the noise. Five of them jostled around the sizzling wick. Their waving bodies cast ghoulish shadows over the walls, clawing at the ground and each other, fighting to wrap their claws around the apparent prey.

Tears streamed down her cheeks, clinging to her pointed chin. "Is this where...?" She trailed off, unable to finish her own question. A question she didn't need to answer.

He nodded. "My first nightmare about us—about you—was right here in this room, but we pushed through. We walked through there and turned the corner. We were mutilated. I remember lying in the dirt and watching them tear you apart." Dean cried, fighting for every word. "All I wanted to do was reach for your hand." He covered his face and sobbed.

Tas placed a hand on his shoulder. "I'm so sorry, Dean." She shook her head. Had she not been so selfish and preoccupied, she would have listened to what he had tried telling her at the brewery, at the hotel. But she didn't, and that was her result, staring at a blinding flare, trapped in the mines.

"What do we do?" she asked, in a whisper.

Dean sniffled back more tears and wiped at his face without lifting his eyes from the ground. "I'm going to make a lot of noise." He coughed sprays of blood into his hand, then lifted his head. His weary eyes met hers, glassy and apologetic. "And you're going to hide somewhere in the dark and wait for the path to clear."

A flood of responses rushed to her, but Tas only managed a simple objection. "No."

"Tas, we died in my dream. Right here." Another tear dropped, and he brushed it away leaving behind a streak of blood dashing across his cheek. "I have to change that and keep it from happening."

"No. There's no way," she said, with a hurt that dug far deeper than the physical wounds that pained her. "We're getting out of here together."

Silent tears are torturous. The therapeutic calm of crying comes from the loud, choking sobs, the release of everything boiling over inside. Quietly releasing a dam through a pinhole creates a greater strain. Every part of her wanted to burst, but the flood had to be controlled.

Dean took the light and shined it on the blood that still dripped from his oversaturated shirt. "Tas, look at this."

She covered her eyes.

"Look," he said, again.

What she saw was a pair of sunken eyes and skin as pale as the monsters that lashed into him. A slight tremor ran through his body. Maybe it was fear. Maybe he was shutting down.

"I can go now on my own terms and give you a shot to get out or drag you down for, what, another thirty minutes and likely get us both killed?" He wheezed and coughed again, grasping at his side. "That nightmare terrified me for months. It was so real. I felt those things and their claws digging into me. My body hurt even after I woke up. But the pain of losing you, watching you die beside me, that was excruciating. I couldn't help you. I reached for you. I screamed for you. But I couldn't help." He took her hand. "But this time, I can."

As if her throat had closed, there were no words to say. He was right. Their hands tightened together as if squeezing hard enough would wake them up from another nightmare. But it was no dream. They stared into each other's eyes, wide and awake.

"I'm so sorry."

"Don't be," he said.

Their eyes never wavered. The glow shimmered behind Tas and the flame's crackling echoed around them. It could have been twenty seconds or twenty minutes as they held hands in silence. Their heads shook and eyebrows raised and furled in a conversation that didn't need words.

There was a tangible bond between them. A bond that stretched and strengthened over distance. A bond that carried them halfway around the world. But a bond that would sever the moment they let go.

"Tas, I..." He faded to a whisper. With a raise of his brows and tilt of his head, she knew every word he was dying to say. Every last one. She nodded back, with the smallest forced smile.

"Go," he said. "You don't want to be late." The saddest smirk crossed his face. She breathed in deeply, held it for a moment, and when she exhaled, let go.

With apprehensive steps, she moved to the side of the room, the archway to her right, Dean on her left. With a final nod she turned off the flashlight and everything vanished. She cupped her hands over her ears and each erratic breath reverberated as if she was listening through a seashell.

Dean's ragged screams rocketed through the cavern but she pictured when they stood atop the Bodie Lighthouse and shouted into the open air, out over the ocean. His face lit up with laughter and a smile so bright it could've been part of the lighthouse itself.

The tortured cries and bloodthirsty growls rushed by her but they sounded distant as if the winds carried them from the lighthouse and to the rolling sands of Kolmanskop above her. She could almost see herself, cradled against the wall, a tiny speck of life dwarfed in an orb of black. So small and so lost.

Everything seemed so far away and for the first time, that included Dean.

Through peeking eyes, the glowing flare was all alone. If she were to move, if her legs would let her, it needed to be then. The screams had fallen silent, replaced by the tearing of flesh and feral sounds of feasting. She eased with painstaking care out of the room and turned on her light as she reached the flare. Standing before her was a steep upward slope, leading ever closer to the surface.

More tears wept down her face. The smoke from the flare burned her nose with every breath. There was no way she could look back. She refused to remember Dean any other way than that day atop the lighthouse. She had to press forward. But her next step and every step after would be different.

She'd be alone.

In solace, she ascended.

The slope fought against her and burned her already exhausted muscles. The gash stretching across her chest made the exertion and heavy breathing a painful challenge, but she pushed until she stood again on even ground.

What waited for her made her heart sink with an utter sense of defeat. The small chamber before her crawled with the contorted bodies that hunted her, rummaging along the ground, snarling and scavenging for any scraps. She hugged against the nearest wall, never taking her light from the prowling monsters. As they grouped near the only other pathway out, she was trapped.

Waiting was an option. Could she sit tight and will them away from her exit? How long before the creatures clawing at Dean made their way back and surrounded her? Or how long did she have before the creatures in front of her searched along her side of the cavern?

No, waiting wasn't an option.

The screen of her phone lit up in her hand. There was still no signal and its battery had fallen to five percent. As a flashlight, her phone wouldn't offer much, but as a distraction, it could make a valiant use of its final moments.

She scheduled an alarm for two minutes and threw it.

The sounds of the phone bouncing across the ground and sliding to a stop piqued the interest of the creatures blocking her path. They moved with purpose, spreading outward as if preparing to flank the next noise they heard.

No two minutes had ever taken so long in her life. Did the phone break from the throw? Did its battery give out?

As doubt crept into her mind, the screen lit up with its cold blue light as the swinging piano melody played. The alarm always made her think of Peanuts. She imagined Schroeder playing the tune while Linus clung to his blankie and Snoopy danced. But in that moment, there was no enchanting innocence that played in her mind. There was only the vision of what would happen if she didn't move. The phone would soon die, one way or another, and she had to be as far away as possible before it did.

She slid along the wall toward the exit watching the phone glow from behind the attacking limbs. Once she slipped into the tunnel, she stared a moment longer with held breath. She had gone unnoticed. Tas put the snarling beasts at her back and moved farther into the tall, stretching tunnel.

What lay ahead looked less like a mine and more like a mortuary. The ground was littered with hundreds of bones. Skulls peered an aimless stare into the distance, broken between their eyes and splintered all around. Scraps of clothing, tattered and ripped, poked out from beneath piles of remains. As if trapped in a forsaken purgatory, death waited behind her and death sprawled out before her.

"The miners," she whispered. The realization shivered through her. She looked over the ground, beside herself. Her light caught a cluster of dull reflections, little metal tags wedged into the dirt. She pulled one free. "CDM, 1119," she read, from the weathered badge before dropping it back into place

Rank odors of deaths long passed hung in the air. Deaths that, in that moment, carried a significant weight. Heinrich's journal talked about those men. She wasn't walking through the tombs of anonymous remains but of people she had imagined. People who were doing a job to provide for their families.

The families.

How many fathers lay beneath her feet? Husbands, brothers, and sons. That mine contained more than the deaths of the men it swallowed but the incalculable pain and uncertainty of the families they left behind. Gone without a goodbye or closure. Gone like they were never there.

Just keep moving, she thought, trudging through the death, trying to leave it all behind.

The walls narrowed and crumbles of dirt fell from the ceiling, piling on top of the mounds that had already formed. Then her light came to an insurmountable wall of earth, a collapse blocking her from moving any farther.

She was stuck.

"No," she whispered.

Her arms and legs tingled with an anxiousness that told her she needed to act. She needed to do something. Anything. That couldn't be the end.

She pulled the knife from her pocket and stabbed it into the dirt, clawing with desperation. Frantic, feverish scrapes that made no dent into the massive wall. She grunted her frustration and fell to her knees, dragging the knife down with both hands. She turned her back to the wall and sat against it.

Doubling back would have meant passing through hundreds of deaths again, including Dean's. No, she refused to face that.

She wouldn't.

Every muscle of hers revolted. She longed to scream, to release everything that built inside of her since stepping into those godforsaken mines. With the collar of her shirt gritted between her teeth, she roared with the malice of a lion. Blood rushed to her face. It flushed, and veins pulsed while her eyes clenched so tightly they may have never opened again.

Silence followed. Her head fell back, and she draped her bloodied hands over her face. Dean's blood. Tears and sweat mixed as her mind fell blank. How could she break down a problem if there wasn't a first step?

A sound struck from behind her, pushing her to her feet in a rush. "Shit!"

Did the creatures hear her?

She stood, helpless, staring at the source of the scraping and digging that moved closer to her from the other side of the collapse. With the knife clenched in her sweaty hands, she looked around the tunnel for any options. "Hide."

A small nook tucked beside a support beam offered her the best chance. She slid away the bones of the men who had seemed to try the same tactic last and hoped for better luck. The digging grew furious and her hands trembled just as strongly.

First in small rolling bits of dirt then in large chunks of rock, the wall of earth came down.

Terror set in when a man's voice called out. "Who's there?" The words were strained and raspy, short of breath. He grunted and fought through the loosening wall. "I see your light. Who's there?"

The last bits of earth fell away and the feeble but driven man stomped his way through. Tas jumped to her feet, high alert, the knife and light jittering in her outstretched arms.

"Tas? Is that you?" Jon lowered his pickax to his side. "Well, I'll be."

Backing away, she desperately sought to keep distance between them. But he staggered forward with his ax doubling as a cane.

"All on your own, I see." A smile stretched from behind the dirt smeared over his face. "It's for the best. You can move faster that way:"

Blood soaked through his clothes, ripped and tattered like a flag that waved high above combat.

"I suppose that means you've found what you were looking for. Well, in that regard, you're not alone." Jon bent down and grabbed a skull from the ground. He spun it in his hands until he stared into its empty sockets. "Heinrich?" He dropped it to his feet and took another step forward, pushing Tas another step back.

"Any of these bones could be his. And these," he said, pulling a metal badge from the dirt. "These tags were used to identify the miners. One of these belonged to Heinrich as well." Jon tossed the badge over his shoulder and stepped closer still. His body kinked to the left, favoring his busted ribs. Each step looked labored, with his shaking arm against the handle of the ax for support.

"See, you came here to get away and experience something foreign, mysterious. Dare I say, macabre." With another strenuous reach, Jon grabbed a long, dirtied bone from the ground. With every step he flipped it, catching it at each end.

"But for me, this was more of a homecoming, like stepping into a place I belonged, a place that welcomed me. I grew up with the stories of these mines and how Heinrich sacrificed to ensure that his family, my family, had a better life. He was a real man. A great man of bravery and adventure. A man I could never be."

He flipped the bone again and let it drop and tumble in the dirt.

"But here I am." Jon stretched his open arm out to the side, basking in the darkness of the mines. "You may think that I, too, am alone here but you'd be wrong. Out there, out in that world, I was alone. Empty home. Anonymous face. There was no connection, no purpose. But here—here I feel connected." His rising words echoed far into the darkness.

Tas slid her feet in the dirt, easing back from Jon with every inch he moved forward. Badges clanged against bone. Dirt clouds hung around her feet. Stones threatened to grab her and send her to the ground.

How far back had he pushed her? How long until the creatures heard him? A terror lurked behind her as unknown and terrifying as the one she faced.

Blood dripping from Jon's wounded hand down the handle of the ax drew her attention. He came to a stop and followed her stare. A twisted chuckle escaped from his menacing grin as he brought his other hand to the ax and swung it back over his shoulder.

"No!" Tas shouted, jumping back farther.

With a snarl of his own, he swung and slammed the ax deep into the ground at her feet. He knelt with huffing breaths as dirt motes danced through the air around the steel head. Tas tensed, realizing she shouted. She was certain her single word was enough to draw the creatures' attention to her, but she had to check to know for sure.

There was risk in shifting her eyes from Jon, but the deepest parts of her core told her to look back, that the greatest danger was the one unseen. With caution, she cast her light over the brutal boneyard behind her. The air hung heavy, and she held her breath as she searched and waited.

The silence of the darkness broke. Bones tumbled and scattered into view followed by four creatures paler than the dried remains they tossed aside. They crawled, like sputtering engines on all fours not yet in pursuit but tracking potential prey.

The first of the bunch came to a stop and rose to stand tall above the others. Its body writhed as if standing stretched its bones into rare, painful positions. Its head tilted back and turned from side to side tracking them with ears conditioned to navigate their environment.

The pickax ripped from the ground behind her and she watched as the creature's head locked in position at the sound.

Attack.

She turned back to Jon, stuck in the middle.

"Get out of here," he said. "Keep right at the split. You'll find your trail from there." The ax rested over his shoulder as he stepped toward the attack. "I came here for this. This is where I belong."

Tas looked back to the creatures, six of them barreling toward her, then turned back to Jon again. There was little fight left in his fragile body. He had spent his life idolizing a man he never knew, a life he'd never lead, but a death he could finally put to rest. His last glance was one of acceptance and solace. He didn't intend to fight for survival. His grandfather died where he stood, just as outnumbered and overpowered.

For him, the trip was never meant to live the same life but to experience the same death.

She pushed herself through the opening as the screams exploded. Ripping flesh and salivating jaws snapped behind her. When the mines split, she veered right where she spotted a bright yellow pebble on the ground with a white M scribbled over its candied shell. Her heart raced, like a jackhammer, pounding within her chest. With long, running strides, she moved between breadcrumbs leading her closer and closer to freedom. To fresh air. To light.

But her next long stride sent her crashing to the ground.

Her light shattered as she fell, plunging the mine into an impossible darkness, a moonless midnight. A set of claws ripped at her legs, each slash searing with pain. She squirmed to her back, sat up, and kicked her legs in a frenzy against the furious claws.

There was no chance of survival in the dark. She needed light. With a seamless twist, her backpack dropped from her shoulders, and she reached for the last flare. She chucked the bag ahead of her, hoping to buy a few moments to pull the lighter from her pocket.

The first flick didn't catch. The second sparked and died. And before the third, a blistering light of pain dug into her. A claw tore into her stomach, pressing deep before twisting out. She gasped and fell to her side.

She tried the lighter again.

Flame.

As the flare lit with an explosive brightness, the creature, monstrous in size, lunged toward her. Its jaw unhinged with disposal-like teeth ready to gnaw through her. Tas dove forward and plunged the blazing flare deep into the creature's mouth.

Its jaws clenched around the flare and it roared in distorted misery. Its pale body glowed with a red hue as the fire ravaged from the inside out. The creature struggled against the burn and collapsed to its back.

Tas took the knife and jumped onto the flailing beast. With both hands, she drove the blade into its chest. Stab and twist until the flowing crimson covered the bright inner glow of the flare.

She wanted to scream. Each stab made her want to roar with defiance. Its warm blood splattered over her, adding to the layers of death she already wore. When her fury died, she drove the blade into the creature one final time and collapsed at its side.

Her body shook. The adrenaline, the fear, the uncertainty of everything boiled over. She jiggled her arms to work out the shakes but her body revolted. Tensed and churning, she crawled away as the flare dimmed and the tortured cries faded into sufferable whimpers.

Darkness.

Seated against the dirt, Tas dropped her head between her knees. She needed to steady herself and reset. She had to calm down. Without her light or bag, her only hope was a clear head.

Warm spurts of blood pushed out of her stomach with each pulse. She pulled her shirt off, trails of fresh blood streaking over her, and tied it over the wound. She pressed her hands against it and leaned her head against the wall.

Where was she and where was she going?

She replayed the attack. How did she fall? Which directions did she crawl? Before she made a move, she had to be sure which direction to go.

It took all of her strength to calm her racing heart and slow her breathing. She needed more time to rest, but every moment she waited worked against her. With grinding teeth and flashes of pain, she pulled herself to her feet. The gash in her stomach forced her into a hunch, unable to stand straight.

Faint growls rolled in from around her. The echoes swarmed, almost without direction, yet she had to move. With one hand clenched to her stomach and the other leading her, she moved with cautious, quiet steps following the trail she could no longer see. She labored through each step, meticulous and slow. The growling of the creatures grew closer, moving with a freedom and quickness she no longer could. She was too slow, too hurt, and unable to navigate safely.

She waved her hand in the darkness, feeling for anything, bracing for contact that never came.

Lightheadedness set in and her knees buckled on the uneven ground. Dirt and rocks dragged around her and haunting echoes followed her.

This is too dangerous, she thought.

It was a matter of time before she tripped and hurt herself, creating the fatal noise that gave her away. She eased back to the ground, hugged her knees into her chest, and waited, listening to every sound without making one herself.

Alone.

She'd never known what it meant to be alone until that moment.

Sydney was gone.

Mike was gone.

And Dean; she had to walk away from Dean, leaving him to accept the fate that loomed over her.

Everything she loved was slaughtered, left to rot away in the damn mines. With only death trailing behind her and mere survival waiting ahead, the full weight of the darkness dropped her heart into her stomach. That's how it felt to be alone. No shining star leading her home. No spinning lighthouse keeping her safe.

The acceptance almost allowed her to relax, succumbing to the realization that the cost of survival may not even be worth it. A Pyrrhic victory. She was too tired to cry. Too beaten to move. Too broken to break the situation down into little pieces.

The mine was alive, filled with scavenging claws dragging across the ground, ravenous growls, and chomping jaws all hidden behind the blackest veil. She squeezed herself tighter and lowered her head. Her focus broke and wandered out into the darkness, imagining the horrors that awaited her. The jagged teeth. Merciless claws. The devilish rage. She sat in the darkness, alone and insignificant in a world she didn't belong.

Disrupting the darkness came a strike of a heavy bell. It's deep, otherworldly tone sent ominous echoes crashing toward her. The creatures hidden from view howled from all directions creating a maddening swirl of terror.

The bell rang a second time, a devilish sound strained with age sent another shock through the mines. Thunderous screams erupted again. Layers of glass-shattering shrieks pierced into her head. Hundreds of beasts stormed through the passages, the deep rumbles vibrating the earth. The screams faded, dying down, to bring a momentary calm.

With the third bell came the volcanic screams again, shuddering through the mines and filling the darkness with feral, unrelenting rage. Hordes of beasts stampeded through the darkness like the dam had burst. Tas covered her ears but the devilish shrieks still reached inside of her with their icy grip to freeze every bone. Chills washed over her. The shakes followed. Her head grew too heavy and wobbled until it toppled her onto her side.

Rusted metal twisted and screeched like broken cymbals, and racing waves of monstrous screams surrounded her as if she were conducting a hellish chorus from the center of their lair. Stomping hooves and clashing claws tore through the lightless underworld shattering everything in and around her.

Her focus.

Her will.

Her.

- 28 -
THE GHOSTS

Joseph was in the office pouring himself a cup of coffee before the first scheduled tour arrived. He stirred in a splash of cream and made his way to the long table where his coworkers chatted before starting their days. It was the same mundane small talk found in any office in any town around the world. They complained about the weather, the visitors, about anything they could. Nothing brought people together like a common enemy.

When he finished his coffee, he dropped his mug to the table with a sigh. “Who’s on cleanup with me this morning?”

There were no volunteers, but then again, there never were. Eyes looked away, and a couple squeaked their chairs across the floor to stand and do anything else.

“Rudi. Come on, man.” It sounded less like an order and more like a favor.

They each took a large bag and a trash grabber and headed out into the morning heat.

“I’ll never get used to the amount of trash people leave behind,” Joseph said. He’d been giving tours of Kolmanskop for a year, and each morning he walked the town picking up the previous day's trash, disgusted at the number of plastic bottles and wrappers lodged in the sand.

"We need to toss a few bins out here," Rudi said.

"Yeah, that would 'devalue the genuine experience,'" he said, mocking the response from management when he'd suggested the same thing.

They made their way by the architect's home, down Millionaire's Avenue, around the hospital, and to the school at the edge of town. They stepped into the building, the floor covered in a thin layer of sand from the night before. The wind and foot traffic throughout the day would bring more inside.

"Check this out," Joseph said. With his grabber, he picked up a snake, sandy in color with a triangular head. He held it out to show Rudi.

"Looks like a sidewinder," Rudi said. "So what?"

"So? What happened to it?" Joseph dangled the snake to show its severed body.

"A bird? I don't know, man. Just bag it so we can get out of here."

They continued through the building, checking the rooms and long halls for more trash. Visitors rarely went as far as the school, but that didn't keep it from hanging onto a few traces of life inside its walls.

Joseph made one last pass while Rudi threw his bag over his shoulder to leave.

"All right, man. I'll catch you back at the office," Rudi said.

"Hang on a minute. We got something else over here." Joseph knelt and brushed sand from a leather wallet. "It's our lucky day."

He opened the wallet and searched the compartments. "Nothing. What a waste," he said, tossing the wallet to Rudi.

"Michael Carver," he said, checking the license. "Just another dumb American tourist."

"Yeah, a broke tourist at that," Joseph added. "Toss it with the others when we get back."

They walked out through the doorless frame toward the office. The light breeze and sunlight made for a beautiful, peaceful morning by any standard. The daylight captured the town in its deserted, lifeless form, but only after the sun set did Kolmanskop come back to life...

If you close your eyes, you can still hear the commotion at the old pub, see the sick and injured lumbering around the hospital, even catch an act performing one final encore at the entertainment hall. Kolmanskop is more than a town of deserted buildings, but a world-renowned ghost town. Only the visitors never ask about the ghosts themselves, the demons lurking in the town's past.

But far below the huge blue skies and sunshine, deep beneath the layers of earth, are the mines that made the town prosperous, the epicenter of wealth and industrialization. The town sits atop the forgotten remains of the men who never made it home and never said goodbye. There was no closure, only unrest and merciless death.

The picturesque town is nothing more than a mask over the hell hidden beneath its foundation where life still courses through the mines, ever so faintly, like a dying heartbeat. They crawl and prowl through their labyrinth, evolved to not only survive but thrive in their tombs, to protect the underworld they inhabit.

Among their legions, she searches for light, disoriented by darkness, and crawling with the irregular movements of a misfiring engine. She knows the world above her carries on as if she isn't there, as if she was never there, and cries silent tears with her face in the dirt. If she could only find light. Any light.

With light comes hope, but with the darkness comes ghosts.

ACKNOWLEDGMENTS

I can't begin this section without thanking my partner, Essi, for being the driving force behind me starting The Mines. You not only encouraged me to begin this story but helped shape the characters and plot points, and provided valuable feedback along the way. You've played a huge part in this, in every aspect of it, and I'm so glad I've been able to share this with you.

It's also impossible to not acknowledge my tremendous editor, Nikki Busch. I still remember the first draft I sent you and when I think of it compared to now, it blows my mind. You somehow helped the story grow while becoming tighter at the same time. You made The Mines a better story and made me a better writer in the process.

I also need to give a shout out to my beta readers who took time to read this and offer me much needed feedback from quite a few different perspectives. And I have to thank friends and family for all their comments, likes, and shares online supporting me through this process. And definitely shout out to my friends here in Helsinki who haven't forgotten about me during the past year and a half of my being a total hermit.

The Mines wouldn't be a thing without everybody and all of your support. Thanks y'all!

ABOUT THE AUTHOR

While growing up in the US, Daniel Yuschick was raised on horror and heavy metal. It wasn't until he moved to North Carolina, though, that his interests in dark tourism, ghost towns, and urban exploration began. After traveling to various dark spots throughout Europe, he decided to stay across the pond and make Helsinki, Finland home. There he spends time researching his next remote getaway with his dog, Abbie, and a hot chocolate by his side.

STAY CONNECTED

www.twitter.com/yuschick
www.facebook.com/danielyuschick
www.goodreads.com/yuschick

Made in the USA
Columbia, SC
11 August 2019